NIGHTMARE IN STEAM

ALLIANCE OF SILVER & STEAM BOOK 1

LEXI OSTROW

Published by
Colliding Worlds Press

Cover art by:
Dreams2Media
Edited by:
CLS Editing

This is a work of fiction. All of the characters, organizations and events portrayed in this novel are a product of the author's imagination. Any resemblance to persons, living or dead, actual events, or organizations is entirely coincidental.

Dedicated to my mom, for all the help and support she has always given and continues to give me as I achieve the dream.

ACKNOWLEDGMENTS

This series blindsided me. I always read steampunk and was either fully enthralled, or shaking with a headache from trying to understand all the amazing things being done in the pages of the story. I reached outside my comfort zone and fell in love with a cast of characters and a story line that I cannot wait to share with the world.

Thank you to my husband for sitting around doing nothing but talking names. Yes, in the end we found a name generator and yes whatever name you picked, like a good wife, I changed later the next day. But your support and willingness to help me figure out the world I was getting ready to live in means everything to me.

Finally, a huge thank you to Dreams2Media. I cannot envision a more perfect cover for every book in the series. I had big dreams, and you matched and superseded my expectations. Thank you so much.

ONE

Lucius looked over the scribbled note again, trying to force his eyes to understand what it was saying. The handwriting was hardly legible. A scrawl at best, but it wasn't preventing him from reading it. Comprehending what it was ordering him to do, that was the issue. As an assassin contracted to a very powerful demon, he didn't have the ability not to do what the note asked. That didn't make figuring out how to do it any easier.

He'd fucked up time and time again, and now it meant he had a debt to pay, or face execution. Lucius wasn't a demon meant for torture. In fact, he was a lesser demon, cloaked in human guise and everything. It meant most of the powerful species of demon wanted nothing to do with him, which made ripping them off in gambling halls incredibly easy because they felt he didn't have the talent to win. It made stealing steamy nights with married women a simple act too, because he oozed something human men didn't, danger.

The problem was, the one time he'd been caught had been by a demon mere pegs down the ladder from the one running the show. People thought Lucifer was in charge of Hell because of a religious myth. He'd been in charge, but only because he had fought his way in and had taken over from the demon that had been there before him.

Hell wasn't his creation; it had always been there, and he wasn't in charge. Sure, he'd been the head for centuries, but an Angel had fallen on purpose to take over Hell and launch revenge on the Pure Angels who'd wronged her. So now, a dainty little slip of a woman, Seraphina, was sitting on the second most powerful seat in the world. The first belonging to the King of the Pure Angels, who was ironically, still just another demon wearing cleaner wings.

Thankfully, she'd enjoyed Lucius' talents in the bedroom and had offered him a deal for sleeping with her favorite warrior's wife. Demon for hire, contracted assassin for whomever she wanted— human, demon, Angel—it was his new job to put them down. A task that was much harder in Victorian London than it had been in the Dark Ages. He was a timeworn demon. Thousands of years had passed, and he'd managed to survive nicely until a hundred years back when he'd fucked up.

For the most part, Lucius enjoyed the tasks. He was a Nightmare Demon, a being who could suck the souls from victims after terrifying them to death. He kept a piece of the soul for energy, but lady Fallen got the rest. Sure, he could invoke whatever he wanted in dreams, he didn't always kill either, but he needed the soul to react to a dream so he could feed. Without a soul, he would die sooner or later. So killing them made Seraphina happy, and it gave him the strength he needed.

That didn't mean he wanted to do what was on the blasted note. Growling, he crumpled the flimsy paper in his hand and tossed it onto the floor. Seraphina wanted him to go after the Alliance of Silver and Steam. It was damn near suicidal, not to mention impossible, since he couldn't function well in the daylight and they didn't fucking sleep at night.

The Alliance of Silver and Steam was a thorn in the backside of demons everywhere. Somehow, they'd learned about the existence of demons, from Pure Angels was his personal bet, and had made it their goal to take them all down. Not necessarily one by one either. Sometimes they just blew shit up and blamed others. Either way, they were more than just demon hunters. They had tools at their disposal that the rest of London hadn't yet discovered. Lucius had never been on the receiving end of their weapons, but he'd seen the secret motorbikes barreling down the back alleys more than once. Not to mention, he'd seen the charred remains of a demon unlucky enough to tangle with those strange guns of theirs.

"Take down the Alliance she says. Kill a guild member to gain access to their memories in their dreams she says." He kicked open the door to his home in Whitechapel and breathed in the scent of despair.

Living in Whitechapel might dent his image as a gambler, but it was perfect for his line of work. Nothing said easy to kill like humans barely hanging onto their pathetic lives by a thread. Disease always hit this borough first, and it wasn't uncommon to find someone dead in the gutter with a blood trail running behind them every few days. Lucius didn't have to don his best clothing if he was going to get around and blend in where he was going, but he sure as shit needed to dress better than he would if he was hunting there. Top hat, frock coat, and cane added the right amount of money look to his drab attire of breeches and a billowing shirt.

He tapped a drunk passed out on the corner with his toe. Yup, good old Whitechapel. Why couldn't he just kill people over here? The Guild of clockworkers that hid the Alliance of Silver and Steam was a pain in the arse of a walk, and he couldn't secure a carriage here. They didn't come to Whitechapel, and Lucius didn't blame them. It just meant he walked a lot and would walk more tonight.

By law, all the guilds of the city were in an industrial section of town just outside Rotherhithe. Couldn't have the pollution getting in the way of the nobles on their Sunday strolls, now could they?

Twenty minutes after he left his hovel of a home, he stared at the grandiose tower of a building that was London's only Clockworker Guild. It stretched only five stories high, but the building was a work of black painted brick and wrought iron work that made it look intimidating, and that was without knowing what lurked on the inside.

He propped his body up against a wall across the street. He didn't sleep to invade dreams, but he wasn't at a functional level of consciousness, and since he needed to be within a few hundred meters of his target, leaning against a wall was the safest way not to draw attention. It was twilight, and someone would assume he'd stopped for a rest on the way home from a local pub. Simpletons really. That's what made humans such easy targets. They had no idea what was crawling right under their noses. Except for the Alliance of Silver and Steam.

Closing his eyes, he let his senses do the work. He could feel people who slept. The Fashion Guild and Textile Guild on either side of the Clockworker Guild held troves of sleeping victims. But his mark? Three people at best.

"Well, that's three more than you thought you'd find," he grumbled to no one at all and let his consciousness search for the deepest sleeper, the one that would be easiest to infiltrate. "Gotcha, my dear."

His target was a sleeping female, older in age than a woman living in a guild ought to be by the days' standard. Her energy pattern felt near thirty and five in age. Her health was viable though, and he felt a small tug of remorse at what he was about to do. He could sense her energy level and know things about her, even though he wouldn't have a visual until he went to work. Wrapping his metaphorical fingers around the energy of the woman, he slowly slipped into her subconscious and ordered her brain to conjure up an image of herself —he hated not knowing what his victim looked liked.

Lucius wasn't ready for the sucker punch when she did, though. This woman, Eliza Kempe Dorley, according to her brain, was stunning. Long locks of blonde hair fell to her waist. Her eyes were round, doe-like and a serene golden brown that almost looked like honey covered chocolate. It may have been her lips that were tempting him the most. They were small, pouty and just red enough to want to kiss. He let his eyes trail down her body and whistled as they did. She was short but had the curves to know how to tempt a man. His prick pulsed to life in his trousers, and he bit the inside of his cheek to stop the erection from forming. Sex was not a nightmare, and he needed to kill the beautiful Eliza.

Slowly, he allowed himself to form in her dream. He was likely not her nightmare, but something was demanding he played with her first. She didn't gasp when he appeared. They never did because he did so at the beginning of a dream, a way to seem more natural than anything else.

He took her hand and placed a kiss on the top of it. His lips felt warm on her tanned skin, even to him. She gasped sharply but did not pull away. Instead, those beautiful eyes landed on his, and he couldn't stop the blood from rushing to his prick. Images spun out of control in his mind about those eyes staring into his whilst her pouty lips wrapped around his cock. He groaned unintentionally, this was going to make killing her harder.

Then she damned them both.

She didn't say a word, simply stepped closer to him, tugged his frocked cape in her hands and leaned up, even as the action tugged his head down. Her lips had slanted against his before he had a chance to jerk backwards, and once they did, the spark that jolted through him ensured he didn't move a muscle away from her.

She tasted of chocolate and the smell of lavender, probably a perfumed hair rinse, drifted up to his nose. His cock was fully awake and ready to be released. She groaned, and the action let him slip his tongue inside her mouth, deepening the kiss. She wasn't shy, but fairly inexperienced as far as he could tell as their tongues danced together.

Lucius wrapped his arms around her back and pulled her into him, grinding his rapidly thickening erection into her body. He could smell her arousal, and the scent of it made him harder than ever before. Her hand trailed up his neck and twisted in his hair, causing them to lock together more. He was hungry for her, and she seemed just as hungry for him. Her other hand ran over the muscles of his stomach and stopped at the bulge in his pants. She massaged him through the cotton of the pants, his shaft her play toy whilst her mouth was his. He couldn't function beyond devouring her mouth with his as her hand drew him toward a climax.

His arm unwrapped from her body and found her breast, perky and firm. He kneaded the delicious body part whilst she began to increase the friction to his cock. Their breathing was loud in his ears and the mewls of pleasure she made, paired with the way her body had begun to gyrate against him, was all it took.

His release slammed through his body, his prick shooting his seed into his pants in spurts. Eliza mercilessly continued playing with him until his orgasm finished, and he smiled against her mouth when he felt her body twitch and buck against him. She'd come to her own release simply from his kiss. Fuck, the power he could have with her, buried deep inside her body.

The thought pulled him back to normal from his lust-induced haze, well almost normal, thinking patterns. He tore his mouth away from hers and almost buckled at the knees when he saw how swollen her lips were and how he'd yanked down her bodice to play with her breast. *Next time I'm going to suckle those rosy peaks into my mouth whilst ensuring her pleasure comes from more than just a kiss.*

He pulled completely from her dream then. Panting, he opened his eyes and let the cool air wash over him. It did nothing to cool him down. He actually checked his pants and was shaken to find he'd come.

He was shaken, turned on and terrified all at once.

There was no way he was going to kill Eliza Kempe Dorley. Not until she'd been screaming in pleasure under his body in the real world, instead of in a dream. Orders be damned. He was going to complete them, but not with her. She would be safe until he could sate himself on the pleasure of her flesh, blood and body.

Trying to shake off the need to storm the guild and take her, he blew out three deep breaths, a calming technique his mother had taught him when as a child. Slowly, he felt the pounding blood in his shaft simmer down. "Go time, number two, Willan. Better make this quick."

The sky was beginning to glow with the first pink rays of a sunrise, and whilst many people slept well past the dawn, his skills were harder to use when he had to focus around the bright light, which made him weak and essentially useless. Without this kill, he'd likely find himself strapped to a table in an underground facility again. Last time had been all the warning enough not to fail again.

Closing his eyes, he found the energy of a male. Good. The male was so young, it almost stopped him from proceeding for the second time, but if he didn't, the allure of Eliza's sleeping energy was going to pull him back to her. He didn't waste time once he entered the boy's dream. It had been easy to seek out his fears in his mind because he was young and had so many to choose from. Usually, he'd play with his victim, induced more than one fear. Not this time, not when he could virtually feel Eliza through the energy she was giving off. A quick and easy run of a vagrant breaking, entering and shooting the young boy for his presence.

Lucius always liked to wait for a few minutes after the kill before stealing the soul. If he moved too fast, he wouldn't be able to get it all. Since he was sharing with a damn woman who only wanted the energy as proof he'd succeeded, he wanted to get it all. The effect of the soul passing into his body wasn't orgasmic or anything of the sort. But it was replenishing, like a cool washing on a sticky summer day or like eating at the king's feast. For a moment, he lingered in the energy left from his kill. Any second now, the energy would deplete, and he'd be kicked back to his curbside location. Yet, something about being there, as the energy drained away, and the soul was stolen, was as erotic as what had just gone down with Eliza.

When he next opened his eyes, he was back outside the guild and was startled to see hunters were filtering through the front doors across the street. The sky was still a mix of pink and black, which meant he was watching the patrols come back from their missions. He'd heard rumors they could detect demon kind with a crystal set to read human versus demon blood. He sure as hell didn't want to get caught up in that, so he turned and strolled casually back down the street he'd come.

He'd passed so many potential victims on the way home, it killed him not to stop and take just a little more. Whilst he loved the kill, partially because it was needed to survive and partly because it made him feel powerful, he felt sick about killing the youth. He made it his goal to generally only take down the older victims. He'd cared too much for life to enjoy snuffing out a young one. He'd gotten slack for it from others of his kind before they were all killed, but he actually enjoyed the humans. They were easier to bed and gamble against than the demons, so he needed them around.

Locking the door to the shack he called home, he tossed the cape and hat onto the dusty couch. He needed to rinse away the feel of Eliza's hands. He loved the rainfall of water from a shower when he bedded wealthy enough women, but it would be all cold water and dull smelling soap this morning. He tugged the shirt over his head and dropped it on the floor as he walked back to the small room he could use to wash. Cleanliness wasn't his forte.

He almost tripped whilst tugging off the trousers because his eyes landed on the minuscule, very dingy mirror he used to shave. Right on his right arse cheek was a swirling mark that hadn't been there before this evening. The telltale sign of a demon's mating mark.

"Shit."

TWO

THE BUZZING of the alarm clock on the small nightstand rang far too loudly in Eliza's ear. She shoved her head under the down pillow and groaned into the mattress. "I'm going to kill whichever one of us figured out how to make a clock go off at a certain hour."

Annoyed, she stuck her hand off the bed and knocked the clock to the floor. The chattering of the symbols powered by the small crystals was even more obnoxious clanging into the wooden floor.

"Ugh! Mother of all that is holy!" Eliza jerked her head out from under the pillow and jumped out of bed. She bent down and slammed the off switch on the clock. She heard the satisfying click that signified the cog and gear grinding together to stop the racket. "Blessed silence."

She closed her eyes to absorb the peace and quiet, and an image slammed into her head. A gorgeous male all over her, kissing her and touching her until she climaxed. His eyes were a soulless black, which made him all the sexier. His hair was a chestnut brown that was cut shorter than society's fashion trends. Everything felt so familiar, so real. Her body even rocked with pleasure as she thought about the orgasm racing through her. She shivered at the idea and realized why it felt so familiar. The dream.

Some deity had decided to bless her with a fantastically handsome and talented dream lover last night. She certainly hadn't even paused when he'd shown up out of the blue, she'd been fantasizing about being with a man before she'd fallen asleep. Her body missed the attention of a man, and she found it hard to find many that her parents would approve of and weren't intimidated by her smarts.

From the corner of the room, the tinny sound of her automaton barking shattered the silence. She walked over to Jessabelle, the metal dog she'd made as one of her first inventions at the Guild. Patting the metal dog on the head, she smiled, remembering just what she loved about her job. Creating things. She'd had a gift for solving puzzles when she was young. It was only when she'd been shipped off to Oxford that she'd learned she wasn't just good at puzzles.

Her parents had sent her because they had no male heir to show off to the educated crowd. She hadn't minded, though. Quite the opposite in fact. She'd had a professor, Mr. Shundot, who had been a worker at the guilds. He'd seen her skills and hadn't wasted anytime opening up the world of the Clockworkers guild to her.

She didn't think she'd ever forget the day she'd crossed into the marble foyer of the Clockworkers Guild. It was as grand as her parent's estate in Halifax, but the energy and life were what had drawn her in. People bustled everywhere, coming and going at a rapid pace. Then she had been shown the true secrets of the guild. Learning about the Alliance of Silver and Steam had thrown her world upside down. The idea of demons roaming the city streets made her dizzy with fear and excitement all at once. Her whole life she had been sheltered and stuck with nothing but her parents holidays to entertain her.

When the Guild Masters and the Guildmaster had given her the elusive purple and green crystals and told her to power metal with them, she'd looked at them as if they were crazy. She had almost refused; not wanting to be associated with what she assumed was witchcraft. She'd peppered them with questions, and they'd ignored every one of them.

For weeks, she had stared at the pile of cogs and gears before she realized that, if she used steam to heat the crystals, it would cause them to vibrate and give off a beam of sorts. In a matter of days, she had tossed together the ray gun the hunters used to take down the demons. It was safer because it was quiet, offered a more precise aim and was just as deadly as bullets. A week later, she had disappointed her parents beyond all belief when she'd accepted a position as a scientist and inventor within the Guild. Her parents didn't understand why a guild would need one, but they were too busy being disappointed to ask too many questions. Almost six years had passed before they even spoke to her again; she wasn't sure if that was any better, though.

Sighing, she knew the day was getting late. If she didn't get to the labs, the clocks they actually sold to the city wouldn't be produced, and none of the work on her hunting creations would be done. They were behind in production, which meant anyone skilled had to work on the clocks and watches for a time — just until their current Acolytes became full members.

Yawning once more, she wondered if her dream lover wasn't really a curse because she certainly didn't feel as if she had slept. Her body ached with tiredness, and she couldn't quite keep her eyes open fully, but she needed to get to the labs.

Her favorite part about working in the labs as a woman was also her least favorite. She was treated as one of the intellectuals, one of the men. So whilst no one belittled her, and she was able to wear more comfortable fashion, she also couldn't seem to find a suitor as most of the men in the Guild were older than dirt or already happily married to a more feminine woman. She'd had as many dates as times she'd been drunk, which she could count on one hand. Some days, she didn't mind, and others she felt as if the guild was the wrong choice for someone who had always dreamed of a family.

Tugging her reflective radiation goggles out of the nightstand drawer, she slipped them over her hair and onto the top of her head and opened the door. The living quarter hallways were dank and cold compared to the resplendence of the grand hall. Voices drifted down the barren, concrete floored hallway and Jessabelle barked again, pushing her way out into the hallway.

"Jessabelle! Jessabelle get back here now!" Eliza's voice was barely above a raised hiss because she didn't want to call attention to herself and shouting in a cement hallway was the best way to do it. "Jessabelle! Bloody hell, come here, you tin mutt!" She padded her way down the hallway and almost stubbed her toe on the automaton when it stopped outside the door to a young apprentice's room.

"He was found laying there when the clock the scientist made kept on clamoring." One voice, a male, didn't even bother to lower his volume as he spoke.

His companion had the sense to whisper. "Jones is really gone? I can't see anything in there."

Her heart plummeted at the news. Young death wasn't obscure in London, and certainly not amongst guild workers, but the Clock-workers Guild had access to incredible caregivers due to being funded by the Royals and the inventions they couldn't share. Those that did die unexpectedly were of demon doing. For the slightest moment, fear slinked its way around her body and caressed her neck. A demon inside the guild, aside from Greyston, was the most terri-fying concept she could imagine. For the first time, she wished she actually carried one of the specialized guns she had created.

"Hurry along now. Get to your assigned duties. There's nothing to see here."

The deep timbre of Master Agardawes' voice echoed off the walls, and she flushed a deep crimson when his wizened brown eyes landed on her.

"Forgive me, Master Agardawes. My dog, she sensed something and ran down here. I'll be running to the lab now, after I return her to my quarters."

"Miss Dorley, I have a new assignment for you. Two actually."

She stopped walking, shocked the Guildmaster was addressing her. She normally flitted under his radar, despite how she always pictured him as a second father.

"First, I need you to start working on a steam and crystal powered transport. I want something faster and quieter than the bikes we've been using. They attract too much attention in the rare moment of quiet in the London Underground. The Royals aren't yet ready to make everything we do a public session. Soon, they assure me, but for now, we must remain quiet with our instruments."

His voice trailed off, and for just a moment, she wondered how weary the Guildmaster was.

"Ahh, but then there is the side project." His hand gently patted Jessabelle on the head. "Felicia has one of these, one of your originals. But yours appears to have some sort of intelligence behind the eyes." To punctuate his meaning, he squatted down on the floor and held the dog's head steady whilst looking into her eyes and then back at Eliza. "I want to know if what you did can be replicated on a variety of automatons—specifically militant ones."

"Yes, Master Agardawes. I can certainly try. It was merely a tinkering with a crystal, embedding ideas onto it typed out by the—"

He smiled and raised a hand to stop her. "Miss Dorley, I assure you this old brain can't wrap its head around that. Just see to it please." He pushed off the ground and walked into the room of the now dead boy.

Her heart raced at the idea. Ordinarily, she was only granted real assignments when they required the whole lab, but this one had been specifically directed at her. She had been acknowledged as the best, but most things were done as a team.

Grabbing the dog's collar, she walked alongside as Jessabelle trotted back to the room. Closing the door with her pet safely inside, she rushed to the labs and cursed as the goggles slipped off her head and thumped onto her nose as she rushed down the stairs, ignoring the lift.

Rubbing her nose carefully, she pushed open the door to the lab.

She was shocked to find it illuminated with a crystal. They had found a form of light could come from them without a candle years ago. It was much like reflecting sun rays off a mirror to cause a heat trail, but somehow, these crystals held onto the light long after they were exposed to the heat. But, it quickly depleted the crystal, and they were hard to mine, and fear of running out always kept them tinkering powering things with steam elements as well. But today, the brilliance of the purple crystals reflected off the steel and copper piping that ran throughout the labs.

With a nod to Stephano, an Italian who had recently been brought on, she slipped behind her desk and grimaced when she tried to prop up on the stool, and the wheels sent it backwards, dropping her on her backside. "Bloody hell. Fucking alarms and chairs, what's next?" She was rubbing her arse and not paying attention to anything else as she stood up. A chuckle reached her ears, and the soft Irish lilt made her spin to see her favorite hunter.

"Cursin' everything tae dae now are ye, Eliza?"

Kellan Doughlas' voice could swoon the knickers right off of her and any other woman, but he was selective, and she doubted he'd ever lain with more than the Royals he rubbed elbows with. Not to mention his strong jaw and hard body complimented the grass green eyes and floppy hairstyle he wore. He oft replaced the Irish accent for a British one, as the nations still weren't the best of friends, but never inside the guild.

"Absolutely, Kellan. Which would include you." She sat successfully on the chair and poked him in the chest as she tucked her legs up onto the small ledge on the bottom of the chair. "Now what brings you down here? I can't remember the last time I saw you down here. Oh, wait, yes I can. You'd just broken—"

"My gun?" He raised an utterly smashed gun and offered a lopsided smile.

She laughed, put her head in her hands and shook it whilst she chuckled. "This looks like a steam bike rolled over it, Kellan."

Again, he offered her a grin that surely had gotten him out of scrapes worse than needing a new gun. "Ye might say that. I donna ken what else could cause such an effect, lass."

"All right, mister reckless and deadly. Pass it over here." Eliza made a motion with her hand, and he dropped the gun into it. She shook it next to her ear and sighed when she heard the telltale sound of cracked and broken crystals. "You broke the bloody power source, Kellan. You know how we're on a budget with these things. Does Master Agardawes know?"

"Eliza, you dinnea ken I could have an accident and not destroy tha bloody crystal did ye? Of course not, I couldnae tell him."

"But of course you can't."

She shook her head, in distress this time, and opened the bottom drawer of her desk. She pulled out a tin lockbox, grabbed a small key from the other desk drawer and opened the box. She stuck her hand under papers and pulled out a new gun. It was modified from the first and had a longer barrel, and the crystal was visible behind the trigger. The guns worked differently, the pressure from the trigger being squeezed caused a kinetic energy that set the gun off. Hold the trigger, use the laser. "It's different, break it, and I'll be forced to hurt you, big guy. I can't make another." *Not until it is approved at least.*

He bent down to kiss her cheek when the shrill scream of the demon alarm pierced the lab. She heard the clattering of many objects and cursed herself. But not Kellan. His eyes turned dark, and he quickly put the gun in its holster before tugging down his goggles.

"Thank ye, Eliza. Donna worry I'll nae break this one. I must be off!" He didn't wait for her to respond but took off toward the lift and the main Guildhall.

Forty-seconds passed, and the shrill alarm stopped. The alarm was certainly the most important thing they had. It still blew her mind how it had been set up. Crystals were scattered throughout the streets and had been embedded with the ichor of demons. When something triggered them, a large magnet would act as a conductor and pull the energy up to the crystal disguised as a bell on the rooftop. It was able to print out coordinates, so a team could be dispensed. Ingenious, but she had no clue as to how the blood in and of itself could be read, let alone how the Alliance would have set it up if they'd been acting alone. But humans didn't do it. Fallen Angels had, back in the beginning, when they'd first appeared. She'd bet people had been shocked. But really, if there could be demons surely there could be Angels.

"Someone should tell me why we had to have the fucking thing scream inside the lab? It's not like we go out and hunt the fuckers."

Eliza grimaced at the language Ambrose used. She wasn't a prude, used it herself, and she was used to the men using it as well. But she still didn't like hearing it.

"Because, sometimes, they are in here. How did you miss Kellan?" her voice bristled. She hated the alarm as much as they did, but it was essential to their safety, to London's safety.

"Right, because every once in a whilst, they grace us."

Ambrose went silent, tinkering with whatever it was he was working on, and she didn't feel the need to continue the conversation as she had two projects specially assigned to her.

"I like the alarms. They're a blessing in disguise," she whispered the words under her breath and meant them. They didn't have many crystals, and they'd recently learned they didn't work on lesser demons, but the more violent ones, the ones with real power, it could pick up on them. That made her feel infinitely better. It meant that there was no way a demon was in the guild last eve. The crystals were all over the guild entrance.

Letting out a breath, she relaxed her body, the tension from the morning's discovery slowly fading. They were safe in the guild after all.

THREE

THE BURN of the whiskey as it slid down his throat felt like heaven. It had been months since Lucius had sought out the comfort of a pub. He'd been in way over his head when the fucking mating mark showed up on his arse. Hadn't believed it, actually. He thought back to the sting he'd had on his arse for the past fortnight. Failed attempts at removing the fucker had left him out of commission. He'd tried it all—rubbing it off, scraping it off, acid removal—not a damn thing worked. Sure enough, when the skin grew back, the circular mark with a heart in the middle remained. It branded him.

Branded him as a sissy and as mated. Both of which had set his nerves on edge. But really, the biggest issue was the pain level from each pathetically useless attempt to free himself from the damn thing. He leaned back in the chair and relished the feel of no pain in his arse as he did so. Lucius slid the empty shot glass down the counter top. Comically, it didn't make it all the way to the drink tender, but rather toppled over and smashed into the floor.

"My mistake." He shrugged at the drink tender and placed ten pence on the top. "This should cover it. Make my next one a double whilst you're at it." Lucius leaned back in the seat and, breathing in the cigar smoke that laced the air around him. The air was so thick with it that he was almost amazed he could see through it.

The shot was slammed down in front of him, and the new payment snatched up as he leaned forward and wrapped his hands around the bigger glass. He had just lifted it to his lips when his eyes landed on the pair of men coming through the doorway. Dean and Arial. They were Seraphina's enforcers and the ones who tradition-ally kicked the shit out of people who betrayed or annoyed her. Both looked like the hired muscles they were. Long black hair, grey eyes and enough muscle to pop someone's head off their bodies if they wanted too.

"Bollucks. Bottoms up." He sloshed the brown liquid back and smacked his lips before setting the glass down and jumping off the stool.

He was doing his best to shoulder his way out of the pub, but it was so crowded with gentlemen and their stupid top hats and polished leather shoes, he was afraid he was going to have to resort to unleashing his power on them. Whilst he normally functioned when people were asleep, he could still plant ideas into their head whilst awake, hallucinations of a sort. But he didn't get a chance.

Hands wrapped around both of his arms, and he felt the sharp bite of demon claws slashing the shirt he was wearing and sending small rivers of blood trickling down. He bit his tongue to not cry out and struggled to get out of their hold. Using his abilities on them would be a waste because he had to go all trance-like, and they sure as hell could carry him off then. He hadn't stolen someone's soul energy since he'd met Eliza, which meant he was weak and definitely not a match for two trained killers.

"If you expose us, we'll take you to Seraphina. Right now." Dean's voice was raspy.

He and his brother might be able to pass as human, but it was barely surface deep. They were the top rung of the useless lesser demons. Stranglehold Demons, named because of their incredible nails and strength. If they got hold of someone's neck, that person didn't stand a chance at anything except struggling and ripping their carotid right out. The threat was real, though. Demons were existing topside only because humans knew nothing about them. If they ever found out, most of the demons wouldn't stand a chance. They were limited in number because of their long lives, and they didn't reproduce oft. Not to mention, for many species the vicious and violent coupling left many dead in its wake. Until Seraphina could figure out the best way to make all of the Angels fall and give their side more power, the humans weren't allowed to know a damn thing.

He launched his elbow into Dean's stomach, the oomph the demon made satisfied Lucius enough that he let them walk him through the pub. No one even gave them a second glance, and when they were through the doorway, Arial sank his nails deeper into Lucius' arm. The pain was like a hot poker, and he grimaced. It subsided just as one of the brothers rounded a corner to a back alleyway that smelled like something the drunkards spit up, and Arial threw him backwards into the building's brick wall.

His shoulder blades crashed into the brick façade, and his vision whited out for a second. It seemed this year of his life was going to be all about hurting, he was getting worse and worse at running away. The pair didn't back off just because they'd knocked him around a bit. Repetitive punches landed in his stomach, leaving him breathless and dizzy with pain. With each strike, the pair sunk their claw-like nails into him until he was sure he'd lose consciousness from the blood loss.

He heard bones crunch in his ears and tasted blood as the sticky fluid dripped from his nose onto his lips. The flavor didn't offend him, but he wasn't interested in spilling any more of his blood. Without warning, he closed his eyes and let a trance fall over him. He could hardly feel the alternating hits and slams of his head into the building behind him. Instead, he was sliding his way around the Stranglehold Demons' minds.

What makes them tick? What sends them running with their tails betwixt their legs? Their brains weren't as simple as he would have assumed, they had more depth than should be possible for a species used as nothing more than lapdogs and errand boys. What they were was remarkably similar. He couldn't tell Dean's brain from Arial's.

He wasn't aware of how much time had passed, but his ability to look in their minds was growing fuzzy. They must be killing him. Killing him and he hadn't gotten to claim Eliza as his, hadn't felt what sex with his mate would be like. *There. There it is.* Just in his path was the answer he needed. Seraphina.

She began to form in the alleyway. Lucius couldn't see her clearly whilst he was trying to make her seem real because his eyes were closed. But he would know her anywhere. One time in bed with her had branded her into his mind. Her hair was long, curled around her knees and a red dark enough to be blood in color. Her eyes were an icy blue-grey and her skin a pale porcelain. For a minute, he wondered if he would be erect thinking about her, but assumed not, given his recent mating and all-consuming sexual thoughts about Eliza. One last touch and he had the fake Seraphina speak.

"Fools. Stop now, or I'll see you killed," the illusion said.

The seemingly unending attack on his body stopped. He could feel the tension around him vanish when the brothers dropped his body onto the ground. The jolt took him out of the trance, and the vision disappeared.

A hand wrapped around his neck, and Arial's deep scratchy voice filled his ears. "You thought you could scare us? You're worthless, a piece of shit."

He felt his windpipe crush just slightly under the pressure.

"Let him go, Arial. It's just as well. We weren't to kill him, anyway." Dean, ever the less violent of the two, was actually his savor. "You're off your game and behind, Lucius. Seraphina has a list of humans, and even a few demons that you need to kill. Top of the list is Greyston Westham and his new lover, the tiny human with odd colored hair. Get better and get them, or she's going to drag your arse down to Hell and remind you of why lesser demon's typically don't live their full lifespan."

Without another word, the two walked away from him and back into the early morning hours. Being Seraphina's go to boys, they could easily transport themselves, which meant someone was going to die for Seraphina to be able to transfer such power.

Carefully, he picked himself up off the ground. They were right about one thing, though. He needed to get his energy back, or next time they came for him, he wouldn't be able to stop them. There wasn't a shot in hell he was taking down Greyston Westham. Greyston was an Incubus Demon who had given it all up to protect humans because most demons hated his kind, found them utterly useless. Most were killed by higher demons and bled dry of their blood so their sexual potency could be dropped into drinks and used to seduce anyone at anytime.

He'd been on amicable terms with Greyston for the better part of the last century, and he'd figure out some way to change the target. Even if it meant he had to break his ties with Seraphina, which he was fairly certain he couldn't do, but he would try. Sure, someone else would go after Greyston, but they also may just leave him alone. Maybe.

Lucius was torn. Half of him wanted to track Dean and Arial and see if the Alliance members would get them. He had seen the Alliance teams work one or two other times, and it was entertaining, to say the least. The other part of him wanted to resume his latest activity, stalking outside the Clockworker's Guild for a chance that his Eliza might come out. No rational part of him was speaking out to remind him he needed to dream hunt to heal properly.

The decision was out of his hands when a blur of yellow and an inhuman scream crossed his path and raced towards the back of the alley. Seconds later, two men darted passed him. His eyes followed and confirmed what he had thought. Alliance members. He took a step behind the trash heap and almost gagged as he inhaled the putrid smell.

He never took his eyes off the two hunters chasing the Thrasher Demon down. Both were foreigners, a Frenchman and an Irishman, he could hear it as they spoke. He watched, utterly fascinated, as they drew their guns. He'd seen them use the strange devices before but was shocked to see a difference in both of them. One was big and clunky, he could see the small purple crystal at the end of the barrel of the gun, he'd no idea how it produced a beam of stinging, burning light, but it did. The other was different, though. It was small and had the slightest puff of steam coming from the butt of the gun. Lucius could hear a clicking sound. The same green light burst forth from it, though, and the smell of burning flesh and inhuman screams returned.

Lucius didn't dare move. He wasn't strong enough to take them down in this state. He was simply going to wait as they disposed of the body. He'd always wondered what happened to the bodies of demons they took down. One began to speak, and he took note of the French accent lacing through the words. The Frenchman began talking into a strange device on his wrist, and he heard people responding. It was surely the devil's work, except the devil was never real. Lucifer, though, didn't have those powers before Seraphina dethroned him. Then the men did the weirdest thing, they sat and waited.

He grew twitchy sitting behind the trash pile. In fact, he'd stopped smelling the wretched scent he'd been there so long. He considered pretending he was a drunk and stumbling out from his hiding spot, tripping all over himself down the street. But he wanted to see what would happen. So he waited with them.

His body was growing numb from sitting perfectly still when the secretive steam bikes pulled up to the alley. Men carried burlap sacks, and he watched, entranced, as the original hunters sliced the demon into pieces and dumped him into the bag.

"Astounding."

His whisper was louder than he meant for it to be, and when they turned their heads to look at him, he lowered himself closer to the ground and backwards into the shadow of the building. They finished their work and passed by him, not seeing a thing.

But as the Irishman passed, Lucius smelled the distinctive scent he'd grown to know as Eliza's. Lavender and sweets. His prick hardened immediately at the thought of it. He had been stalking her outside the Guild, but he hadn't gone into her dreams. He made a guess that sexual torture at the hands of his mate wasn't a good idea. The first two nights, he had gone in, and she'd driven him wild with lust. But she'd never allowed him to fully fuck her, and he didn't have the strength to not devour her a fourth time. So he'd been relegated to stalking.

Not tonight. Images flashed through his mind. His own fears—images of her wrapped in the Irishman's arms and the man's body covering hers. His nails bit into his flesh, and he cursed. "Well, what are you waiting for then? She doesn't even know you're real, so fix it."

If she was with the other man, she would certainly come out and greet him when he returned from the dangers of hunting. And if she did, he was going to have to figure out how to tear them apart. If she didn't, well, then he was going to show her exactly what it meant to be mated to someone like him. But not tonight, tonight he would simply watch. Then he'd find someone's dreams to haunt so that he would be ready for her.

FOUR

SHE CHEWED her lower lip as she tried to reach her fingers all the way around the seat of the transport motorbike to tighten the cog on the improved upon engine. Eliza's tongue slipped out betwixt her lips in her intense concentration.

"Come on, come on just a little more." She touched the gear necessary and slipped off, the rough edge stinging as her finger slid over it. "Bloody hell!" Her curse rang out through the lab, and she heard the snickers around her and promptly went back to reach for the gear again. "Stupid hands, stupid short arms." Her fingers kept flailing just out of reach of the item, and she continued to curse her physical appearance.

Most women in the ton had long slender arms with delicate fingers to match, but not her. Her arms were long, sure, but her fingers were far from slender or delicate. Ten years working in the labs with cogs, gears and all manners of metals had left them chubby and swollen.

She leaned forward and pressed her breasts into the side of the transport. No doubt the men around her would be judging her for not having the intelligence to test the capacity of the steam and crystal to work together before placing it inside the bike, but she had never been the most logical of thinkers when she was working. Sure, her brain matched wit and formula with all the men in the room and even the few women in the normal levels of the clock making, but that didn't mean she went about it the easiest of ways each time.

"Aha!" Her finger grazed the gear, but this time she was able to wrap both her index and forefinger around it and give the necessary tug. It barely moved, which either confirmed she had done it properly the first time, or was an indication into her lack of strength. Either way, she was done trying. Her knees ached from being slammed into the floor all day, and her breasts were beginning to ache from the pressure of being against the seat.

She rose off the floor and brushed any dust off the tan breeches; oil would never come out and she had long since stopped trying. She felt the familiar cracking of her joints in her back and grimaced a little. She needed to speak to the Guild physician about such matters before she could no longer stand up right. Ignoring the discomfort, she turned to her desk and frowned when the little golden key was nowhere to be found. Her eyes narrowed as they ran over everything on her extraordinarily unkempt desk, and she did a mental catalogue. Files, spare gears, oilcan, charcoal drawing sticks, ink, quill pen, her pocket watch, her communicator, but not a key to be seen.

"What could I have done with it?" Her eyes dropped to the floor as she peered under the desk to ascertain if it had fallen below her workspace. "Perhaps it bounced off?" She let her eyes scan around her as she put her hands on her hips and let out a frustrated growl.

"Lose something again, Eliza?" Douglas, another lab worker, had a playful tone in his voice as he teased her.

It wasn't uncommon for her to misplace the smallest of things, but it still grated her nerves. She'd been working on the project for over a fortnight, and this would be the first time it was complete enough to even check if the bloody thing would cycle on.

"Of course I did, Douglas. A day should not pass that I do not live to infuriate myself with such small, and yet crucial, mistakes."

Perhaps more dramatically than was needed, her body flopped into her chair, and she shut her eyes trying to visualize where she had last seen the blasted skeleton key. The cushion protected her from any real pain, but the motion still jarred her a little, and of course, Douglas chuckled again.

"I think I may be able to cheer you up. Maybe be your knight in shining armor."

She popped open one eye and raised a brow at him. For years, he had toyed around with her that way, yet he'd never made so much as a move on her. In fact, the only man who had ever made a move on her was a drunken noble at her family's holiday ball three years prior. The rest had simply seduced her for the fun of it and left it alone. None wanted to marry her, and she'd accepted that. If someone was going to use their charms on her, she supposed Douglas was handsome enough with his thick bushy hair and deep brown eyes covered by silver wire spectacles. He was lithe, but not terribly tall.

"Well, don't you want to ask me how that will be possible?" He wiggled his brows at her.

She flushed that she'd fallen into one of her waking fantasies. "Oh, but of course, Douglas. Anything you might be able to do to brighten up my sour mood would be most appreciated. I fear I will have to go to the clockworkers' level and have them create a whole new lock and key and install it before I can see if I've done what Master Agardawes has wished." She could hear the grumpiness in her tone, followed quickly by her mother's incessant chiding that women of the upper echelon do not use such tones.

She was lost in her thoughts until Douglas cleared his throat. It took her a moment to focus on the gleaming item in his hands. The small, gold, skeleton key.

"Oh Douglas! You found it!" She leapt from the chair, swung her arms around his neck before she realized the impropriety of her action, and hastily pulled back. "Forgive me. I wasn't thinking of anything but that you saved me from certain failure just now."

His cheeks were ruddy with a flush too. He merely nodded and cleared his throat. "I happened to watch you bump it off the desk a few moments ago. Grabbed it in case it really did go missing."

She smiled again. "Thank you, Douglas."

"Any shot you two might get back to your assignments and stop chattering? Some of us need the quiet to work if you don't mind." Stephano's accent was laced with annoyance.

Eliza had to put her hand over her mouth to cover a chuckle. "Sorry, Stephano. You know us women, we can't do anything without chattering away."

He grumbled something in confirmation and she looked back at Douglas.

"What do you say to seeing how my calculations played out?"

She could feel herself giddy with energy. She'd established herself as top in the Guild many years before but wasn't oft given projects because she had a tendency to make dire mistakes. Not this time. She'd checked her calculations multiple times. The request had been a speed boost to their current transports.

At present, the little steam bikes were running purely off a combination of kinetics and steam. They'd been given money from the Royals to reproduce a steam engine's pieces, but on a much smaller scale. They had been in place prior to her becoming a member of both the Guild and the Alliance of Silver and Steam. All together, she had found them quite proficient. But her opinion meant nothing, she was never the one on the back of one, her hair tousled about in an array as she sped off in chase, or fleeing from one of the many demons that lurked the streets. No, she was merely the scientific mind behind the items, except when she was testing them.

The new bike would be perfect, but a slight bit louder than its predecessor, which was the exact opposite of the request, but she hoped the advanced speed would overrule the noise problem for the time being.

She'd figured out a way to amplify the current engine with the introduction of a crystal, just as she had done with the ray gun Kellan had been boasting was "sheer perfection" since she had given it to him. The kinetic energy from turning the key would set the cogs moving, the cogs would, as always, generate the power needed to keep the gears and cogs moving and power the device. However, the addition of the crystal meant that the steam would heat it up and cause heat energy to pulse throughout the steam bike, amplifying the already working power source. It was quite ingenious, and she wasn't terribly certain why it had taken her so long to put the engine together upon realizing the crystal was the perfect beacon of energy.

Douglas smiled and winked at her before setting the key in her palm. "She's all yours, Eliza, I wouldn't dream of starting her up for you."

She smiled back as she wrapped her hand around the key and turned back to the steam bike. Taking a deep breath, she slipped the key into the hole and turned. As with the other bikes, she could hear the slight *clink* and *clong* as the gears began to grind and twist together. Within seconds, the steam began to swirl behind the bike, white puffs of air that she watched float over Douglas' legs.

"Come on, come on," she chanted quietly under her breath as she waited for the steam to start to power the crystal. For the moment, the bike was simply as it always was. She bent at the waist and placed her hands on her knees, searching for the telltale glow of a crystal. She could just barely make out the faint purple color through the steam circulating. Sighing she stood upright and glared at the bike.

"Um, Eliza? This appears to be doing exactly what it always does. Produce steam and probably chug along." Douglas' voice held confusion and defeat for her failure.

Her eyes narrowed, and she glared at him. "Thank you for pointing out my failure. I'll be sure to notate to Master Agardawes that you noticed such before I went back to the st—"

She didn't get to finish her word, let alone the sentence. A large *boom* rocked through the room. She lost her balance and shifted slightly, her hip slamming into her desk. Curses were floating through the room, all seemingly aimed at her. Rubbing her hip, she looked at Douglas then the bike.

It was on fire.

Orange flames licked up from the inside component of the bike. She hadn't the foggiest what had gone wrong. Perhaps she had allowed the crystal to overheat. Or mayhap it was too large a size. Frustration spiked, and the room before her was speckled with dots— something that always came with her intense frustration. She didn't move an inch. She merely stood back by her desk and watched as the bike continued to flame.

"Turn the bloody thing off, Eliza!" someone shouted from the other side of the room.

She shook off her frustration and stupor because he was right, if she didn't turn it off, the room would fill with smoke. With a sigh. she leaned forward to pull the key out and growled when she neglected to twist it. The metal somehow bent, most likely made malleable from the heat of the flames.

"Damn it! Move out of the way, I have to get this outside," she shouted, even as she put her hands on the handlebars and started walking the bike toward the exit. The labs were deep within the guild on a sub level to conceal them under the many workshops of actually clock working, and that was going to spell disaster.

She hit one of the desks on the way out, and her hand slid down the metal handlebars that were heated from the flames. A streak of pain shot through her palm, and she smelled burning flesh before she pulled her hand away. The bike almost toppled to the side as she pulled her hand back. Disgusting pockets of skin bubbled and rose off her palm, a burn more serious than most she'd obtained from her failures.

Apprentices and guild workers tripped over themselves to get out of her way as she pushed through the small hall to the steam lift at the end. The pain from the burn was white hot, but she couldn't afford to push it with only one hand. She knew Douglas was pushing from the back because she'd seen him when she rounded the corner and stepped onto the lift, but she didn't want to make things harder.

"Eliza, the crystal—" Douglas' voice was shrill, laced with panic.

She whipped her head around, even as the lift was opening, to look at the crystal. She had never seen anything like it. The deep purple crystal had lightened in color, and she would swear it was actually glowing. But what caused her to pause were the tiny fissure cracks running up and down it, beautifully lacing together like a spider's web.

She felt the bike move, and she blinked, remembering where she was even as Douglas fought to push forward. The flames still licked out from the engine component of the bike, dancing across the metal and reflecting in it. Perhaps if it weren't also leaving behind a growing cloud of black smoke it would be pretty to look upon.

"Move! Get out of the way!" her shouts echoed off the walls in the grand hall as they raced through it.

The sound of scurrying feet and the thumping of her and Douglas' steps almost drowned out the shattering sound from within the bike. Eliza didn't have even a moment to realize what was occurring as the shattering and cracking sound came again, coupled with an explosion of flames that knocked her into a wall and caused pieces of the beautifully made bike to fly apart. She cringed as her head smacked into the wall with a loud *thump*. Blackness threatened to take over, but not before she saw what had happened.

The grand hall was littered with pieces of burning metal. She briefly saw Douglas to the left of her, blood trickling from his leg. She tried to push herself up off the floor, but it only intensified the pain in her head. The shouts and screams resonated with a sickening tone, and she couldn't hold onto consciousness any longer.

FIVE

"MISS DORLEY. Miss Dorley, might you be able to hear the sound of my voice?"

Words reached her ears, mushed up sounding and hard to decipher, but she recognized the voice. It belonged to Tate, the Guild's head of medicine. Accidents weren't unheard of, and as with all guilds, the Clockworker Guild took care of its own. She hadn't seen him oft for problems, but he was an old friend of her parents, and she had grown up in his company at balls and feasts.

Her eyes slowly cracked open. The rush of candlelight to her right elicited a groan, and she snapped them shut again.

"Miss Dorley, please. I can see you have regained consciousness, and I must impress upon you the urgency of checking your injuries for something more substantial than a bump to the cranium."

She felt Tate's hands gently rocking her shoulders, and she pulled away, turning to the right. She cried out as a slice of pain tore through her shoulder, hot and blinding. She panted, and her eyes flew open. The candlelight was further away, and she sighed in relief for that small blessing.

"Careful. You have sustained a fair amount of injuries this afternoon. Thankfully, a sore shoulder seems to be the worst I've been able to see, aside from that terrible burn. Do try to remain still."

She saw the candle flame move back and forth in front of her eyes, and she growled low as her gaze became transfixed on it, following the dancing flame side to side.

"Ah yes, magnificent, no signs of a bleed." Tate stepped back from her.

She pushed up, forgetting the burn on her hand, and hissed. "What happened?" Her voice sounded strange as if she was speaking into a cone or something and coming out amplified.

"Well, to be frank, you had an experiment quite literally explode in your face."

Images of racing through the Guild with a flaming steam bike crashed into her consciousness. "Bloody hell," she groaned.

"That would sum it up. One moment and I'll be back. Master Agardawes wished to be informed when you awoke." Tate turned and left the room, but left the oil-burning candle with her.

Her stomach was a mess of nerves, there were consequences for failures that endangered lives, and she knew she would be in for something fierce for this. Thomas Agardawes was not known for being a particularly harsh Guildmaster, but with Alliance members, well, failure was a poor option for the team of secret workers.

The sound of a throat being cleared pulled her from her thoughts of the various punishments that were about to be placed upon her.

"Miss Dorley, how are you feeling?"

Master Agardawes' voice was soft, quiet, and it made her more concerned. Calmness meant anything he said came from a level head.

"I am afraid I could feel better, sir."

"I suppose you could. Douglas was released an hour or so ago, his injuries were mere slashes to his legs, and he shall be fine."

Bile gathered in her stomach like a lead pit, she hadn't even thought of Douglas or his status. She was a poor companion to him.

"Do you remember much?"

She nodded and flinched, biting down on her lower lip as the pain surged through her. "I was working on the faster cycle you had asked for. I - I did something wrong. Something in my calculations must have been off, and I'm ashamed to say I don't know what. I promise I can find out." The words rushed out as they oft did when she'd broken something as a small child and had sought forgiveness from her parents.

"It exploded, well it caught on fire first, and then the crystal just exploded." Her head slumped a little at the thought, lives had been endangered, the great hall and a crystal were in ruins, and she'd ruined her first solo assignment in years. Her head continued to the thud, the blood pumping an audible force that caused a wave of pain with each sound.

"Yes, that would be accurate. Add in a significant bump to your head, a minor burn and some sort of damage to your shoulder, and you shall have the complete picture."

His eyes locked onto hers, and she swallowed. If ever there was a time she wished for an invisibility device, now was such a moment. She could almost feel his disappointment as if a cloak had settled over the air betwixt them, heavy and constricting.

"Miss Dorley, it brings me no pleasure to do this. But once physician Tate has cleared you, you are on a leave of absence. I want you to leave the Guild, go home, go visit a college mate, but you are to vacate the premises and clear your head. I cannot have such mistakes being made within these walls again."

Tears stung her eyes. She forced them to remain unshed, blinking rapidly to hide them. Even in the dim candlelight, she did not wish to be seen for the child she was. The condemnation stung as much as the burn on her hand, and she bit her lip to stop it from trembling before pushing out long deep breaths.

"Do you understand, Miss Dorley? This isn't permanent but leave your destination with my assistant, along with your communicator. I will send word for you when I feel you have had enough time away."

She forced herself to keep taking the deep breaths. "Yes, sir. I completely understand." The wavering in her voice betrayed her pain, and she wanted to smack herself for such a show of weakness.

Agardawes nodded before patting her gently on her right forearm. "I am glad you are well, Eliza. I will see you soon." He turned away from her and began to leave the room. "Tate, she is ready for you. Thank you for your care."

She heard voices indicating the two men carried out a conversation of sorts, but her thoughts buzzed in her head so loudly, they drowned all else out. A suspension from the Alliance was unheard of. She'd always strove to be perfect, to make her family proud, and if they heard of this, they would quite possibly disown her as they had when they'd learned she'd stepped away from a position offered to her by his majesty to pen documents.

Tate administered cream to her hand, and she hissed as the sting blocked her thoughts for mere seconds. She also knew he said something about being careful with her head as he helped her off the narrow cloth covered table. She heard him say that she could travel in three days time. But nothing truly penetrated. Her mind was in a fog, a blackness with nothing but fog rolling through it. Her feet carried her to her chambers, and her hands even petted Jessabelle when the metal dog barked at her.

Dismissed

The word echoed in her thoughts even as tears slowly slipped down her cheeks. She had never been good enough back in Halifax, and now she wasn't good enough at the guild. Her vision blurred, and she hardly felt Jessabelle's cold steel tongue dragging over her clothed leg, trying to get her attention.

Eliza slid the communication device from her wrist and tugged at the protective goggles that someone had put in her pocket when they'd brought her to the medical rooms. She felt the snag as the metal loop that connected the strap to them caught on her breeches, and a tearing sound sliced through the chamber.

"Damn it, Eliza!" she snarled and yanked at the goggles, further tearing the pants before slamming the goggles onto the ground. Jessabelle whimpered and immediately withdrew from her attempts at attention, slinking away to the corner. The tears blurred Eliza's vision so terribly that she almost missed how upset the metal dog was.

Sighing, she dropped to her knees and stuck her hand out. "I'm sorry, sweet girl. It was an accident." Jessabelle's metal eyes just stared into hers, and for the first time, Eliza noticed how truly lifelike the dog was capable of being. She left her hand outstretched, hoping her pet would accept the apology.

"I'm not useless. Look what I've created. I can do this. I can fix that bloody bike, and I damn sure shouldn't be dismissed!" The fire in her words was back, and she threw her hands up in the air and pulled back from the dog.

"Fine, Jessabelle. Cower. Live life afraid of everyone, terrified they'll hurt you and send you packing." She pushed off the floor and walked to the closet to pull out her Italian leather carry bags. "Fat lot of good it's done me. I'm thirty and three with no prospects for a family. I've been momentarily sent away from my job, and, oh yes, I'm talking to a tin can!" Eliza slammed a pair of wooden dress heels into the bag. Anger rolled off her in waves. Pain made the room spin, but if she had to leave, she had to pack.

But she was only angry at herself. *Taking it out on a poor invention isn't making you a better person, Eliza.* She didn't look at Jessabelle as she continued to pack her bags for a journey home. Her eyes lingered on the communicator on her bed stand, and she snatched the device up and tucked it safely betwixt her undergarments and blouses. Heavens knew there would be demons where she was going. They were everywhere.

For a time, they had thought the demons were only in London, but they had quickly learned better when strange attacks had been in the papers. Besides, something about having the device close by, to call the guild should she need, made her feel better. *Not as much better as being able to handle the nasty buggers myself would make me feel.*

The packing was monotonous. Over and over, Eliza looked at her work clothes and then grabbed something else. Her parents would have been appalled if she showed up in anything less than splendid silks. Unfortunately for her, she did have two such dresses at the guild. Her mother had seen to sending them when they'd decided to forgive their only child. She couldn't be rid of them, or when holidays came about, she would never be free of the harassment from her mother. There was no excuse in the Dorley house for improper dress.

Her eyes drifted to the clock on her bed stand when she'd packed the last of her belongings. Two twenty-seven in the morning. A yawn escaped her, and she dropped down onto the bed. At some point, Jessabelle had forgiven her and climbed onto the bed. Her cold steel paw was underneath Eliza, and she gently pulled it out and stroked the dog's head.

"I'm sorry, sweet girl. I'm just so upset. That man! He just decides everyone's fate, and it isn't fair! It simply isn't fair." She was cut off as another yawn pushed past her lips. Her eyes drooped with the need for sleep, and she pulled the covers back without even undressing. "I must be tired if I'm willing to sleep in my clothes, huh, sweet girl?" Eliza yawned again and placed her head on the pillow. "I just have to make it through a few weeks. A few weeks, and I'll be back where I belong." She exhaled, long and dramatically, and even Jessabelle sighed with her before she closed her eyes.

He was in front of her. The same man she kept running into, at this same pub. He'd vanished for some time but was back. Her mouth went dry at seeing him once more. His eyes lingered on hers for a moment, and she felt the same rush of heat and desire that always accompanied his gaze. His eyes appeared to hold no pupils, which she'd learned from another scientist at the guild was impossible, the eyes could simply not be black. But his were. Eliza supposed she should be frightened by him, but she wasn't.

Instead, all she felt when she looked at him was a hunger. She wasn't bedded oft, and this man had tempted her every time she'd seen him. And every time she'd pulled away before sleeping with him. She'd known plenty of women, Felicia even, who slept with demons for intel. She'd always thought bedding a man was important, not something to be taken lightly.

His hand was small for a man's, and he set down the glass he'd been holding. She could tell from the dark amber color, it was filled with whiskey. It was her father's drink of choice, and she would know it anywhere. Her eyes watched as he ran his hands over his hair, the brown strands were now shoulder length, and she had the strangest urge to run her fingers through the strands.

More like tug your hands through his hair whilst he sinks deep inside of you. She flushed at the vulgarity of her thoughts and looked down at her drink—gin and tonic, neat. She stared into the colorless liquid and lost herself in its depths, trying to ignore the seductive call of the man only a few places down from her. It should have concerned her that she was out in a pub. Respectable women such as herself did not do that.

"Perhaps you're not as respectable as you would like everyone to think."

The words were whispered against her ear, and the warm breath of the speaker sent a shudder through her. She turned to give him a piece of her mind, not even realizing he had read her thoughts but stopped when she saw who'd spoken.

It was him. The man that oozed sex from across the bar top. She twitched nervously in her seat, hoping he couldn't see the lustful flush on her cheeks or notice as her eyes dropped immediately to his crotch. His erection was undeniable, and rather large if the bulge in his straight-leg trousers was anything to go off. Instinctively, she squeezed her thighs together as a wave of desire passed through her, so intense she thought she would wind up in his arms from the intensity of it.

"That, sir, is not how you speak to a lady." Her voice was confident, not betraying the sinfulness in her thoughts.

He grinned down at her, his lips twisted into a playful smirk, and she almost laughed at how charming he looked.

"We were actually discussing just how much of a lady you might be." He ran the slightest touch of his fingertips over the nape of her neck before placing a kiss at the base of the column of her throat.

She gasped. His actions were outrageous. She would be looked upon as a common whore if she didn't immediately pull free from his grasp. But she couldn't. His hands were gently massaging her shoulders whilst his mouth nipped, and then kissed, her right shoulder. Eliza closed her eyes and sucked in a breath, it was all she could do not to moan in pleasure. Little tingles of ecstasy raced through her body wherever his lips touched, and her mind wondered what it would be like if he touched her where she was craving it most.

"Sir, please. I am not that kind of a lady. I do not even know how I came to be alone in a pub."

He kissed her shoulder once more before pulling away and sitting beside her. "The answer to that, Eliza, is quite simple. A dream."

She stared at him, her mouth agape, and laughed. "Really, sir, I think I would know when I am dreaming. They have a certain feel to them. A certain emptiness that this situation is not warranting." As if to prove her point, she picked up her drink and tossed it back, gagging slightly at the bitter taste as it went down. "See, as such, I am not a gin drinker, and the taste left something unpleasant behind. Dreams do not have tastes."

Her eyes watched his as they moved from side to side. She wasn't certain, but she had the feeling he was looking at her, assessing her even. She looked down and saw that she was still in her work attire, a loose cotton top, and a man's breeches. Nothing that would make her appear to be a lady of the night. He paused, simply stopped looking at her and smiled again, a smile that sent both chills and a round of desire through her.

"They do when I make them." He stood up from the stool beside her then and pushed it out.

He reached his right hand out to her, and she hesitated, looking at it before slipping her hand into his. There was something about him. She couldn't put her finger on it. At moments, his eyes seemed to lack a soul, and others, they appeared to be so full of passion and playfulness she couldn't imagine what had sent chills through her the moment prior. But a dream? She opened her mouth, was going to question him when he let his head tuck down and placed his lips over hers.

The minute he kissed her, everything flooded back, like a damn wall was crumbling from the pressure of a slamming rush of water. She'd seen him before in dreams. It was never real. Never ever real. For nights now, she'd dreamed of this man, and how she'd forgotten, she'd never know.

"A dream," she whispered, completely unaware the words had slipped out. She had no clue how a dream could feel this real, or why he would claim it was his doing.

"Yes, Eliza, a dream. A wonderful, sensual dream that should it not be you here with me would end in death." His words held no malice, but his eyes had that soulless look again.

She took a step back toward the bar top and cried out as her ankles hit something and she landed on her arse. On a bed.

Startled, she jerked her head from side to side. The pub was gone. They were in a lavish room, akin to something they might find in the guest quarters of her parent's home. The bed linens were a rich golden color, and too many fluffed pillows lined the headboard. The carpeted floor looked lush, and she wanted to squish her toes around in it just to see, but she refrained. Light streamed in through the windows, and her confusion deepened.

It really would have to be a dream, places don't just disappear, and she was certain this man, this deadly sexy and perhaps just deadly man, hadn't slipped her anything. It truly was a dream. Of course, it would be, though. Men like him never showed the smallest hint of interest in a lady who liked to roll around in grease and oil all day. So, of course, it would have to be a dream for him to look at her as if she was the tastiest morsel in the room.

"That's where you're wrong, Eliza. I would want you anywhere."

She let her eyes drift over to him, and she stopped breathing. He was fully naked, muscles hard and taut, all exposed for her to see. She didn't waste any time lowering her gaze to his crotch. The bulge she saw at the pub was nothing compared to the mouth-watering erection he sported now. Easily twenty-five centimeters long, he was thick and round, a drop of wetness seeped from the tip of his prick. She had the strangest urge to lick it off to see how salty he would taste and then take him into her mouth.

She shook her head, trying to get control over herself. She'd been in this position with him before, but never with him stark naked in front of her. Her eyes peeked at him again, and she inadvertently sighed, wanting to touch him.

"I want that, Eliza. I need that. Look what you've done to me."

Slowly he turned, exposing his arse to her, and her mouth watered at the tight, firm butt cheeks that he presented her with.

"Do you see that blasted mark? That infuriating little circle with a little girl's heart in it? Well, it's your fault that it's there. And frankly, I'm tired of not getting everything that should come with a mark like that."

"How . . . how do you keep doing that? Reading my mind and answering things I know I'm not saying out loud?" Her voice shook with her barely restrained lust dying to break free. He'd proven his point. It must be a dream. She'd never seen him unless some sort of sexual play was involved, and there was no such thing as magic, nothing that could've made a room disappear and a new one appear.

"Why not? There are demons aren't there? And besides, I've answered that question. Twice now I believe, and I'd like to think you're a smart enough girl not to need it answered a third. But just in case, just this once, I'll oblige you."

She had no idea what he was talking about and didn't even care. She was utterly lost in a haze of lust and wanton thoughts. He'd turned around and started walking towards her. Each step made his cock bob, and when he took himself in his hands and squeezed the head of his prick, she almost came undone. He pressed his lips to hers and kissed her hard, his tongue pushing impatiently past her lips as he ravaged her mouth with his. His cock pressed against her hands, and she itched to wrap her fingers around it as she had so many other times. He bit her lower lip, then licked it and pulled away.

"Because it's a dream, Eliza."

That was all it took. One final confirmation that there would be no consequences to her actions. Three bed partners would likely be enough to set her parents on edge, a complete stranger would kill them.

"But it's a dream, Eliza."

She dug her hands into his hair, twisted and pulled him down to her. "Yes, yes, it is." She went to kiss him, to lose herself in the taste of whiskey that lingered in his mouth, but he pulled back.

"Lucius. You need to know my name because it's going to be crucial to you when I'm pleasuring you to the point of seeing stars."

She didn't doubt that he could do that to her. *Lucius, a respectable name. He could be from a family with wealth. Someone my parents would certainly approve of. If you weren't about to fuck him purely for the way he set your insides to a molten heat level.*

"Yes."

She wasn't sure why she said it, but his lips curved into that smirk again, and she didn't want to wait any longer.

Her body crashed into his, and she felt his hands tear the shirt away before they grabbed onto her breasts and began to knead them. His hands, the ones that had seemed so small holding the glass, were perfect and warm as they touched her. He shuffled slightly, his cock dragging across her breeches, and she bit her lip not to scream with need. He stopped then, his body a warm wall of heat behind her, and tugged her backwards into him. Her arse hit his cock, and she suddenly realized that she was naked and froze for a moment.

"Shh, shh, now. It's all a dream. Of course, your clothes are off, Eliza. I want them off. I need them off."

His mouth trailed close to her ear, and she wanted to turn and claim it, take control of the situation because she felt so helpless, so lost in her need for this Lucius.

But he hadn't kissed her again, not yet, and she whimpered, wanting to feel his mouth on hers. His breath was warm against her neck. His lips were soft, barely a whisper along her skin as he kissed a fiery path. He placed gentle kisses along the long column of her neck.

He was so cold, so brutal and calculating out of the dream. She could tell from the soulless look in his eyes, the look he sometimes got when he thought she wasn't looking anymore. Yet, there, in the dream room, he was heat and desire as he stood behind her. Match for match as her own selfish heart called for his touch, knowing that it was nothing more than a dream. She didn't let the details concern her as she felt him press against her, naked flesh to flesh. His cock, a rock hard reminder of what would come, pressed into the small of her back.

"Come with me Eliza, let me please you. Let me take you this time. No holding back, no forcing yourself awake. Just you and me. Here and Now."

His voice was so beautiful, so familiar, and it curled around her as she assumed a real lover might. The city was so stunning. She was startled for a moment as she realized she could indeed see the flickering lights of the city. *How can that be?*

"A dream, Eliza. Nothing more than a dream. You like the city, the way it gleams in the night, and so I created it for you. I created this window with which you can look out whilst I take you because I cannot wait much longer, love. I need to be inside of you like I need to be in your dreams."

The sentence confused her and stole her breath at the same time. He was a figment, a made up persona to be what she wanted him to be, and yet, she would give him anything he wanted.

As she stared out the window, she saw his hand raise and land slightly above hers on the solid glass window. She must have touched it to confirm it was truly there. His low growl in her ear as he nipped the bottom of it sent wetness betwixt her legs. She squirmed, pushing her backside against his cock and shuddering when he reached betwixt them and held himself. She could feel him stroking his shaft, feel as his hand stroked up the thick length and bumped the small of her back.

"Come now, Eliza."

His free hand wrapped around her waist and turned her to him. Her startled gasp changed to a sigh of pleasure as he turned her and ran a finger along her clit. Her hips bucked, even as her hand fell from the window as she turned to him. The motion caused his finger to slip inside her folds. His growl was more like a purr as he stroked along her inner core.

"Damn, Eliza, you're wet enough to bring me to my knees to taste you and see if you taste of chocolate to match your smell."

Her head fell back as he used his knee to push her legs further apart. She trembled under his touch, shook with need and longing to complete what she wanted. Sex. It was a dream, no one would ever know, and she wasn't a virgin, anyway. She wanted it all with Lucius, and she wanted it in this dream. The heat, the desire, the pulsing of her sex when she came screaming his name.

Small whimpers escaped from her as he rubbed the head of his cock against her entrance in small circles that had her seeing a multitude of colors instead of him. Reaching down, she ran her finger slowly down his cock before wrapping her hand around him. She could hardly close it around his thick cock, and the thought sent a wave of liquid betwixt her legs. He grunted and pushed her until her arse pressed against the cold window.

His hips bucked against her, and he dragged his teeth along her neck before he swirled his tongue over the same spot. Her cry was a tangle of pleasure and need whilst his fingers stroked her. The head of his prick nudged her entrance, and she spread her legs wider, sliding down a little as she got lower to the ground.

He hesitated as she pushed against him, taking him deeper. His groan echoed in her ears, and he took control back again as he buried himself balls deep inside her. His hand traced a path down her chin and pulled her eyes to his. She rolled her hips, urging him forward, knowing that if he stopped, she would shatter with or without him.

Lucius' hands grabbed onto her arse and pulled her up, her legs wrapped around his lower back impulsively, and she cried out from the sensation. Eliza's head spun from wave after wave of pleasure that built within. His roar caught her off guard, and she felt his cock jerking inside her. Her body responded, seeking out release, and she clenched around him, clenched and unclenched to drag out his pleasure and threw herself over and lost herself in her own release. She felt her body begin to throb with her release, and she cried out his name. She let her head fall onto his shoulder as their combined breathing filled her ears. The sound was so loud, she could not rid her ears of it as it grew louder and louder . . .

———

GROGGILY, Eliza's hand found the clamoring alarmed clock and shut it off. She sat upright on the bed and rubbed her eyes, trying to force them to focus. She was in her room. There wasn't a big window looking out at the city, there weren't any deeply luxurious sheets or sexy naked men doing wicked things to her. She groaned, hid her head under her pillow and let out a scream.

It was the morning of the third day, the beginning of her temporary dismissal.

"It really was just a dream. Whoever Lucius is, he's just a figment of my imagination. Probably a product of working too hard and not looking for a husband." She threw the pillow across the room with a curse. "And I have to go to my parents today. There is nothing worse." Tossing back the covers, she gasped. She was naked, head to toe in the nude. When she'd passed out, she'd still had on the smoke smothered clothes she'd been wearing. "However did that happen?"

She shook off any ideas that there had been a lover in her room to undress her. She'd been hot and removed them. She may have even awoken, no way of knowing now. She turned her head and snapped her fingers at Jessabelle. The dog happily jogged over to the bedside and sat next to it, awaiting some petting.

Giving the dog a quick pat, she focused on the clock. "Six in the morning. Of course, I wouldn't have set one for the train schedule."

Her shoulder still hurt if she moved the wrong way, and she grimaced as she did so whilst petting Jessabelle. The burns on her hands were the only true lingering pain, though.

She continued to pat Jessabelle's head as the dog followed her through the room as she dressed for the train trip. The corseted top was enough to make her want to die. She hadn't worn one since last Christmas at the festivities, and it was early May, a long time past. She sucked in a deep breath and continued to snap up the front laced corset she'd invented shortly after realizing she couldn't tie the blasted things on her own. The frilled skirt itched at her legs, and she silently cursed the man who decided women ought to be tortured in such a fashion. Men liked women naked. She knew that, so why they buried them in heaps of clothing was beyond her realm of knowledge. Adjusting the small, black-jeweled hat that sat on her head, she stared at the mirror.

She saw her mother staring back. Her hair was coifed in the back, her face freshly scrubbed in the small sink in the room before she dressed. Her eyes looked older, more mature than she'd last remembered them. But the lines of unhappiness that settled in just around her mouth were what reminded her of Maria Dorley. Her mother loved the finer things in life, but when no one was looking, it was easy enough to see the annoyance in her eyes over many of her father's actions.

Another reason she was grateful for the initial cut off from her parents. They couldn't have created an arranged marriage for her because they didn't care about her. Now, she was passed the proper marrying age, and her parents had given up any hope for it. It made the once a year trip home all the more pleasant. Grabbing her work goggles off the dresser, she tucked them into her bag and turned to look at Jessabelle.

"Time to get you to Felicia and Greyston, sweet girl." She grabbed the twine leash off the hook on the wall, and Jessabelle whimpered when she latched it. Eliza sighed and kissed the metal dog on the forehead. "I'm sorry, sweet girl, but you cannot come with me. There are rules against showing off the technology we create to the world, and you would stick out like a red herring."

A cold, hard, metal tongue ran over her hand before Jessabelle barked once and stood up.

"That's my sweet girl."

Eliza grabbed the few bags she had packed and closed the door behind her. If she was going to get Jessabelle in and out of the guild's carriage without notice, she didn't have much time to spare, and she wanted to check over things at her desk one last time before the train.

SIX

Lucius wrapped his fingers around the corner of the brick wall in the alleyway. His body trembled from his release in the dream, and more so from the shock that a sexual release in a dream gave off any flicker of soul energy. He'd bedded women plenty of times in their dreams, and he'd never gotten the energy high he had now. More importantly, he couldn't remember the last time his body had throbbed so hard from the release and had already hardened back up at the thought of doing it again. His breaths punched in and out of his body as he tried to calm his thumping heart.

"Fuck. Is this why some demons are racing off to acquire the mating mark? Can't say I blame the blokes."

He forced himself to stand upright. That close to the guilds, when all the members would be coming back, he didn't want to be detected as anything. Who knew if they would come over to help a man who appeared to be in a drunken stupor. He'd shown up that evening ready to claim Eliza. He was going to knock on the damn Guild doors and pray they didn't get in his way. He hadn't been certain he wouldn't have used his talents to kill them all if they had. But when he'd gotten to the Guild, all the lights had been blazing.

The building looked as if it had suffered a catastrophe of sorts, and coppers were lining the sides of the road. By the time it had all cleared, he'd watched seventeen hunting teams leave the Guild. When he reached out to be certain she was in, he'd been greeted with the energy of her in a deep sleep.

But he hadn't been able to walk away.

He was so juiced up thinking about finally being with her that the only thing he could do was demand she be with him in her dreams. "And she took the bait." His words pulled from his mouth before he'd realized it. His words caught the attention of a young boy, probably someone from the thieves' quarter, running by with a loaf of delicious smelling cinnamon bread. Lucius had a soft spot for the pastries and turned away and down the alley before he accidentally grabbed it from the boy. He didn't kill children. Period.

The walk was anything but relieving. His prick ached as if he hadn't just slept with Eliza in some form. Sure, the sex hadn't been real, but the sensations and the teeth chattering release he'd had were. The stain on his silk pants was more than enough confirmation of that. But he couldn't get the idea of bedding her out of his mind.

Would it stop once I do? Would it get a thousand times worse until I do nothing but sate myself on her day in and day out? Lucius growled and kicked at a glass bottle in his path. "Stupid fucking mating mark. Why the hell isn't there a handbook on this some-where?" He shoved his hands in his pockets and snarled. Of course, he couldn't actually reach his erection from the shallow pockets, but he'd damn sure been wanting too.

The sun would be coming up over the city in two hours. Streaks of pink would muddle the black night into a muted grey, and he was no closer to being able to get Eliza off his mind than he had been before spending a night with her. He hadn't realized it, due to the discomfort of walking with an erection, but he hadn't headed back to his little hovel. In fact, he was standing outside of Greyston's, and the light was peeking through the night sky already. Yet he wasn't tired as he oft was closer toward morning. How could

NIGHTMARE IN STEAM   49

that even be possible? He shrugged and looked up at the sprawling mansion.

"Well, I'm in front of the door of perhaps the one demon who can answer my questions. No harm in knocking."

Looking down at his wrist, he wished he had a watch or pocket timepiece made by the guild. He'd walked so far, he had lost all sense of time, and he'd rarely been outside past dawn.

Taking the front steps two at a time, he made quick work of the eight-step entrance and pounded on the door. The knock echoed through the empty street, and he winced, hoping no one would be too angry.

Greyston Westham was Captain of the Royal Guard. As such, the company he kept when he stayed outside the palace oft had their panties in a twist over the smallest of things, like not getting enough beauty sleep to make the paint the women slathered on their faces cover how ugly they truly were.

He lifted his hand to bang again when Steven, another Incubus Demon that lived with Greyston, opened the door and looked rather annoyed.

"Ah, Mister Willan, what sort of trouble did your nasty habits get you into now?"

He pushed past the annoying demon he'd never gotten along with and walked into the parlour, dropping down onto the suede, green sofa to wait. "None that would be any concern of yours. Where's Greyston? I've got business with him." He thought about adding that part of the business was the leader of Hell wanted him dead. Better to save that for after he had the information he needed about being mated to a human in case Greyston didn't believe Lucius wouldn't kill him.

A sharp moan cut through the air, and it sent a wave of lust through Lucius. He crossed his legs uncomfortably. Steven looked at him with a smirk and started to walk out of the room.

"I suppose that's all the answer you need. When the moaning ceases, feel free to knock. If I were you, I'd just wait. He's very thoroughly pleasing his betrothed." Steven chuckled and walked out of the parlor and back up the stairs.

"No, I don't want a bloody cuppa tea, but thank you for the offer you louse!" He growled low in his throat as another passionate groan, Greyston's this time, echoed off the walls. His hands balled into fists, and if he wasn't careful, he was going to be stroking himself right there in the parlour. When he inhaled, he smelled lavender and chocolate. His Eliza had been there.

THE BRUSH PASSED SMOOTHLY through the dark red strands of her hair. It always did. Even as a Fallen, her hair could never tangle, and her looks could never be anything but perfection. Angels were always perfect, always beautiful and always masters of seduction. She'd heard rumors from the humans, rumors that Angels were chaste and pure. A smile curved on her lips at the ridiculous thought. Even when Angels weren't Fallen, they were anything but chaste.

There also wasn't a supreme deity pulling their strings. They simply existed. Just as all demons did. They fought to keep demons from hurting humans purely because they felt it was their duty to protect those that could not protect themselves. But sex and seduction were always something they had been known for before religion had been added into their mythos. Along with the ability to be the perfect bed partner to whomever they were with. Because again, they simply were perfect. A Fallen Angel was no different in their sexual habits. They just felt no love towards the humans and wanted them dead.

Seraphina was no exception.

She'd fallen hundreds of years before, at the turn of the seventeenth century, and she would never feel shame in her choice. Not anymore. She was never in love with the idea of protection, even before she'd fallen. She'd wanted the Angels to make the other, less important races their slaves. There had been no reason not to, but she'd held her tongue for the sake of her lover, Demetrious. He had been head of one of three battle sects, Angels that specifically sought out demons acting out.

Seraphina closed her eyes and briefly thought about Demetrious. His large, white wings were the first thing she pictured. Then his strong pectoral muscles, the way his purple eyes had looked at her whilst he pounded his body into hers, or the way he'd looked when he laughed. The jar of sleeping powder she held in her hand shattered as the images brought pain and hatred flowing through her.

Her face morphed into an ugly snarl, and she threw the glass pieces at the mirror, not bothering to move as one bounced back and slashed across her cheek. The blood dripping down her pale cheek was as dark as her hair as it dripped down her pale cheek. She kept watching as the skin stitched itself back together, but not before a drop of blood splashed on the floor near her feet. Angel ichor was decadent, even the smallest drop could intoxicate someone, and even as Fallen, they were careful not to spill their own blood.

Demetrious had shared his blood with her oft, not in a vampiric way, but a few small drops before battle. It strengthened their communication whilst fighting and had given her a boost of strength. But, that connection had come with a price.

She'd felt it as the human's stupid knife slammed into his stomach as if it had been her own. Her knees had given out, and a scream had torn past her lips so loud that many of the combatants near her had ceased to fight.

She hadn't been able to get to him, hadn't been able to force her legs to move. The pain had run lines up and down her body, and she guessed the disgusting humans had continued to jab their weapons into them. She'd felt the life drain from her lover just as the will to stay conscious had left her body. When she'd awoken, he had been gone. Dead. When Angels died, they went to Hell, a special section carved out just for Angels like in the nasty underworld. However, they didn't remain long. Once their energy drained from their soul, they merely ceased to be, in any fashion.

So she'd fallen to find him and restore his soul in another's body.

Seraphina had torn her wings from her back that very morning after seeing his body, bloody and broken from a bar fight that demons had tricked humans into participating in. The pain as she had torn each and every feather from her back during a six-hour period was always with her. Always a source of motivation to go on when things felt too hard. Nothing was harder than falling by choice, and she'd done so for love.

When she'd found Demetrious, he'd been disgusted. He'd told her she was unclean, and he would never touch her again. Rage had consumed her. She'd launched herself at him, strangling him, and trying to wring the last life out of his soul as she'd slashed at him with her weapon. She'd succeeded, and when her body had crashed into the ground because his had vanished, she'd sat there for what felt like days. Sat there and plotted.

She was going to take humanity down for what it had done to her. The only way she could do that was to get rid of and make all of the Angels fall so they couldn't stand in the way. A century had passed before she'd managed to seduce the idiot to his death, and now she commanded all the demons in Hell and above ground. It wouldn't be long until she took down the Alliance and began her reign of terror on the humans as she slowly killed every one of them on the planet.

A snore passed over to where she stood, and Seraphina looked up at the mirror, smiling wickedly. Her latest bed partner, an Ice Demon, lay exhausted on the bed. The pleasant thrum in her body from a delicious round of sex was the only reason she hadn't slaughtered him when she'd finished coming. He'd been a willing partner, as so many were for a taste of Angel blood. She would let him live for his accomplishments, but only after she woke him, and his tongue pleasured her from inside out to stop her from worrying if the coward Lucius was doing as he had been ordered.

THE VEINS IN LUCIUS' neck were threatening to burst. He'd been waiting a little over forty minutes, according to the clock on the wall.

For twenty of those minutes, he'd been doing everything humanly possible not to stroke himself to release in his friend's front room. But the sounds of sex had been too much. He'd slipped into a trance, not to invade anyone's dreams, but simply to have his own. He hadn't dreamt of Eliza or anyone for that matter. He'd simply tranced out to avoid pissing someone as strong as Greyston off by having him walk down to a demon pleasuring himself in his home. Footsteps on the stairs had jerked him out of it. He was always acutely aware of his surroundings whilst in those states, his safety required it.

The footsteps grew closer, and he pushed himself off the couch. Greyston was almost halfway down the staircase; a small red-haired female was tucked behind him, fully clothed, but still obviously in his protection. He heard the slap before anything else.

"Honestly, Greyston, get out of my way. I hunted and fucked demons for Gods' sake, I can walk down the stairs first when you think there's someone in here."

He watched, with a smile tickling his lips, as the woman who could only be Felicia, shoved past. Greyston's growl was deep and angry, but he didn't get to respond before his eyes landed on Lucius.

Lucius could see the visible sigh of relief in his friend. He'd never minded a visit before, strange that he would be so nervous now. Even if he had a mate to protect.

"Lucius. What are you doing here?" his voice was tight, his eyes laced with concern and he tried to shove Felicia behind him again.

"Really, Greyston, if it's someone you know, I'd think you'd let me walk down the stairs like the adult that I—" Her voice cut out mid-sentence as a strange buzzing filled the room.

Lucius had no idea where it was coming from. It was soft, barely audible, but her eyes shifted at the sound.

His eyes darted around the room, from the ridiculous lace curtains he hoped Felicia had put up to the clock ticking harmlessly on the wall above the mantle.

"Demon!" Felicia snarled and hurled herself down the staircase before he'd even processed him being a demon was a bad thing. Her fiancé was a damned demon.

She came at him, her body slamming into his and knocking him backwards and down onto the sofa. He did his best to shove her off without damaging her. Whilst he wasn't a champion fighter, he was still by far stronger than a measly human female on any given day. With his energy up as high as it was after dream fucking Eliza, he could certainly do damage to a petite human female.

Felicia clawed at him, even as her foot wrapped around his ankle once he stood up. Taken off balance, he crashed backwards and flipped over the bloody couch. His head rang from the smack on the floor, and he tried to stand, but Felicia slammed her foot down onto his throat. His windpipe crushed under her slender, barefoot, and he wondered how she was doing it. His hands wrapped around her foot, and he slammed upwards, knocking her backwards and off his neck. She thumped into the ground and was back up on her feet at the same time he was.

If she didn't stop, he was going to have to hurt her and scare her into stopping. Her fingers wrapped around his neck, and he felt them as they dug in. It wasn't painful like the Stranglehold Demons nails, but the pressure didn't feel too right after she tried to stamp him to death.

"Greyston—" his voice squeaked out, barely getting past Felicia's fingers, "—come and remove your woman before she kills me without me getting to tell you what I came to inform you."

His vision was getting hazy, and he closed his eyes, dropping into a trance when Greyston's laugh sounded next to his ear.

He opened his eyes and saw his friend holding the tiny scrap of a woman back with one hand. She was infuriated, her eyes dilated wide, and she kept swinging her arms at Lucius, trying to land a punch.

"Felicia. Stop. Stop it."

She strained against Greyston, and Lucius had to admire her

determination. Apparently, being mated to a demon hadn't changed her desire to fight them with her Alliance family.

"Felicia, he's a friend. He's a good guy."

He peered into Greyston's eyes, and his friend shrugged his shoulders.

"Okay, that's a lie, but he isn't someone to kill. If I let go, will you let me introduce you before you go and choke his brains out?"

She frowned and nodded. A second later, Greyston slowly unwrapped his fingers from her forearm. She looked tense, ready to spring at any moment, but she didn't move.

"Pleasure to meet you, Miss Felicia Gannon. I've heard a lot about you in the underbelly of the city." Her eyes spit fire at him, and he took an inadvertent step back, raising his hands. "I come in peace. I have information, information on Seraphina. But I have questions too."

"He's not saying anything that's making me not want to kill him, Greyston. And who the fuck is Seraphina?"

Her fierce gaze was on his friend, and he idly wondered if she thought it the name of an ex-lover. Luckily for Greyston, Seraphina really wasn't.

"Calm down now, little grasshopper. I promise she is nothing to me, but everything to your Alliance. And since he's too daft to protect himself, I'll save his arse for the hundredth time again. Felicia, this is Lucius Willan, a Nightmare Demon."

Her eyes grew wide, and he could see the tension in every muscle of her body. She wanted to jump on him again, but she was holding back.

"Yes, he kills people. Bad people if he can make it happen."

She maintained her glower on his. "You left out who Seraphina is. Now, Greyston."

Lucius coughed to hide his laugh. Greyston was a dominant, for Felicia to be speaking out in such fashion meant she clearly knew that she was the only one his Incubus Demon friend would ever be able to get it up for again, and she took advantage of it.

"She's the ruler of Hell. The big bad boss lady who keeps dispatching the demons that you keep killing. And no, I don't mean Lucifer. Seraphina tossed his arse into the pits of Hell over a century back. She's running the game, and she hates humans."

Lucius watched as the wheels in Felicia's head slowly turned like the cogs and gears in a clock. Understanding dawned quickly on her face, and he admired Greyston for finding such a competent mate.

Greyston swung his gaze onto Lucius. "Now, what are you doing here?"

He contemplated skipping Eliza for a moment. Things were bad enough, and the warning really should come first. Should have, but didn't. His eyes locked on the mating mark on Greyston's wrist, and he couldn't ask anything, not until he asked about Eliza, more specifically about sex with Eliza.

"Right, thanks for not killing me, by the way." He inclined his head quickly toward Felicia. "I want to ask something first."

Greyston looked less than thrilled as he crossed his muscular arms over his bare chest. "Quickly, Lucius."

"I want to know about Eliza Dorley."

Wrong question to ask, well, wrong statement to lead with. Felicia had her forearm under his chin and slammed him into the wall so fast his head spun from it. Greyston had to be training her. That was the only answer. Whilst her arm dug into his throat, she lifted her knee and ground it into his crotch. He grimaced and clamped his mouth shut from the pain. The air whooshed out of his lungs, and Felicia's face was close enough to his to bite his.

"What about her, demon? And be careful what you say. I may not have my weapon on me, thanks to feeling safe in my own home, but I can still take you down without it. It will just be much slower. Much, much slower, and with an added degree of pain."

Lucius tried to swallow around the death grip she had on his neck and choked. His eyes bored into hers, silently requesting she let him go if he was going to answer her question.

"Felicia, ease up a little. He can't answer you like that, and I'd very much like to know how he has the name of the only female inventor in the guild." Greyston raised a brow and leaned against the back wall. He almost looked casual, but the anger radiating out of his green eyes matched Felicia's.

Lucius felt her hand ease up on him a smidge, and he coughed, his throat raw and angry from the second chokehold.

"You may want to let me go. If I can't give you proof, you'll never listen to me, and I'm not sharing my damn information until I get an answer from your lover, hunter."

Felicia made a sound much akin to a growl and let her hand go completely. Her eyes trained on his, and Greyston shifted to block the door. Lucius was stuck.

"She's my bloody fucking mate."

Felicia's mouth dropped open slightly, and she snapped it shut almost as quick. Greyston, however, chuckled.

"What's so funny about this?" Felicia's anger hadn't simmered a bit.

"This isn't something he'd lie about. Lucius is known for being somewhat of a Casanova in demon circles. He wouldn't make up being mated. He certainly would come running, tail betwixt his legs, with questions to the only other person he knows that's mated to a human."

Greyston laughed then, long and hard, and the seconds it encompassed began to grate on Lucius' nerves. The energy he'd had from his liaison with Eliza was fading, and he had questions to ask.

"All the same, Willan, care to prove this?"

It was his to turn snort out a laugh. "You won't like where it is, honest." He didn't wait for a reply, simply undid the silver buckle on his silk trousers and let them drop to the floor. He heard a distinct feminine intake of breath, followed by a growl. He turned and stuck his arse up into the air a touch. "See the fucking mark, Incubus? Happy?"

Both Felicia and Greyston were in stitches laughing so hard. He muttered to himself as he tugged up the pants.

"My questions now."

Greyston chuckled and coughed, trying to force his laughter to stop. How Lucius wished someone had been there to laugh at him a few months back.

"First, what did you come to tell me? I'll take pity on your poor soul and give you a few bits of information, but we're different species, you know mating in Incubi comes with a much higher," he cleared his throat, and his eyes shifted to Felicia, "price." He looked at the floor as he said the word, probably trying not to piss her off.

Lucius bit his tongue, wanting to force the information from Greyston. He had the powers, but he lacked any physical prowess that could compare with the big demon, and he wasn't in the mood to fight. He wanted to find out why he smelled his mate and leave. Greyston gestured to the sofa, and they sat, but Felicia seemed content enough to leave the room with a kiss on Greyston's cheek.

The sound of barking, almost metallic in nature, cut him off before he could answer. Banging accompanied the sound, and not one, but two metal dog-like creatures bounded into the room. One appeared to mimic a Labrador, the other a hound. But they had none of the right colorings, and their movements were harsh. They really were creatures of metal. *But how?*

"Fido! Jessabelle! Down pups!" Greyston's voice boomed, and the dogs quickly hushed.

How are these dogs? What happened to them? The one that resembled a hound slunk away from Greyston and rested its head in Lucius' lap. He smiled, he had a soft spot for dogs, and if this were a dog, it wouldn't get any less affection from him. The other, however, jumped straight onto the sofa and into Greyston's lap.

"Fido! Get off me, you tin can," Greyston growled.

Lucius couldn't believe how far the alpha demon had fallen.

"He is not a tin can!" Felicia's shout came from the upstairs.

Lucius chuckled as he patted the hound's head. It was an odd, cold sensation, but the creature seemed to like it. "I suppose you must be Jessabelle then." The cold slide of metal over his palm had him look down at his hand. It had licked him.

"Your mated one created these. She's brilliant really. Felicia said she's the only one at the Guild with such skill with the metal. If you look closely, you'll notice Jessabelle is alert, not just a set of motions and behaviors like Fido. She's much more alive, and it creeps the fuck out of me. Eliza was sent off to her parents, she leaves for Halifax around half past nine actually, so the contraption stays here, with Felicia's."

"So that's why I smell her. Greyston can I stay here for a few hours? Traveling in the day is rough, but I need to meet her."

"Excuse me? Meet her? You had to have already fucked her to have a mark like that."

"Yes, about that. I haven't. Not really. I was sent to kill an Alliance member. Seraphina wanted dream intel. As you can guess, it didn't wind up going down that way." Greyston didn't say a word, so he kept going. "We didn't even fuck in the dream. What we did, well it was enough to trigger it I guess, but now I can't stop thinking about getting her under me. About feeling her warm skin under my body as I claim her for real." He looked down, somewhat embarrassed. He didn't mind talking about his bed partners usually, but this just felt wrong.

Greyston patted him on the shoulder. "Sorry to hear that. It's not going to go away. It gets worse for my kind once we have found ours. Different species, different rules. Too bad Seraphina went on a spree and took out your people."

He ignored the sympathy in Greyston's voice. It wasn't a secret that he was the last of the Nightmare Demons. Everyone knew it was his fault too. Refusing her and tormenting her had occurred from him and his king. Along with her bargain had come a death sentence to his kind. To show him who was in control. That night, he'd fucked her, filled her dreams with nightmares and had run. She'd been paralyzed enough to give him some leeway, but he'd wound up on a slab for almost twenty years as payback.

"Well, there aren't. And thanks." He had three questions, but he knew the answers wouldn't matter. There was no outrunning a mating mark. He was going to have to find some way to court Eliza Dorley. He sighed and rubbed his hand over his face.

"I'd love to tell you that was the worst thing I came to share with you. You're on Seraphina's hit list. She doesn't appreciate you running around helping the Alliance take down her demons." No point in sugar coating it.

Greyston had been helping the humans for around eight years, and any loyalty he would've felt to the demons had been squashed when Seraphina had passed the law that all lesser demons, all that could remind her of humans, were to be punished and kicked from Hell on sight.

"I see." Greyston sat there and stared at the clock on the wall before turning to Lucius and asking the question that was going to be impossible to dodge. "You're the hit-man I take it?"

"I'm not going to do it if that's why you're thinking. I'll find someone else, another demon masquerading as a human, and they'll just have to do." He hoped his friend saw the sincerity in his eyes or else he was likely about to experience a lot of pain.

Greyston nodded once and shoved Fido off his lap. "Good. See to it. You should be able to get a few hours sleep. The quarters is up the stairs, five doors on the left. It's yours. Be quiet on your way out." He looked at Jessabelle and laughed. "I was going to tell her to go with you, guard your sneaking arse, but it looks as if she'd likely help you murder me in my sleep." He walked to the stairs and stopped a few steps up, but didn't turn around. "Thanks for the warning. I'll repay the favor someday I'm sure." With that, he went to his room.

SEVEN

"GET HIM OUT! Greyston, I want him out now!" Felicia's voice pierced his ears and jolted him out of his trance.

He couldn't help but laugh quietly to himself. Felicia had been such an easy target. All tucked in bed and already worried the news meant someone wanted to hurt Greyston.

"Lucius!"

Jessabelle jumped off the bed and bolted out the doors. He heard Greyston's steps running down the hall, and he grabbed his shirt and tugged it over his head. Sapping energy from a small dalliance in Felicia's dream had not been his best plan. His shirt was stuck over his head when the door swung up.

The shirt stuck over his head, Lucius sailed across the room before he could tug it down. His back slammed into the wall, and he cried out, unaware of how strong Greyston really was. *Note, do not piss off a mated Incubus Demon. Ever.*

Greyston wrapped his fingers in the shirt and lifted him off the floor. Lucius' feet dangled as his friend punched him straight in the face and dropped him. Pain shot through his body from the impact, and he swallowed.

"You ever think to touch my female again, and you won't need to find another mark for Seraphina. I'll kill you myself. Get out, and the next time I hear from you, it better be you collecting on your favor. So this is a free pass. Show up again, and I will kill you, Lucius."

There was nothing but cold fury rolling off Greyston in waves. Lucius did his best to pull himself off the floor, but he had to brace himself on the bed, and still, the pain vibrated throughout his body. Greyston hadn't stuck around to get an apology, which was good. Lucius wouldn't have one. He was a Nightmare Demon, and he couldn't ignore prey out on the table anymore than an unmated Incubus Demon could ignore the scent of arousal.

Jessabelle had crept out of the room earlier, and he was oddly disappointed. Grabbing his boots, he stepped into them and headed out—he had a train to catch.

ELIZA'S SHOULDER felt as if it would give out under the weight of her two travel bags. It wasn't healed enough to be carrying the amount of weight she was attempting. The Guild's carriage had taken her to the train station, but she needed to get her ticket still. Great Western Railway had only been operational for a year. The technology they used in the guild was a reconstruct of the steam engines used to make the trains run. But these were giants, beasts of metal, and only the wealthy could afford travel on them.

She struggled to make her way to the ticket clerk and wondered briefly if she would be better able to carry her belongings had she been a hunter, not a scientist. She didn't bother to mask her troubles as she simply dropped the two cases to the floor at her feet.

"One ticket to Halifax, please."

The man behind the window was young, and she wondered how he'd gotten a job at the rail station instead of as a merchant or soldier. The war with America had taken many of their militant forces. She personally never knew if peace was truly upon them or if, one day, the demon threat would get so big that the secret of what lurked below wouldn't be announced to the people of London, of all her majesty's territories.

"Three pounds please, miss."

She flinched at the cost. It wasn't oft an Alliance member had to pay for things. As such, they made a meager wage, and the fare would all but clean her out until they allowed her back.

It's not as if you have any place else to go, she thought as she placed the currency under the small glass circle and retrieved her ticket.

Eliza groaned low as she bent to grab her bags again. Slowly, she hefted them off the floor. Her head was still slightly down as she started to look for her gate, and she gasped as she crashed into something.

Her eyes traveled up. No, not something, someone. A man dressed in a simple pair of silken trousers and a grey-dyed silk shirt. It clung to him slightly, and she took in the muscular tones of his arm and knew from the impact that the impressive muscles extended to his chest. She'd felt them and had mistaken him for a wall or lamppost. She swallowed hard as her eyes continued to make their way up his body, and she felt as if she might faint as they took in his face.

Two dark, black eyes looked down into hers. *Lucius.* Her heart pounded in her chest so loud, she almost missed him apologizing for their collision. She blew out a breath and thanked God that she hadn't said his name aloud.

Don't be foolish, Eliza. Lucius is a dream! This man is just similar. She looked at him one more time, and the heat in his eyes was a dead mimic for how Lucius had looked whilst stroking his cock in her dream.

Wetness pooled betwixt her legs as desire almost took her to her knees. She stumbled, and the man reached out and caught her. Where his hands touched, she swore she felt some sort of shock occur. His grip was light, but it felt to her as if he hung onto her for dear life. As if she was the only thing keeping him from falling, or as if she was the air he breathed. The thought caused her to sigh and lean against him, wanting to feel him, but she managed to stop herself —just barely before reaching out to touch him. Women did not go leaning upon strangers. Not women of her social circle. Well, her parents' social circle.

"Please forgive me. I'm afraid my bags were far too heavy, and I wasn't looking." She could feel a flush warming her cheeks, like when Kellan would compliment her, and she darted her eyes back to the ground.

"Never apologize. I love when beautiful women bump into me."

His voice burned into her soul. It was Lucius' voice. She was going crazy. She had inhaled something when that cycle she'd been working on went up in flames. So this man was real, but her hearing and seeing Lucius had been a hallucination conjured up in her mind. His words didn't even register, and she just kept staring at the ground.

"Are you okay, love?"

Love. That was what Lucius had called her in the dream. She shook her head so hard to be rid of the thought that she almost made herself sick.

"Yes. Sorry. I'm going to visit my parents in Halifax, and well, we aren't the best of families. I suppose I'm just in my own head." She finally lifted her head and looked back at him. Those deep black eyes called to her, set her body on fire. She wanted him to touch her again, but his hands had already let go when she'd righted her balance.

"Halifax you said?" His eyes continued to bore into hers, and though she was standing up on her own, she felt as if he was still holding her, still touching her somehow.

She nodded slowly, not trusting that her voice wouldn't come out as lust laden as her thoughts. The smile that lit up his face gave depth to those eyes of his, amusement seemed to flicker in them, and she felt a pang of desire in her gut. This man couldn't be the one from her dreams. But how else could she explain him? She hadn't eaten more than toast and jam that morning after leaving Greyston's manor. Could that induce hallucinations of this level?

"Perhaps you'd like to ride with me? I've got a private car." He must have sensed her hesitation because he lightly touched her on the elbow. "Think of it as a way to make up for nearly plowing you down on my way to the tracks. Plus, I can manage to carry these bags of yours."

She noticed that he didn't seem to have anything on him except fine clothes that almost appeared to be slept in.

She looked from her bags to the track location. They weren't numbered, but it was easy to tell which was which. Lugging her belongings might only lead to another head on collision, and perhaps the next time would be with someone who wasn't such a gentleman.

"I don't know about sharing a car, sir. Yet, perhaps you can carry my things the short distance whilst I make up my mind?"

"It would be my pleasure, miss." He nodded and grabbed her bags off the ground.

"Miss Dorley." She trotted behind him to keep up and was a little ruffled that his response to her name had been merely to look over his shoulder and wink. All she'd needed was his name, something to prove to her that he was not the fantastic dream lover from the past weeks. He'd not answered once.

"I'm to the right, two train cars in. Have you decided to take me up on my offer?"

He flashed a dazzling smile in her direction, and again, she felt an insane need to be with him. To take a stranger up on an offer. She was grabbing her ticket from her bag, wanting to check on the status of her own seat. She had a private car as well, but there was no need to tell the gentleman that. Based on their dressed attire it would have been easy for them both to make assumptions about the social status of the other.

The sound of the communicator jerked Eliza's hand, and she dropped the ticket on the floor. She cursed because she was stepping into the car as the ticket fluttered lifelessly to the ground below and there wouldn't be any time to rescue it prior to departure. She snarled at no one at all and pretended she didn't hear the ringing of the communicator. The device was still secretive to the people of the

London, and if she made a grab for her bag, the gentleman would seemingly inquire what was going on. As it was, a few people heading to their cars turned in her direction. She prayed a flush wasn't creeping up her cheeks.

"I don't suppose I have a choice now do I?" She tried to force her voice to sound on the side of casualness but feared the tension she was withholding had leaked out, anyway.

He grinned again and winked, making it the second time now she'd seen playfulness in him. The man in her dreams had been all hard body and hot kisses. He'd never appeared friendly before.

See you're letting your lack of bedding get to you, Eliza. Really.

He offered her his arm, and she lightly placed her hand in the crook of his elbow. The small streak of lust chimed again, and she glanced up. The man was gazing down at her, all playfulness gone from his eyes. She was behaving foolishly, but if she could sit with her carry bags on her side of the seat, she would be safe. She'd slipped the crystal gun she'd always had hidden away in her room into one. Her aim was likely to be dastardly, but in close quarters, if this man proved to be anything more than a kind stranger, she had a feeling even she wouldn't miss.

He stopped and carefully removed her arm from his at the door to their train compartment. "Ladies first, Miss Dorley."

He smiled again, and once more, she melted. If she didn't find a way to get her dreams out of her head, there was no telling what would occur in the car. The journey to Halifax was a little over six hours, and if he continued to prove to be such a temptation, she was going to have to find a new place to stay.

She watched as he carefully set her bags down on the bench along the right side of the room. But he didn't sit. Instead, he twisted his bow tie and smiled warmly at her.

"I know it's early, but I find starting a train ride in the dining car is best. Not as many people clamoring for the food. Would you like to accompany me?"

Eliza's mouth spoke before she'd had any time to process the idea of a formal meal with a stranger. It could be akin to courtship, and there was none present that would not castigate them as sinners for sharing a car, but it hadn't stopped her.

"Yes."

"Magnificent! I will go arrange something for us. Shall you meet me in the dining car for some tea in say, ten minutes?"

She fumbled for the pocket watch she owned. All clockworkers owned one as a means to show off the work, but the hunter's pocket-watches contained a small crystal shard, which matched the ones on the street designated to pick up traces of demon. Hers, however, was just a pocket timepiece, since she wasn't a hunter. Her stomach grumbled as she checked the time. It wasn't even ten past ten, but she was hungry now that he'd mentioned it.

"That would be wonderful. Please let me change out of my traveling hat and coat, and I shall meet you."

The man said nothing, simply turned and walked from the car. She blew out the breath she'd been holding. Whether it had been to release some of the sexual tension streaming through her body or simply one of exhaustion, she wasn't certain.

"You've lost your mind, Eliza. This is positively ridiculous." She pulled the white gloves from her hands and shoved them into the bag closest to her. "Really, though, it's not as if he can do any harm to you in a public car, and he certainly hasn't cornered you to pick-pocket. You have no pockets." She rambled on with reasons to run, and the one reason she couldn't as she took off her coat, hung it over the seat, removed her hat and placed it on the shelf above her. She wished there was a mirror to check her hair, but she just had to hope that removing the hat hadn't pulled the pins down and ruined the up-do.

She strode quickly to the dining car, eager to get the man's name and show herself how foolish she had been. Smiling to the attendant as he opened the door, her eyes found her companion quickly. He was handsome, even from a distance. Absolutely striking in his silken clothes. She was staring so intently, she bumped into the table closest to her, and the man jumped up as if to catch her. She offered him a small smile and laughed.

"Please sit. I am not the most graceful of women when I must wear such finery." She hadn't meant to let on that she didn't always dress to those standards, but it had slipped out.

He sat, but not before assuring she had reached the table. If she wasn't mistaken, she thought she heard a low growl from him as the dining attendant pulled her chair out for her, but that was foolish. It must have been the wheels grinding on the track. Perhaps it needed some oil.

He smiled and thanked the wait staff as their glasses were filled with chilled water and a pot of steaming water was set down for mid-morning tea. Eliza couldn't help but realize how graceful the man was. The turn of his body, the tone of his voice, all of it. Perhaps graceful wasn't the right word, charming. Charming was the proper term. This man was well and truly fascinating, and she was sitting in a mostly empty dining car having a spot of tea with him. Her heart fluttered when he looked at her over his water glass.

"I find cool water helps when I am tired. Please, have as much tea as you would like." As if to indicate his sincerity, he picked up the white porcelain pot and poured it into the waiting teacup. "I do not presume to know what type of tea you like, Miss Dorley. I assume you can handle that." He winked and picked up his water glass once more.

She carefully looked over the three tea satchels on the plate and selected a sachet of Chamomile; hoping it would still the attraction he kept stirring in her. "I've never done this before," she blurted as she picked up her tea mug. He raised an eyebrow and chuckled. "I mean, I've never taken up with," she leaned in and lowered her voice considerably, "a stranger."

It only made him laugh louder, and she knew she flushed as two elderly women at the table nearest to them, turned in their direction.

"Well then, I shall consider myself honored. How can I put you more at ease?"

His hand reached over and laid over hers, and she sucked in a breath at the sensation. His thumb began to rub small circles over the topside of her hand, and she briefly wondered if he was the well-intentioned man she had thought. It wasn't as if she was outside the guild oft enough to judge men other than the scientists, clockworkers and hunters.

"Your name would be most appreciative. I don't think anything about this situation is entirely in the realm of proper, but a name would help." She saw something flicker in his black eyes, something akin to panic, and she pulled her hand out of his. She was beginning to lean more and more towards the idea that he was not a good man. But then, he smiled at her and leaned back in his chair.

"My name is Willan."

Inwardly, she frowned. So it was true. He wasn't the real life embodiment of her fantasy come to life. She wondered if her look of disappointment was mirrored in her eyes and quickly tried to banish it.

Honestly, shouldn't you be happy he isn't? How crazy would you be if you told a man you just met that you'd had nights of wild encounters with him in your sleep?

"It's nice to meet you, Willan. Thank you for that. I do think that will help put me more at ease and be a less uptight companion." She flinched at the word companion. It sounded as if she was offering herself up to him. Wouldn't she, if he actually asked, though? The answer made her nervous, and she hastily picked up a tart.

"Now, give me that smile again. Make me think you are having fun, so I do not throw you over my shoulder and take you away to ravish you." He grinned and waggled his brows.

She laughed, and he smiled. The way they interacted was strange as if they truly did know one another. The small morning meal continued in that fashion. Cups of tea were drunk, and she'd even loosened up enough to laugh at his jokes and attempt one of her own, which he politely laughed at.

All the whilst, their knees touched under the table and her body heated with an urge to actually go and be alone with the strange man. Her body was humming with need, and when he stood, she did as well. God help her when they made it back to his train car because the look he gave her as she rose with him shot chills through her that only sent her desire soaring. Three hours to go, and if her body had any control over her brain, she would be his before the train stopped in Halifax.

EIGHT

Lucius pushed open the door to the train car and almost ripped it off the wall. He wasn't the strongest demon around, but with how energized his body was, it hadn't seemed to matter. For the past hour and thirty minutes, he'd sat across from Eliza, barely refraining from shoving everything off the small table and taking her in front of everyone. She was a vision in her blue gown, even if he knew how many laced and hooked undergarments resided underneath. All he could focus on was taking it off her and undoing all the frivolous bottom pieces with his teeth.

He left the car door open, wanting her to feel safe. A strange idea, since he was usually in the habit of setting off every fear a person possessed, but he didn't want that with her. She'd looked at him and seen him, the man from her dreams. It had been a risk he'd been concerned with. But many did not remember their encounter with him the next morning.

The look in her eyes when they'd first collided had betrayed her memories. Delight. Lust. Confusion. Worry. When she'd asked his name, he'd felt the blood drain from his face. Telling her that information would have been no problem if he was starting the seduction from scratch. But he wasn't, he needed to be a different man to her, just for now. And he hadn't lied. He might have only produced a surname, but she hadn't pressed for more. So for now, he would be Willan. He just hoped he could convince her of everything he needed to.

More importantly, he hoped she didn't react to him as Felicia had.

"You may close it, Willan. I know I expressed fears prior, and perhaps I am naïve, but you've been nothing but kind to me. If you wish for privacy in your own car, I will not infringe upon it." She sat down on the side he'd designated for her and went about pulling at pins in her hair.

Without warning, the blonde locks cascaded down her back, and he felt the strongest need to grab her by it and smell the lavender bath oil he could scent from a few feet away. His prick pressed up into his trousers, and he debated betwixt fixing it and ignoring it. Her eyes were looking at something in her lap, and he used the time to adjust himself. The problem was, the movement of his hand across his hardened cock caused a choke of pleasure from him. When she looked up, he couldn't help himself any longer.

"Miss Dorley, I think it might be proper if we got to know one another better since we are traveling to the same destination in the same car. We might run into each other there and knowing one another would be much nicer." He sat across from her, his eyes locked onto hers waiting for an answer. He could sense her heart was pounding and that it wasn't fear. There was a distinct difference in the way the heart jackrabbited when it pounded in fear and the quick, deep beats of someone on the verge of a sexual liaison.

She swallowed deeply, and he watched the muscles in her neck. He wanted to drop his lips to her skin and taste her, but he couldn't. So he clenched his teeth instead.

"I couldn't agree more. Please, Willan, call me Eliza. I know it's a bit informal, but as you said, we are sharing a car and need to know those things, should we need to prove we are a proper couple."

Her eyes blinked rapidly, and he didn't find a reason to stop himself as he changed sides of the car. Their legs pressed together, and even through their clothes, he felt the heat.

"A wonderful point, Eliza. If we are to be able to pull that off, well then, perhaps—" He didn't wait for permission.

His lips touched hers, and his body exploded with passion. Eliza went still for a moment, and he feared he'd made a mistake. She sighed and leaned into him. She didn't hesitate to open her mouth as he ran the tip of his tongue over the seam of her lips. She cried out and pressed closer to him. Her breasts connected with his chest, and he let one hand wrap into her hair. The other, however, trailed down the bodice of her dress and stopped on her thigh. He was careful as he pulled at the blue dress fabric. He feared any movement that was too quick would alarm her and send her running.

But she made no move to stop him. Only small moans of pleasure and panting came from her. His cock was ready to burst, but if he was going to seduce a woman of such good breeding, he was going to have to see to her first. There would be time once she'd accepted him for him to sate his needs. He knew from her dreams, she would be more than perfect wrapped around his cock when the time came.

Lucius slipped his hand under the gown and slid it up her thigh. It was covered in stockings of course, and he cursed the idiot that felt women should wear so many layers. He nipped at her lower lip as he did his best to tug aside the frocked underwear she wore. His finger moved over her, and he found her wet, ready and his for the taking. He pushed a finger inside her tight body, and she arched off the seat, even as her mouth sought to tangle faster with his. She was needy, and he was going to give it to her. His finger moved in and out at a slow pace, dragging across her clit and wiggling whilst inside her, touching the spot that held the most pleasure. She mewled, and his hips bucked with need as he added a second finger. She was tight that he groaned, knowing the reality of how her inner walls would grip him when he finally sank into her body.

The lavender smell was intoxicating, and he pulled his mouth free from hers and dropped to the floor of the car. He had no reason to think she'd let him taste her, but he was too far gone to stop himself. Her whimper sliced through the compartment when he pulled back, and he quickly tugged her dress up.

"Willan!" Her voice was strained, infused with lust and a pleading for him to continue.

He knew she wasn't a virgin from their dreams, but knowing he could do this to her sent a buzz through him. He hooked his thumbs in her underwear and pulled them down to her knees before leaning forward and placing a kiss across her core. She bucked against him, and he could picture the need in her eyes as he licked a path from top to bottom and suckled her clit.

She tasted sweet, not quite like the chocolate she sometimes smelled of, but still a rich taste on his tongue. He growled low and slammed his tongue betwixt her folds, driving it in and out and swirling it inside her. Her hips bucked, riding his tongue. As he darted it in and out of her wet heat, he ran his thumb over her swollen bud, increasing her pleasure.

His cock throbbed and pulsed with need, and he had half a mind to stroke himself as he went, but his thoughts were too addled with the delicious taste of her to see to himself.

Her breath was coming out in hard pants, and her hips were bucking hard against the seat to reach her orgasm. With one last lick, he began to gently rub her clit. Back and forth, faster and faster, until her cry broke across the train car.

It wouldn't have been so bad if his hadn't been louder as he came from the sheer act of watching her release. His breaths were ragged, and he wasn't sure he could handle any more. He was getting ready to slip out from her skirts and see that she was all right when that same loud buzzing noise from before went off.

She tensed, and her knee knocked him in the face. He pulled back, and the look on her face warred betwixt pleasant and terror. She hadn't been ready for him, not mentally. His urge to claim her faded, like water thrown onto a winter's fire.

"Eliza, I'm sorry."

The damned shrill noise came from one of her bags again, and she jumped back. He knew it would be a guild device, but she was trying hard not to check whatever it was. Lucius could only hope it wasn't a device to let her know she was with a demon. He'd planned to tell her that later, after a few days of getting to know one another.

She looked pale as it sounded a third time, and the smallest sensation of fear gripped him. He stood up and walked out of the train car. He wasn't sure where he would go, with an impossible to hide the bulge in his pants, but he needed to give her space for a few moments.

HER HEAD WAS SPINNING AROUND and around, the train car barely able to come into focus. What had she just done? "More importantly, why do you not feel guilty about it?" Her voice was breathy, and she could feel her heart pounding so hard in her chest that she thought it was going to explode out. The shrill awkward chime of the communicator went off for the fourth time, and she shook her head, trying to remove the lust induced haze but failing. "Who on Earth could bloody be calling me? No one even knows I took this damned thing!"

Which wasn't entirely true. Felicia and Greyston knew.

She hastily unzipped her bag and shoved her hands in, carelessly pushing clothes aside until she found the brass device—glowing a faint green in the bottom of her bag. She snatched it up and pressed one of six buttons on its face. To anyone else, it would appear to be a watch with a few more dials. To any person in the Alliance, it was sometimes the only thing betwixt a dead hunter and a dead demon. They worked the same way as the magnets that lined the streets, only they resonated betwixt magnetic pulses that could be assigned to the crystals by polarizing them. The process was the only one at the guild she'd never understood, probably never would understand either as it wasn't her area. Nonetheless, the devices worked and allowed a very remote and sometimes broken sounding communication betwixt people.

"Felicia?" That was the only excuse for someone calling, the only person who'd known she had illegally taken Alliance tech out of the guild that morning.

"Eliza! Thank goodness I've reached you. Why have you been ignoring your communicator?" Her friend's tone was laced with both relief and annoyance.

Eliza felt her own irritation bristle at the idea she had to answer to anyone, especially when she'd just been discharged from her life for an unspecified amount of time.

"Well, think about it. I am on a train to Halifax . . . a train that, by design, mimics our technology and half of London rejected as bollocks and magic when it was first unveiled. Let's think about why I wouldn't pick up a device that was allowing me to talk to a woman over two kilometers away!" She hadn't meant to raise her voice, Felicia was most likely only worried, but it had happened anyway.

Thankfully, Willan had closed the door as he'd left and no one could hear her crazy shouts.

"Right, sorry. Look I need to talk to you. Are you alone?"

Eliza didn't respond, she let the stupidity of the question hang in the air. Felicia was impulsive but rarely so addled minded.

"Dumb question. You wouldn't have answered. Have you been alone this whole time? No compartment mates of any kind?"

"That's an unexpected question. I actually lost my ticket betwixt the train carriage and the ground the first time my communicator went off in public. Luckily, there was a nice gentleman ready to step in and help. Without him, and I presume thanks to you, I would have been waiting for the train tomorrow and been knocking on your door for a place to stay."

"Eliza, it's important. What's the man's name?"

Bile churned in her gut. What could be so important that Felicia's voice hitched in pace?

"Willan. I suppose that could be his proper name or his surname,

I didn't think to ask. It hadn't seemed important." *But perhaps you should have before you allowed him to kiss you in such a place.*

Eliza almost missed Felicia's response as her head swam with images and sensations of what she and Willan had just done. It was unlike anything she'd ever experienced. Though she knew she should run screaming from the compartment, all she wanted was for him to come back so she could explain to him she wasn't angry. Oddly enough she hoped he would consider courting her properly.

"Fuck! Bloody fucking hell. Greyston this is all your fault! Now she's alone with him!"

Eliza was confident the last part wasn't meant for her, but the first?

She tried to keep her voice calm and steady. Throwing it all into a tizzy had never helped in the lab, and it wouldn't do any good in a crisis either. "Felicia, who am I stuck with and why is this a problem?" She had misjudged Willan, and she somehow knew it without Felicia telling her. But what could Felicia have known of the man?

"Eliza, that man, was he tallish with shaggy brown hair and eyes that look like they're solid black?"

She said nothing.

"Eliza, damn it. Answer me now!"

"Yes." The word came out soft, barely audible even to herself, and the train car spun again. Something was truly wrong with Willan, and she'd not only allowed him to touch her in the most intimate fashion possible, but she'd been wanting more of it.

"His name isn't Willan. Well, not completely. It's Lucius Willan. Eliza, he's a fucking demon."

It was as if the train car slammed to a halt. She felt her body jerk and slip from the seat in shock. Blackness threatened the corners of her vision, and she squeezed her eyes shut tight, hoping to stop the dizziness from taking hold. Lucius, the man from her dreams. It was truly him, and somehow, they'd connected in reality.

And he was just as wonderful at making my body turn to jelly with passion as in the dreams.

"Eliza, did you hear me! He's a demon. You need to get away from him right now."

"Felicia I heard you. I'm having some problems. What kind of a demon is he?" Maybe he was an Incubus like Greyston. She could think of worse ways to die than being seduced and having her energy completely drained. It would explain the nature of their interactions and her intense need for his touch.

"A Nightmare Demon, Eliza."

"A What?"

"Exactly. According to Greyston, there is a Fallen Angel named Seraphina who eradicated all but five or ten of them in the last century. I'm sure there will be a briefing about her. She's a player it would have been nice to know about a long time back."

Eliza could almost picture the glare Felicia must be giving Greyston at that exact moment.

"All Greyston knows is that they're capable of killing—both whilst asleep and whilst you're awake if they aren't distracted. They get inside your head, access what terrifies you most, and they let it get you, Eliza. They open up a Pandora's box of fear, and they let it come and consume you. It's how they eat. Like a Kappa Demon. The soul lets off energy as it leaves the body, and apparently, not only do they need the energy, but they can capture the soul. They can claim it and make use of it however they see fit."

A chill raced over Eliza's body. It almost sounded as if the Fallen Angel had done the world a service getting rid of such a powerful bunch. Lucius hadn't given her nightmares, quite the opposite. Did it matter, though?

"But, then why hasn't he killed me? I hadn't said it before, but well, he's most certainly been in my dreams."

She heard Greyston's laugh through the communicator, followed by an intake of breath, and she wondered what was going on. The power would drain out quickly, and they would be disconnected, leaving her with so many unanswered questions.

"Eliza, you aren't going to like this. Trust me, I didn't at first either. Eliza, you're Lucius' mate."

The world stood still for the second time in a span of minutes.

"M..m..mate?" She wasn't one to ever stutter, but the idea disgusted her. Yet, at the same time, it explained so much. "Felicia, Greyston is a demon, and you're with him. You wouldn't be calling to warn me, so I know what I'm getting involved with, would you?"

"I wish, Eliza. I really do. But Lucius is not a good guy. He's a gambler and a whore among men. Most importantly, Lucius met you in your dreams to murder you. You were lucky the mating bond kicked in so to speak, or who knows what he would have done. He works for Seraphina. He kills for her all the time. Humans, Eliza. He kills humans for the supposed Queen of the Demons."

She couldn't stop herself, her head turned away from the communicator, and retched. Her shoulders heaved, and she couldn't bring herself to care about the crushed velvet seat or the lush, expensive carpeting beneath her that was now covered.

"He's a trained killer? He's exactly what we hunt. What you hunt." She hadn't been speaking to Felicia, not really. Her mind was spinning, going up and down with thoughts and possibilities. They all led back to the fact that she'd engaged in promiscuous activities with the monster they hunted, with what preyed upon the citizens of London and worldwide.

"Eliza, you need to get away from him. I don't know where he is, and I don't want to know what you've done. I know what a mating feels like, and I don't blame you if something did happen. I blame myself for not going to the train station myself to meet you the minute Greyston kicked him out for fucking with my dreams."

Eliza felt as if she'd stepped off a cliff and had fallen into a bottomless pit. Detail after detail left her brain running and her stomach churning with disgust.

"I'm sorry, Eliza, but you can't be with him. Get away from him once you get to Halifax. I'll try to persuade Master Agardawes to send a team or two to bring him in. He's a lackey for the person responsible for letting demons out onto Earth, into the streets of London. He needs to be brought in."

She nodded, knowing full well that Felicia couldn't see her, and pressed the button that would tap the crystal and scatter the magnetic pulse that was allowing her to speak to Felicia.

Her mouth was bitter from being sick, and she forced herself to take a few deep breaths and lean back into the seat. What had seen done? It wasn't like when the hunters seduced demons for information or to corral them into an easy to kill location. She'd done this because of the buzz that hummed in her blood and the pulsing betwixt her legs when he'd touched her—even the smallest of touches.

She pulled the timepiece from her pocket. "One hour left."

She didn't know where she was going to go, but thanks to the small pane of glass near the top of the door, she could see Lucius wasn't merely outside waiting for her. She was his mate, but she had no idea what it entailed. She'd never had the nerve to ask Felicia, but she knew one thing. If Lucius opened that door and slanted his mouth over hers, she would never be able to get away.

She pushed off the floor and felt momentarily guilty again about being sick all over the car, but knew she didn't have time to find one of the attendants and tell them. Lucius—God it really was him—could come back any moment.

She was hoping he'd left because guilt had eaten away at him. But she suspected it was because he'd heard her communicator and had known what it was. Looking through the glass panel, she confirmed that he wasn't there and hastily grabbed her bags. She cursed as clothing fell out of the one the communicator had been in, and she bent to shove them back in as quickly as she could.

Throwing open the door, she forced herself to breathe. She couldn't go running through the train. It would cause a commotion. Lucius had the only ticket that was needed when one had a personal car. If she got caught running, they were likely to assume she was a stowaway and toss her out of the moving train or take her for a trial.

Eliza could just picture her mother's face if that happened. She couldn't tell anyone aboard either. It wouldn't matter if she mentioned a man had forced himself on her. Without a ticket, she was a criminal.

And if Lucius wasn't a killer, there would be blood on her hands, and that wasn't something she could handle. She wasn't a hunter no matter how badly she wanted a taste of their lives. Death did not fascinate or excite her.

She took a step out of the private room, one foot in front of the other, and looked down both ends of the hall. Lucius wasn't standing anywhere. He may have found a facilities car, or perhaps he'd gone for a smoke. Her last bed partner had always lit a cigar after they'd finished so he might do the same.

Slowly, she walked down the hall toward the steam engine car. It would be smarter to go upfront. There was always a Constable on board, and if Lucius came after her, perhaps the combined efforts of her crystal gun and the Constable's gun would be enough to take him down.

Her feet stopped moving at the thought. *Could I take him down?* She was certainly not able to be with him, but if she was his mate, the one person he was meant to share his life with, could she be the one to pull the trigger?

"Stop it. You have no idea if he'll even come looking for you. Although, why wouldn't he? Man makes your whole body quiver with release, and you run out. No shot he'll think you just feel improper, Eliza."

She sighed and kept walking. The train was quite stable for being such a new mode of transit—far less rocky than the cycle bikes they rode in secret.

Eliza passed through two cars before finding her saving grace in the third, a baggage compartment room. Once again, she looked, this time for train attendants, before opening the door, going inside and closing herself off from Lucius.

NINE

THE SCREAM WAS LIKE AN APHRODISIAC. LUCIUS' whole body thrummed with excitement as another pierced the air. He was standing, rather casually, along a brick wall in the dream of an Alliance member. Lucille, to be exact. A hunter who was honestly far too old to be running the streets of the London Underground. Her deepest fear had been simmering right at the surface—being outrun by any of the demonkind they fought. Lucius hadn't even had to try to create a truly horrifying nightmare. Lucille was damaged goods. She'd been attacked by a Kappa Demon earlier in the year with the Alliance.

So he'd manifested a good ten or twenty of the vicious little buggers and had stepped back out of the way to watch. Her screams echoed off the brick walls, and he couldn't wipe the smile from his face if he tried. A part of him had been reluctant to seek out an Alliance member. Killing a potential friend of Eliza's wasn't going to help them along. But he couldn't control how he felt when victim responded to a nightmare.

It was who he was after all, and it was quite apparent Eliza wasn't going to see him. He'd tracked her down quickly, mated mark and all that. But she clearly knew who he was, what he was because she hadn't slept during the night. Maybe she hadn't slept at all. He couldn't tell. It had been two days, and he'd been rocking an erection everywhere he went to the point of pain because all his body wanted was her. It seemed Greyston had been right about what touching your mate caused.

A thumping sound shook him from his thoughts. Darling Lucille was down on the ground, down and out. He couldn't see her too well, but every once in a whilst, he got a solid glimpse of a Kappa Demon latching onto her. Typically, they only bit to turn a human, but for this dream, they bit to kill. Over and over again. Her body twitched and convulsed, red rivulets of blood ran down her arms and over her face. He watched the rise and fall of her chest as best as he could until it stopped. A moment later, her soul was departing her body. Souls were pathetic really. Walk up and grab them, and poof, they were gone.

His hand grasped her soul, and as with every kill, it melded itself to his body. Seraphina stripping them hurt like hell, and the only nice thing about the bitch was that she only wanted her proof once a month. She could always tell when he got humans, anyway. Hell was Hell. The Underworld. The afterlife. Didn't matter who you were or what you believed, you went to Hell. Some people just got nice cozy rooms, whilst other people were left to roast in Hellfire for all eternity. Either way, she knew.

He felt a nasty pain in his stomach, and he gagged. Another pain, in the same place as before and he gasped, jerking out his trance. Arial and Dean had found him a few hours earlier. Kicked the living shit out of him, but not enough to leave him unable to do Seraphina's bidding at the moment. They were back.

His eyes flew open in time to watch as Dean's huge hand landed across his face, snapping his neck and making stars dance in his vision.

"It's done, you mother fucker. Stop fucking hitting me. I bloody well did what the bitch wanted." His words were strained, but he'd still made a mistake. Never call Seraphina a bitch to her lap dogs.

Arial's hands were around his neck so fast, he wouldn't have even known it, save for the warm trickle of blood he felt running down his neck where the demon's claws punctured. He coughed, tried to choke out any meager attempt at drawing air into his lungs and failed. Black touched his vision, and he felt as his head lolled to the side.

"Arial! Stop it before you really do kill the demon."

Hands slipped away from his neck, and he gasped, drawing in all the air his lungs could handle but still feeling as if it wasn't enough. His chest rose and fell rapidly, trying to aid in sucking in the air. His vision was blurry, and he wanted to puke, but he wasn't in any position to get off the wet cobblestone he'd been dropped onto. He laughed. Hitting it hadn't hurt nearly as bad as some of his attempts to get the mating mark off his cheek the entire month before.

A boot slammed into the side of his head, knocking him off balance and sending spittle and blood onto the ground.

"Next time, don't make us come after you. Seraphina doesn't like expending energy sending us up here after tracking you down. She'll be waiting for Greyston Westham's soul within the week. Don't forget." Without another word, the two Stranglehold brothers popped out of sight.

Lucius pulled his upper half off the ground and stood on shaky legs. Thankfully he wasn't as bad off since he'd just made a kill, but it didn't mean it didn't fucking hurt.

He spit to the left of his boot and grimaced that the dark red blood, that landed on the stones contained no white, frothy spit. He wiped at his mouth with the back of his hand and was thankful he'd put on a deep russet shirt. There'd be no evidence and no copper coming up and asking him questions.

"Try that again, pricks. When I'm paying attention, you won't get away with it!" He probably sounded like a drunkard shouting into the night, but he didn't care.

Arial and Dean had snatched him earlier as he'd left his lodgings. He hadn't killed anyone in weeks, so he'd been an easy grab. Either way, he may have been prey for them since they were stronger, but they had a habit of knowing when he was weak. Probably Seraphina's doing since she'd put a fucking tracker on him somehow. Angel magic, he supposed, but he wasn't sure. All he knew was that the brothers had pushed him into doing what he didn't want too, and he'd loved every second of it once the fun had begun. Nightmares were literally in his blood, and he'd been trying to be better for Eliza. Then they'd been back to check on him, something that made his blood boil.

He was trying to only murder those Eliza might find unsavory. Too bad he wasn't too good at figuring out which ones they were unless he caught them. Whilst he'd been trying to connect with her the past few months, he'd found a man forcing himself on a barmaid and someone mugging an elderly man. Those had been a piece of cake. He'd even realized he liked hearing them scream even more. He relished the way the evildoers had felt when the tables were turned.

One didn't run from a deal with Seraphina. He knew that, but he couldn't help it. He could claim all he wanted that Greyston was too strong as a mated Incubus Demon, but sooner or later, she was going to smell the shit through the flowers. Greyston wouldn't be any harder than any other demon to take down, the exception being Fallen Angels. The ding-dong twins hadn't specified who to kill, and there had been a team of Alliance hunters patrolling Eliza's house, probably trying to protect her from him. He didn't think Seraphina would mind having another Alliance member off the street and added to her soul collection. Not that he knew what she did with them. All he knew was she stuffed them into a wall, and he didn't ask what her plans were for them. Only Angels could truly play with souls, and if a Fallen wanted them, then those souls were damned.

He stretched, and his muscles pulled slightly but felt vital for the most part thanks to the soul. He felt the kick to his head, though, probably would even after a good night's sleep. Demon's healed quicker than humans, but pain was still pain. He leaned his head to the side and heard the satisfying crack more than felt it.

Injuries aside, it was time to seek Eliza out. He had tried

knocking the first day, and the butler damn near drove him off. Yelling at him about showing up without a requested audience. He hadn't realized just how much money Eliza came from until he realized her father was closely aligned with the Duke of Halifax. The house alone would have been easy enough for Eliza to hide in if she wasn't his mate. But going inside hadn't worked, so he'd resorted to waiting outside until she walked out or snagging her in her dreams. Whilst Lucille might be missing, there were still two other Alliance hunters watching over her, and it made that a bit harder.

His feet knew the way to her house as if he'd been walking it his whole life, not a mere two days. The manors sprawled before him, and large green trees loomed from yards. Wrought iron fences tucked most of the residences safely away from anyone walking on the street. Lawns were as green as dyed silk, and some sported white porcelain fountains with naked cherubs or something equally as asinine.

He'd been intimidated two days ago. He lived in squalor, but it was an act. He had masses saved up and had even registered himself as a lord at one point in the Middle Ages. He did like his rundown home. It fit his lifestyle. Seeing where she lived, how she'd grown up, he'd been immediately nervous that, even if he could undo whatever damage someone, most likely Felicia, had done, he would never be enough for her.

His toe bumped into the brick column that marked the entrance to her home. He almost shouted with joy at the energy he felt from within. Not only were her parents sleeping, but so was she. Her energy was still and seductive. All he needed to do was pray that she wouldn't do something stupid in her dream whilst trying to wake herself. With him present, and his powers working just enough to bring him into her mind, she would be able to kill herself.

Lucius retreated across the street. A large oak grew on the premises, and he walked around the back of the massive trunk and stood. He was concerned the landowners could see him, but the windows were so far from where he stood, they would most likely assume their eyes were playing tricks on them rather than thinking they saw a man. Especially at such a late hour.

He pressed his back into the bark of the tree and closed his eyes, letting his power work its magic. He slipped easily into her dream.

"Lucius."

His name was a mix of barely controlled venom and desire. Her voice sent a pang of lust through him, and he inhaled her chocolate and lavender scent before he could stop himself. He looked up and found her honey colored eyes blazing fire up at him. She looked as if she was prepared to fight him.

"I knew you'd find me." Her voice lacked the fire it had held a moment prior, even if her eyes didn't.

"Eliza. Let me explain. Please let me explain."

She reared back as he put a hand out to brush over her face, and he felt as if someone had slapped him. She didn't want him to even touch her.

"I don't know what you were told, but please, listen."

"I got a message this morning. From Felicia. Lucille was found dead. An Alliance member they spared to guard me whilst I'm on this ridiculous leave is dead. Please, explain that one."

Some of the heat had returned to her words, but she was all the way across the chamber in her dream. Probably her room. It looked a lot like the room he'd fucked her in during the last dream.

Wrong thought ole boy.

His cock surged to life, and she looked down and snorted in disgust.

"Tell me you didn't do it."

He wanted to lie to her because he knew it would be the only way to save them. But he couldn't. "I killed her."

She recoiled again and shut her eyes. When she opened them, they were filled with tears ready to fall over her lashes and stream down her cheeks.

Her voice was barely above a whisper, but she didn't break her gaze on his. "I wanted her to be wrong. I wanted them both to be incorrect."

She turned, ready to walk out the door of her dream room. Her hand pushed on the imposing wooden door, and she walked out. Only to walk right back in. The startled look on her face would have made him laugh in any other scenario.

"You can't control this, love. Just like that one night, I'm the one in charge in here. The only way out is to wake up, and fortunately for me, you don't have that kind of control over yourself. You could if you practiced, but you don't."

She lunged at him. A fury of skirt and blonde tresses. Her nails raked across his chest, but he felt nothing through the thickness of his shirt. He did his best to wrap his hands around her shoulders and hold her steadily away from him.

"Eliza, please just hear me out."

"I don't want to hear anything you have to say. Fuck you being a demon, Felicia and Greyston are happy. But you lied to me! You lied to me, seduced me, and all but took me in the train car!" Her voice was high pitched, and her cheeks burned pink with anger.

The flush was turning him on almost as much as the way her body had smashed against his during her assault. His fingers dug into her shoulders a little deeper, to hold her still.

"I. Did. Not. Lie. My name is Willan. You never asked for more details than that, and you did nothing to stop me on that train. You didn't even pull away. In fact, you melted against me so perfectly I wonder what would happen if I touched you again, now."

He pulled her into his body, letting her feel the thick erection barely restrained in his pants. He watched as her eyelids drooped a little and her mouth parted to form an "o." He ran the back of his palm down her cheek, and her sigh as she pressed her face into his hand was the only thing he needed to know.

He lowered his head in one smooth motion and captured her mouth in his. For a split second, her body tensed and then relaxed against his, and her mouth opened for him. His tongue laved hers slowly, and he released her shoulders and let his hands travel up and down her back. She moaned into the kiss and pressed herself into his erection before pulling back. He looked down at her, at the picture of wanton desire she was before him. Her hair was still perfectly straight over her shoulders, but her eyes smoldered with hunger, and her lips were rosy and plump.

"I hate you." Her words held no conviction, and she pulled his arms, tugging his mouth back to hers.

His body was on fire, and his shaft throbbed to be inside of her, but he knew it wasn't the time. He was aware that Eliza was certainly not as put off as the airs she put on. She cried out when his lips left hers, and he felt his own grow cold without her touching them.

"That speaks quite the opposite, love." His voice was deep and husky. He was dying to grind against her.

She didn't say anything, just took a small step back from him and pouted her lips.

"Let me explain. I've had chances to kill you, both in your dreams and on the train, and I didn't. I wouldn't."

She was quiet and looked everywhere except into his eyes. The time dragged out, and he worried if she would ever answer or simply leave them standing there, locked in silence.

"Tomorrow morning."

He flinched. Morning would leave him weak, and if the Stranglehold twins came looking for him, she would be in danger. "I'm weaker in the daytime." Honesty was the only thing he could use in a situation like this.

"I know. It wasn't hard to figure out. Of course, a creature of dreams would thrive when most of the world dreamt. I want to believe you, Lucius. But you just admitted to killing someone I knew, someone who did good. I need to know you'll trust me when you're at your weakest."

The impact of her words hit him like a cannonball. *Trust.* She wanted to trust a demon, which meant she wasn't ready to be done with him. Whilst he certainly wouldn't say this was an emotional tie, it was a sexual one, and the more he spent time with her, the more he admired her. All he knew of her was what she projected into her dreams. She was smart and passionate. She was looking for something she didn't have, and she cared deeply about the Alliance. All things he wanted to know more about, and he wasn't even annoyed that he wanted to. She fascinated him.

"Morning. I'll be out front." He bent down, took her hand and placed a kiss on the top before severing his connection to the dream and sending them both spiraling awake. Her, back in her room, and him leaning against the bark of the tree.

He opened his eyes as the sky was slowly fading from the dark of night. He couldn't find the timepiece he'd stolen before meeting her at the train yard to check the hour, but if he wanted to have any semblance of energy he needed to get back to the inn and rest.

"That's not all you need to do, Willan. That's not all."

THE SUN SHONE into her room, and she groaned as she rolled over on the bed, clutching the duck feather pillow. If there was only one good thing about being home, it was the bed. She'd slept fitfully after Lucius had departed. The idea that she was remembering meetings that essentially weren't happening concerned her slightly. If Felicia hadn't said his breed was basically eradicated, she would have attributed every dream, every nightmare, in the past thirty-three years to a demon. With a groan, she forced her eyes to open, first the right and then the left. The light assaulted her, and she grimaced, tempted to turn back over in the bed but knowing she had things to do.

She grabbed for the pocket watch on the table, and her eyes took a moment to adjust to the small black numerals. "Twenty past eight. Right then, I'd better get up." They hadn't set a meeting time. Actually all they'd said was morning.

She had a distinct feeling that if she randomly told her mother she was going for a morning walk, she would never make it out of the house alone. "Perhaps I'll just ask if they would like anything from the baker," she muttered to herself as she got out of bed and pulled open the large cherry wood armoire doors.

Her dresses all hung, waiting. All the blues, purples, lush greens and yellows from her past. She'd known her mother would never discard them, but somehow, seeing them reminded her of being a young child, of all the times she'd earned someone's scorn simply for being a child. Eliza pushed the thoughts off, pulled a green dress complete with white skirts from the closet and laid it on the bed.

Her eyes drifted over the row of corsets hanging to the right, and she frowned. "I don't suppose he'd mind terribly if I skipped the dreaded contraption." She'd always despised corsets, and her attire at the guild had never called for one. Only during festivals and balls did she don the torturous device. In fact, none of the women at the guild wore them if they did not have to. It probably made them very improper, but many did not look upon the working class, anyway.

Her mind drifted briefly to the other reason why she did not wish to wear one. She wanted his hands on her, wanted him to have access to the swell of her breast through the thick layers of fabric. It should have disgusted her, but it didn't. She may not trust Lucius Willan, but she wasn't going to deny her baser instincts enjoyed his touch.

She stepped into a pair of green slippers, dyed to match the fabric of the dress, and walked over to the window, grabbing her opera glasses from the top drawer as she walked. Her hand slowly pulled the thick, pale blue curtain to the side, and she raised the opera glasses to her eyes and peered out. She wasn't certain if she expected to see Lucius or not. But there he was, a hundred yards across the perfectly cared for garden and looking perfect for the society ladies in the area.

He donned a black suit with what appeared to be a silver vest and white bloused shirt. He looked handsome, if not a little overdressed. Eliza pulled back from the window when his black eyes seemed to connect with hers from such a distance.

"Get a hold of your emotions. He may not be honest. This could all be a trick, a mission of his." Nodding her head to no one in particular, she let the curtain fall back into place over the window and left her room.

As expected, her mother and father sat in the parlor. Her mother, in a beautiful floral pink gown, and her father, in a cream-colored suit. Both had a cup of tea on a saucer before them, and her father had the *London City Press*, which was a week old due to transit times to Halifax, opened whilst her mother sat with needlepoint.

"Good morning, Father, Mother." Eliza kissed both of them on the cheek as she entered. She tried to force her breathing to be calm, to make this seem like nothing other than a sweets run. "Would either of you like something from the baker? I fear I have a craving for sweets."

Her father made a noncommittal grunt from behind the paper, but her mother stopped what she was doing.

"Whatever would you go out for? We have servants who can make such a run for us." Her mother's tone was haughty and held a clear disdain for the habit her daughter must have picked up of running to the bakers.

"It's such a beautiful morning. I just thought it would be a nice time for a walk in the park." Her hands twitched, and she wrung them together, cursing the sweat forming under the blasted white cloth gloves.

"Well, it's not like anyone will fancy you. You're well past your prime, and the whole of Halifax knows your dowry is allotted for other things by now."

Her mother's comment sliced through her, leaving her raw and exposed. Words caught in her throat as she tried to form a response, but she couldn't. Tears stung in her eyes, and she mentally chastised herself for letting her mother get to her. She just nodded and turned to walk out the front door.

When the door shut behind her, she gasped, and the tears she'd been holding back fell. She would never be what her mother wanted, and she'd known that for the past ten years. But hearing it stung every time. She stood, her back pressed against the door for a few moments.

When her eyes cleared from the tears, she noticed that Lucius was pacing in front of the gate.

"Let's go play with a demon."

She felt as if the walk down the gravel path to the gates took an eternity, and when she stopped, his eyes met hers. She felt a mixture of emotions, and she wasn't sure if they were hers or his, but they slammed into her. Lust, concern, wanting, curiosity.

"Are you well? Your eyes are bloodshot. What happened after I woke us up?" His hands planted firmly on her shoulders, and he his eyes bore into hers.

She wished she could raise her arm and wipe away the fresh tears forming, but because of the way he was holding her and her healing shoulder, she couldn't. He just couldn't be what Felicia and Greyston said, not with the amount of concern that radiated behind the black depths of his eyes.

Eliza sniffled and sputtered a bit before shaking her head. "I'm fine. I don't quite meet with my mother's standards on a daughter. It's a touch of a sore subject, and since I showed up unannounced, I believe they know something is wrong at the guild."

Lucius growled, and she wondered if it was on her behalf or something else.

"About that—"

"It's nothing. I'm an inventor, and sometimes even my mind needs a little time off." She looked at the ground and hoped he got the message—topic off limits.

His hands let go of her shoulders, and he offered her his arm, just as he had done on the train. She looked at him then, betwixt his eyes and his elbow, and there was nothing she could do but put her hand in the crook of his arm. He had plenty of explaining to do. Lust wasn't trust, and she could be okay with that for now.

"Now, my lady, I'm unfamiliar with Halifax. If you can believe that. Where can I take you that won't cause rumors of courtship?"

For a moment, she felt her stomach drop at the idea that he didn't want it to look as if he were courting her, and she chided herself for her stupidity. One man paying her mind did not excuse that he was a killer, and not like those in the hunter parties.

"That is a rough question. This area is high society, we may be outside of London, but this land has grown prosperous, and many have holiday homes here. Simply walking down the street could signal such a thought, and since you did not speak with my parents, I fear it may not be a good idea. It has been about eleven years since I've truly lived at the estate, but people will still recognize me."

"Well, how about I will walk slightly ahead of you. There is something I wish to show you. Then we can use the same procedure to come back here and sit somewhere on your estate. If you do not think your parents would take notice of us around the back of your property. You have a beautiful tree back there, perfect for hiding behind I would think." His lips were smiling, and he winked at her.

Her heart squeezed at his playfulness. Another thing a killer really shouldn't have. But Kellan did, even if he only killed the bad things. She let Lucius' offer roll over in her mind. Her parents rarely looked outside if her mother wasn't hosting a tea, and it was too early for the servants to be drying the linens.

"Yes, I actually think that may work. But first, where would I be going?" She didn't like surprises. It was the intellectualist in her. The idea of something being fully unknown to her was an obstacle she didn't appreciate.

"Just follow behind me. It's about one hundred meters from here, betwixt two of these gigantic manors. I have a gift of sorts for you."

He piqued her interest, and she motioned for him to lead on. She didn't look back to see if anyone had seen her talking to a man, and she did her best to stay a few yards behind him at all times and appear to be focusing on the trees. It was times like this that she loved the guild more than anything, and she was sincerely jealous of how the working class lived. Yes, there were still rules of propriety, but they could co-mingle whenever they wanted, except in the chambers at the guild. It wasn't even uncommon to have mixed sexes in the pubs. It was a much more freeing lifestyle, and as this outing would determine the fate for her and her mate, it seemed foolish they had to go to such measures to stay separate.

Lucius stopped three residences over to the Powell's. Their house was an imposing mixture of turrets that looked as if they were trying to mimic one of the keeps of the medieval ages. He walked down the side of the house, and she stopped following him. His choice made sense now. The home was big and made of grey brick, it cast a heavy shadow over the side of the house. He could do anything he wanted to her, and very few people would notice.

He, however, didn't stop. Eliza stood in front of the house, probably appearing daft to any who saw. But she wasn't going to follow him in. A moment passed, and he walked back out of the small side area and stopped a few paces from her. Nothing in his eyes gave his emotions away; they were cold, dead black pits.

"If I were going to kill you, I would've in your sleep. It takes a lot for me to manifest anything, and whilst you're only a female, I'm still not the strongest at combat." He turned to go back to the alley but stopped mid-step. "We won't even discuss the rage it's building in me to think my mate thinks I could ever harm her."

He marched back betwixt the houses, and she was left standing, the sun warming her skin. *Can you trust him?* She didn't have the answer to that question. Everyone lied, she was certain of that. But he'd crossed a line when he and she had engaged in carnal actions, and he hadn't told her the truth.

With a sigh, she picked up her dress in case the grass was muddy and looked behind her once. There would be no one to see her slip betwixt the houses, no one to potentially save her if needed.

"Get on with it, Eliza. He's said more than once that he won't hurt you and how weak he is now if he wanted too."

She walked, still rather slow, behind the houses and gasped when she saw what Lucius' gift to her was. Three Rusha Demons sat tied together, all alive based on the rise and fall of their blood red chests. The demons weren't the nastiest the Alliance had fought, but they were deadly. One scratch from their nails caused toxin to flow into the victim's blood, and there was no cure as of yet for it. They'd lost a handful of hunters to the creatures, and it made capturing them as opposed to euthanizing them rather hard.

Their whole body was a deep crimson red, and they had two arms and two legs, each with three fingers and three toes on them. Their hands were shaped like elongated spheres, and whilst they had eyes, there didn't appear to be a nose above the mouthful of tiny, razor sharp teeth.

"How? Why?" she asked as she walked as close to them as comfort would allow.

Their eyes were closed, and she was grateful they could not look at her. Perhaps they were asleep, but she'd guessed Lucius had done something more sinister to them.

"I wanted you to know. To see that I can do the right thing every once in a whilst."

"Lucius, that's not fair."

"Oh, but it is. Felicia and Greyston weren't wrong. I headhunt for the most powerful demon alive, and she has a vendetta against humans. Which means I kill them. I torture them with their darkest fears in their sleep, and I like it. Love it even. The way it feels knowing you have the power to draw such primal reactions from someone is like none other. I suppose it's akin to how you feel when you triumph making one of those deadly weapons of yours."

She took a step away from him. His words bled with truth and sent a chill through her. His admittance unnerved her.

"But that's not the point. The night I found you, I'd been sent to kill a guild member inside the guild, simply to raise panic."

"Is there some point to this? Or are you trying to scare me away from you because that is all you're succeeding in doing at this point."

His smile was cold, wicked even, and it didn't reach his eyes. "Maybe I am. Maybe I want to show you exactly what I am before I explain to you exactly who I will be." He paused, as if allowing her to throw her two pence into the ring, but she said nothing. "I found you, and the minute I saw you, I wanted you. I chose that other boy to spare you. Because what Seraphina wants, she gets. But that isn't the end of it. Her next kill was to be Greyston."

She did gasp at that, and he chuckled, though the situation held no humor for her.

"Obviously, I haven't done it. Felicia would have been here to kill me herself if I had. In fact, I've warned him so he can be prepared. Do you know why I killed before Seraphina ordered me to, Eliza? Did Greyston share that with his betrothed to tell you? Well, it's how I live. Nightmare Demons need the fear given off just prior to death to survive. You can call me what you wish, but I cannot change my basic chemistry any more than you can change your intellect level for your mother."

His words stung as if he had slapped her. He may have been right, but killing innocents wasn't ever going to be justifiable. Ever. "That doesn't make it right. It just means it has to be accepted." Her voice was quiet.

"Exactly. I've never taken a young's life, and I hope to never have too. I have taken a Royal's before. I've taken the coppers, the merchants and whores. But not since I've met you have I taken anyone that wasn't a direct order from the Queen of Hell, and again, you don't disobey her."

Curiosity would be her second greatest downfall next to desire for this demon. His body was so close that, as menacing as his words were, she could feel his warmth. She wanted his arms around her, even whilst she wanted to run away and never look back.

"How have you been surviving?"

"On vagrants."

She sighed in relief, not realizing how much she needed him to be less of a demon.

"I've been taking only those who've done something unjust. A rapist and a pickpocket who didn't live in squalor and wasn't doing it to survive. It's been harder, but I won't lie, there is something even sweeter in their fear when they realize the end has come. So why did I tie demons up for you? Because I'm trying to prove to you that I am a dangerous demon, but I don't always have to be. If I can figure a way to payback Seraphina and no longer serve her, I could swear to you, I would only kill those that deserve it. I've given you demons in hopes that three of them off the Halifax streets are a peace offering."

He took a step closer, ran a hand through her hair and tipped her chin up. "Mates don't have to be more than sexual, Eliza. But I can't help but think there's so much more than just lust betwixt us. I want the chance to try. Greyston got that chance. Proof that even a hunter can open her eyes."

Quiet descended on them. He stopped his speech, and she didn't know how to respond. She didn't know if she could cope with a murderer. What would she see every time she looked at him? Would she see the man who brought her to the edge of passion or would she see the soulless eyes of a demon finishing a kill?

She closed her eyes, and an image of Lucius popped into her head. He was clothed in as elegant a suit as he was now, and where cloth didn't cover his skin, his body gleamed in some sort of candle-light. His hand outstretched as if to ask her to take it, and she knew her answer. She would never see the killer in him because he'd never shown that side of himself.

If he was willing to change who he had been, then she would let him. She wouldn't admit it, but the idea of who and what he was fascinated her at the same time it disgusted her, and his gesture wasn't unappreciated.

"Let me call this in." She stepped back from him and pulled up the sleeve of her dress, revealing her communicator.

"Oh, I have some questions for you, love." Lucius seemed playful again, all traces of violence drained from his voice.

"Felicia. I need you to do me a favor. Don't send any more hunter teams up here to watch over me. You'll never believe this. Lucius brought me demons."

"He did what?" her friend's voice was incredulous.

"I don't have time to explain. Just get the Alliance to dispatch one of their teams already stationed here to bring them in. Or kill them, whatever it is hunters do." She didn't let Felicia answer before she pushed the button to disrupt the vibration pattern.

"We are going to need to have a little talk about all those inventions of yours, love. Some of them seem downright entertaining. Others deadly. I hope you don't have one of those guns stashed under that dress."

She grinned at him. "You're not going to find out. At least not right now. You've got your chance, Lucius. I want to get to know more about you, and then I'll decide if you are sincere here. I want you to be sincere." She hadn't meant to voice that last part aloud, but it was too late.

"I am. I will be an open book. But something tells me the cover of night will make our interactions by far easier. What would you say to a round of demon hunting?"

Her eyes sparkled, and she bit her lip. He couldn't have known that all she'd ever wanted was a night out in the field. Or could he? The list of questions she needed to ask him kept growing.

"Will you protect me, Lucius?"

"Always."

She nodded, placed a quick kiss to his lips and began walking back to her parent's estate. "Then meet me, half past nine round the side of the house."

He reached out and grabbed her wrist. Her body jerked backwards into his chest, and he spun her around and kissed her. His lips pressed against hers, and his hands tugged at her hair. Then he was just gone, walking down the road and she was left standing there, fully ready to tell Felicia and Greyston to fuck off with their worries and give herself to a demon.

TEN

"Don't you think it would be by far easier if you would just commit some atrocious act, Muriel?"

Seraphina walked around the other side of the Angel tied to the chair and viciously jerked one single feather from the female's wings. She was a warrior, though, and there was no howl of pain. To achieve that, Seraphina would have to work much harder. Something she didn't mind at all.

The Angels hadn't obliged her when she'd asked for help retrieving Demetrious. In fact, they'd warned her of what falling would do to her and how she would never come back. Well, they'd neglected to mention how she'd have the power to make them all pay for ignoring her. Had they just come with her, perhaps her love wouldn't have found her grotesque. Truly, it was the Angels' fault the humans would die. Had she gotten Demetrious back, she might be a different Angel. But alas, she was a Fallen, and she would never look back, not until every last human lay dead on the ground and her army could move their true battle against the Angels.

"You are pathetic, Seraphina," Muriel spat in her face.

In response, Seraphina twisted a hand, grabbing at least six feathers, and pulled them out. A quiver went through Muriel's body, and Seraphina chuckled when she felt it. The sound echoed off the rock walls and the stone floor.

"Ah, but not so pathetic that I haven't found plenty of ways to capture the most elusive demon of all, the Angel."

"I was in the right place and the right time. You have no master plan worked out. We will not fall, and by the time you are done with me, instead of aligned with your cause, I will be broken, bloody and dead on this floor. You are nothing." She did her best to raise her eyes and look into Seraphina's.

"It always amazes me how self-righteous Angels are. No wonder humans sought to raise you above the demons you really are."

She nodded toward Ian, the only Asag demon to ever exist and the basis behind a silly Sumerian myth. His snake-like tongue flicked out as he tucked his black skin-like wings against his body and wandered through the small door, his big horns scraping the rock as he did so.

"You see, I thought you'd feel that this was a fool's errand. I'm so sorry to be the one to inform you that it is not. Angels can fall by the will and workings of others. You'd be amazed what it feels like to have the blood seeping down your back and your shoulders screaming in pain as the rooted feathers, the final ones to go, are pulled from your body."

"You're speaking nonsense. I am sorry to see what has become of you. I know now why the blood drinking was forbidden. If it turns the strongest fighters into this, there would be no way to stop your kind of demon from taking over." Her blue eyes shone fiercely.

Angels were always protecting what they loved—humans. They were still demons, but they liked the comforts of the human race and would most likely always fight to keep them from being extinct.

Izazal entered the small holding cell, and a bare-chested warrior with black eyes followed behind him, arms over his chest.

"Thank you, Ian." An intake of breath from Muriel sent waves of enjoyment through her. She turned to look at the Angel even as the male walked toward the chair. "Well, I see introductions aren't needed then. So glad you could recognize Izazal without his wings. You'll also notice one important detail. He's loyal to me."

"No. No, it can't be. Izazal we thought you were dead, but we never knew you were here."

The ex-commander of Angel justice leaned his neck to the right and left, cracking it as he did. "Well, you lot never would have bothered to look."

Whilst he spoke, Seraphina brought down a scythe from the wall. "You wouldn't believe how good he is in bed now that he's Fallen." She winked at the horrified Angel tied to the chair and swung the scythe in a large arc, slicing through feathers and cutting all on Muriel's right wing in half.

"You see, I don't have to simply pluck the feathers out. In fact, I never do this all in one session. You'll notice something as you sit there." She paused as she brought the scythe down on the left wing and then threw it into the wall after slicing off the feathers. The blade crashed to the ground, and the Angel twitched. She was finally shaken.

"Your powers are primarily contained in your wings. You won't be able to do much of anything until the blood clots on your shoulders, and the magic rests within you once again. I will be right on the other side of that gate, though, and I would be honored to watch you try, Muriel." She turned to walk away, never intending to fully break the Angel in one go around.

"This will not work. I might not be dead when it's all over, but you can't stop me from taking my own life the moment you set me free."

She didn't need to turn around to know that Izazal had stroked a hand down his ex lover's face before he spoke the next words. "When you have the blood of a Fallen Angel coursing through your body, you'll see things differently. It works similar to Pure Angel blood, except with a Fallen, it forms an addiction that leads to madness without a steady supply. A madness that you'll do anything to sate. I promise you, when I'm busy fucking you as you feed on my vein, you'll be begging Seraphina to release you from your cell."

Seraphina heard the female Angel whimper and smiled again. It wouldn't matter how many feathers Izazal tore from her back. They'd spent centuries as lovers before Seraphina had captured him. She'd bet he'd have Muriel begging for him to fuck her long before he even touched another feather on her back. She walked gracefully down the hall and nodded as she passed Ian. The Asag Demon was one of her most loyal subjects, and as so few records existed of him. She'd enjoyed setting him loose on the world and seeing what the humans thought of him.

"Seraphina." The raspy voice that signaled none other than a Stranglehold demon shouted out to her from across her office just as she stepped inside.

"Arial. Dean. What?" She sat in her chair and folded her arms over her chest. She despised working with these two. However, there were none better to act as enforcers than demons literally around for nothing more than to strangle things. Their intelligence left much to be desired, however.

"Lucius. He isn't following your directive," Arial spoke and bowed his head to the floor, keeping his eyes there like the good little pet that he was.

Her vision went red. The Nightmare Demon was becoming a thorn in her side. He'd been loyal for the most part until he'd found his mate a few months before. The idea aggravated her beyond belief. Angels were the only demons who had a human form that did not have a mate, whether they were Fallen or Pure, not any longer at least. So, learning that her favorite bed toy and assassin was not only sexually tied to another, but ignoring her was not the news she wanted. A glass vase went sailing and smashed into the wall, shattering glass over where the brothers sat. Her palms slammed down onto her desk, and she pushed off, standing behind it as she dared them to look her in the eyes.

"Would one of you imbeciles care to explain why you are not dealing with it yourselves?"

They exchanged a look before Dean spoke. "You ordered us not be seen by humans in large numbers. He has been surrounded by them day and night. We are unable to use force with him unless you have changed your mind."

She blew out a long sigh. If humans learned about the existence of demons before she had time to quell their numbers, it would be a disaster. There were hundreds of humans to every one demon. All they needed was the knowledge that they were there, and the whole thing would be over before it started. She supposed the Alliance kept its secret for the same reason. They probably felt the knowledge meant people would run amuck, and that there were more demons than humans.

Her nails dug into the wooden desk, and she bared her fangs at the duo. "Do not question my directive. But never wait to report to me. I want Greyston Westham dead for his betrayal. I want his soul trapped in the wall of my chambers, waiting for the day when I release them to torment the remaining humans." She sat back down slowly and forced herself not to attack the idiots where they sat. "Get out of my sight before I decide your incompetence is punishable by execution."

They jumped up and comically slammed into one another as they rushed out of the door. Seraphina leaned back in her chair and snarled. "It's a damn good thing your mate could be useful, Lucius, or this visit would be far more than social."

ELEVEN

His nails bit into the palms of his hands, and he had to unclench them to grab the shaving razor. It was an endless waiting game it seemed. Wait for her to fall asleep, wait to meet her awake, wait to meet with her. Rage simmered just below the surface, and Lucius was grateful they would be out hunting. He needed any excuse to demonstrate who he was to her.

"A Casanova with a gambling addiction and a murderous streak, fantastic plan." He grimaced as he dragged the straight edge over his face. A small trickle of blood slid down his chin and dripped into the washbasin.

He wanted to be more than that to her. He wanted her to see more than the charm he held, more than the way he could charm the undergarments off ladies or some of the things he'd charmed gambling mates into doing. Lucius wanted to be better for her, to be someone she would allow to court her. It was the most foolish thing ever.

He'd spent less than a day in her presence whilst they were awake. Yet, the spark of life she gave off was infectious and made him want to be around her long enough to soak it in. Her intelligence lit her eyes in a way that made him smile just being near her, and he wasn't even touching upon the way the swell of her breasts pushed against her gowns or the way the blonde locks curled around her face, framing her like a portrait. She was everything a human male would want in a wife. Yet, they all ignored her because she liked to play in the grease and could probably outwit them during a game of chess. The thought angered him, though he should probably feel grateful to them for allowing him the chance.

Lucius owned two proper suits because of his desire to decieve humans into thinking he had nothing, and he'd worn them both in her presence already. The last thing he wanted was for her to be appalled by both his low societal rank and his species. His eyes traveled over to the inn's bed where a chocolate brown suit with a pale green shirt lay across it. Fourteen pounds hadn't seemed to be an issue to him when he'd purchased it. But he'd only thought to bring a mere twenty pounds. He ran a hand over the silken suit and realized he'd spent a colossal waste of coin. But it was important to impress her.

The way her fear had wrapped around him near that manor had pissed him off like nothing else in his life. The look in her eyes was a combination of dread and disdain. He couldn't help but wonder if Felicia had ever looked at Greyston that way and assumed she probably had. He grabbed the suit off the bed and stepped into the pants, tugging them up carefully so as not to damage them in any way.

"I do much prefer you removing those garments, Lucius."

The voice was sultry, like melted chocolate or the slide of fine wine down one's throat, and it made his blood run cold. "Seraphina," he hissed her name as he quickly turned to face her.

There was no way he had the ability to confuse her. Angels were hard enough to trick when they were asleep, but to cause any mental frustration whilst she was awake, well it would take a far stronger demon than he was.

"My, my, my isn't that a little unwelcome." She walked up to him and slid her hands down his bare chest.

His body shivered, and a grotesque look crossed his face. He didn't like her touching him. It had to be the effect of the mating mark. *Or maybe you simply like the touch of Eliza compared to pure evil.*

Her hand continued to trail over his chest, and he did his best not to flinch as it ran over his cock through the thin pants and gently massaged a circle.

"What do you want from me, Seraphina?" He spoke through clenched teeth as a feeling of nausea crept up through his body. She didn't let up, and thankfully, his prick stayed flaccid. That was the last thing he wanted, to be aroused by her.

She ran her tongue over his ear and blew against it. An action that, at one time, would have him coming in his trousers. But not now. Now his body shuddered, and he felt his cock try to shrink away from her touch. For a brief moment, he wondered if she meant to dismember him, starting there.

"You'll do best to not speak to me in such a tone. You are a lesser demon whom I've allowed to live because your cock suits me and your skills are not one a Fallen Angel can possess. But do not ever think you can speak to me in such a fashion. Especially given our past."

She let go of him completely and took a step back, perching on the edge of the bed. Her beauty rocked through him. There was no trace of the evil that lurked within. Her eyes even still shone with life and innocence. It was only when she smiled that the darkness seeped out for people to see.

"I'm here because we have a contract, and I believe almost a week has passed since I demanded it of you."

Greyston. She was talking about why he had yet to murder Greyston. "I haven't had the chance."

"Oh, don't be ridiculous. You think I don't have eyes watching you? You think the beautiful whores you've bedded and the fine gentlemen you've swindled weren't Fallen Angels? Well then, I suppose this is an awakening for you, Lucius Cooley Willan. I've always watched you. Just because you only saw Arial and Dean, doesn't mean there aren't more." Her voice was cold, calculating. "So I know that you were with Greyston three nights ago. But more importantly than that, I know about a particular blonde inventor who you've become taken with."

The blood drained from his face, and the room spun. His legs gave out, and he found himself arse first next to Seraphina on the small bed. Eliza was in danger. He had to get her out of the city, out of the country if he could. Seraphina could follow him everywhere, but if there was a shot an Angel would help transport Eliza from inside the Alliance, she would be safe. Seraphina couldn't follow her if she was moved without her seeing it happen because whatever bound her demons to her, she didn't have anything from Eliza. Seraphina could only follow him, and he would not go with her. No matter what he wanted.

"Before you even think it, there's no chance of getting her to leave. An Angel may have told the Royals about the demon infestation a few decades back, but they will not get involved unless they are in danger."

So that was how the humans had come to know of them.

"Plus, I have no intention of harming the woman. For now."

"Why?" Asking her questions rarely led to answers, but he was too stunned by her admission of Eliza's safety to think.

"Because I find you more useful now than ever. You will have a way in." Her red painted lips curved into the sickening smile that could make grown men and even higher demons cry.

"I don't have a choice?" He would find a way to thwart this newest attempt, but he would need a way completely out of her grasp. A way that would only come with an Angel, and aside from what she'd just told him, he'd already known they don't help demons. So it wasn't likely the fine, feathered demons would come to him.

"You already know the answer to that. It really is a marvelous plan. You have to earn Eliza's trust, of course. You won't learn any of the secrets if she believes you to be as deceitful and underhanded as you truly are. So you may have the day to change her mind. I will even supply a way for you to do so." Seraphina rose off the bed. Her dark red hair trailed behind her, and the white silken dress she wore to mock a Pure Angel's garb flowed effortlessly behind her.

"Remember, though, I'm watching you at every turn, Lucius, and if you dare to cross me, she will be the one that pays the price. Your penance will be a life without her as I am not yet through with you."

"If I do this, if I betray my mate and give you everything you need, will I be free to be with her?" He would never do it, but Seraphina wouldn't need to know that. He'd already frayed the nonexistent trust betwixt Eliza and himself, and he wouldn't do it again. But if he could make it seem like he was doing so by feeding Seraphina a little false information, a little misguidance, then he would play the game. Even if Eliza turned him away, he would have his freedom, and she would be forever safe for as long as her human life continued.

She bit her lip and chewed on it. The silence was deafening, and he itched with need to wring his hands around her neck, but that would be futile.

"Yes." Nothing more was said, she opened whatever transport system Angel power granted her and vanished from the room.

Leaving him with more questions than answers.

He finished dressing in silence. There couldn't be too much longer to wait. The sun was kissing the tops of the shops that he could see through the window. How could he pull off the biggest con he'd ever run when he had no way of telling his partner in crime that they were running a ruse? He rubbed his hands over his eyes and grabbed the tortoise shell walking stick he'd bought with the suit because he thought it made him appear distinguished and headed out of the room. He wanted to be there when the sky turned black to get as much time with her as he possibly could.

He nodded to the kind older man sitting behind the inn desk and strolled out onto the street. The night air was warm, even for summer, but he didn't mind. His mind was far too focused on his only chance to free himself and save Eliza to worry if he might develop a musk from walking to meet her. Betwixt thoughts of escape and thoughts of how there would be no other end to this patrol except with her screaming in pleasure beneath him. He walked quicker than he realized and found himself staring up at the familiar iron gate to her house. He decided to be bold and pushed open the gate. He would meet his mate at the door, even if he had to put her family in a trance and make them believe he was the wealthiest lord from some far away nation.

Just as he reached the door, it swung back, and Eliza bumped into him. His prick hardened immediately as he took in her scent. The chocolate scent seemed to have vanished. A sign that she had been eating sweets prior to their last meetings, but the smell of lavender was never stronger. He put an arm behind her to steady her should she lean back or lose her balance. To his dismay, she didn't.

"What are you doing at the door?" she whispered in a rush and stepped out, closing the door behind her. "Do you have any idea how terribly difficult it was to convince my mother that I was a grown woman and could attend an evening dinner at a neighboring house?"

He laughed. He really enjoyed this spitfire side of her. He had yet to see this personality prior and was quite intrigued. Inventor, scientist, intellect and spitfire. He chuckled again.

"I see nothing funny in this, Lucius."

"You look beautiful."

She glowered at him, but it did nothing to change his mind. She was lovely with her blonde hair tugged back into a fashion that held it high on top of her head and draped down her neck, much akin to a horse's tail, really. She wore a beautiful, vibrantly colored red dress, and he could tell from the way her breasts sat, she had forgone a corset once more. Intoxicating.

"Forgive me. And stop walking off, Eliza. But, you forget, I am a Nightmare Demon."

"Hardly." Her statement was dry, and she rolled her eyes.

"But I have brought you far more than Nightmares." He assumed if there had been more light, he would have seen her cheeks turn red. "I can control people whilst they are awake. Make them see what they fear most, or what they desire most. Something tells me that your parents would be elated for a rich suitor to come and ask to court their daughter."

She huffed. "I'm glad you're in such a talkative mood. I have questions, and not just personal ones. I want to know all about your species long before we get to the stuff that concerns you and me."

"I'm happy to oblige. More than happy. Just don't forget the point of this. I want to show you I'm on board with the Alliance. I'll never work for them. But if it makes you think I'm not a threat to your relationship and standing there, then I will do what I can."

She stopped walking and spun to face him. "I lied. I want personal first. Why would you do that? Felicia explained to me when she first accepted her bond with Greyston that a mating isn't romantic. That it's animalistic, raw, mind blowing."

Her voice rushed out on a gasp, and his cock was throbbing hard. Her words were like a hand wrapping around it and stroking it. He wanted to lean down and kiss her, to press against her and prove her words were right. But that wasn't what she was looking for.

"Because, sometimes, they are more than that. Because, at times, romance makes the mating worth it." He carefully stepped past her, gritting his teeth together to stop the pounding of his cock. He would take her tonight, but he wanted to show her there was more in the works than just a mating bond.

"Oh." Her voice was quiet, but she quickly picked up the pace to walk beside him again, and he offered her his elbow.

They walked in silence, the crickets the only sound around them. The questions that passed betwixt them were trivial as if each one of them was testing the waters. Seeing just how far the questions could go. He knew her favorite Shakespearean play—*A Midsummer Night's Dream*—and he knew her first love in life would be tinkering in a garden. The pair of answers seemed wholly unuseful. Yet, paired together, it showed that she lived with her head and heart partially in the fantastical and that she liked to care for things. Things that were hardly worn on her sleeve as an inventor at the Alliance.

He studied her profile, the way her hair spilled down her back, the pointed curve of her nose and the full pout of her lips. They weren't going to discover anything meaningful about one another if someone didn't push the societal boundaries and ask some unaccept-able questions.

"Bed partners?" The words choked out, but he couldn't look at her.

Her laughter was boisterous and infectious, and after a few moments, he chuckled with her.

"I presume you seek to find out how many times I've sinned, Sir Willan?"

"Well, I suppose I was, Miss Dorley." He tilted his head and smiled at her.

"I am not inexperienced if that is what you wish to know. But I do not whore myself out for the Alliance's cause nor sleep with just any superbly handsome gentleman on a train."

So she could be playful as well. He nodded. "I cannot answer if you ask, so you know. Felicia was not spinning tales. I am a Casanova. I have enjoyed the pleasures of more women than I could ever hope to count, and now I wish to focus on the one woman who matters."

She flushed and kicked a small clump of dirt that was before her but said nothing, and the silence returned.

"Tell me, why join the Alliance?"

"I belonged."

For a moment, he thought she was going to leave it at that, but then she continued.

"My parents wanted a son to pass the family name on to. There are no children as of yet, as my father's brother and my mother's sister's family passed of a fever years ago. So they made the mistake of sending me to Cambridge to show their child off. Only I fit in, and I fell in love with science.

"A professor introduced me to the guild. I knew only that they had funding to work on projects far beyond the realm of most. It wasn't until I'd worked for them for longer than a year that I learned what they truly did. What they fought." Her voice dropped, and she looked at her feet, possibly embarrassed due to him being what they fought. "Then once I found out, how could I not help? I remembered then, about the Halifax Slasher. Did you hear of it?"

He nodded.

"It turns out it was far more than self-mutilation. A demon was controlling those humans. The Alliance never found out why, but he impaled himself on a spear in his haste to get away once the hunters had cornered him. They brought him in, and I was allowed to see him. A Mumbasta Demon, he was blue and had scales like skin covering his body. But it was the blood red eyes that scared me most."

He knew as much before she'd said anything. That breed of demon was able to mind control if he could get someone to look into his eyes long enough.

"I knew then that I was where I needed to be. That someone needed to get such creatures off the streets, and if the Alliance of Silver and Steam was the only faction doing so, I wanted to help.

"My turn. Explain your powers, more."

They rounded a corner, and the gas lamps of the central Halifax area started to flicker in the distance ahead of them. "There isn't much to tell. You already know all demons have powers. Mine are over dreams. I am sure, at some point, there were factions of my kind that did various dreamscapes. But I am very old, and I can assure you that, since my childhood, all we've dealt in was nightmares."

"How old?"

He looked sideways at her and grinned. "Over a thousand years."

"God."

"He doesn't exist. You know that already."

She frowned. "We can't know for certain deities don't exist. Demons certainly do, and I'd like to believe there is some balance betwixt you."

"The Angels."

"What?"

He stopped walking just as they would have passed a pub. "Nevermind. It is not my place to speak of other demons. As I said, my intent is only to show you that I will be loyal to you, not that I plan to help the Alliance in any way. I will protect you with my life, Eliza, but I will not protect your guild." He pulled away from her and stuck his head down a corridor. No sign of anything. He heard her footfalls as she raced to catch up to him. He expected her to comment on his harshness, but she didn't.

"How do I know you aren't just working for Seraphina? How do I know you didn't put that mark somewhere on you? Which, by the way, where is it?"

The questions and suspicion caught him off guard. He wanted to tell her that he was something of a conspirator, but he was on her side, and he was going to be doing everything for her safety and his freedom. There was no telling what matter of demons Seraphina had littering Halifax now that she knew for sure he was there. He'd bet she'd transported a few dozen to watch him.

"You'll find out when you decide you trust me." He grinned at her, and then suddenly stopped and put a finger to his lips. "Shh hold on a moment."

He squeezed her arm before taking off at a trot down the street. He'd felt demon energy. It wasn't always the easiest thing, but typically, all demons could detect each other when they were close enough—even if they didn't know just what kind they were. He heard her trailing behind and wanted to shove her backwards, but he'd been the one to ask for a demon hunt. Rubbish really, he should've known something would be out there. They lurked in all large cities, and Halifax, whilst it wasn't grand, was by far larger than it had been twenty years prior.

She caught up to him and grabbed his hand. He tried to ignore the warmth of it and looked down at her. Words stuck in his throat when he saw she was holding one of the crazy weapons. Hers was emitting a faint green glow.

"Bloody hell, woman. Why do you have that thing?"

"Because you invited me to go demon hunting, and I should hope for some protection should we come across one." She sounded rather cheeky for a woman who must know demons lay ahead.

"I hope all human women aren't as crazy as you, Eliza. I've never gotten to know one before, and I can easily see you driving me quite mad." He pointed under the gas lamp to a couple. Two women stood, barely touching, underneath it. "Do you see that pair there? Well, that's an illusion. They're Illusion Demons, ugly little buggers really, but I can't find a way for you to see through the guise."

He started to walk forward, and she called his name.

"Lucius. Don't take another step." He looked back to see the barrel of the gun pointing square in his face. "Those look like ordinary people. I don't have anything that can sense a demon's structure like the hunters do. If you're to hunt them down, in proper Alliance fashion, I should like proof that you're not about to have us slaughter an innocent couple."

He wanted to kill her. She was questioning him again. They were never going to get anywhere if she painted him the villain every step of the way. It didn't help that he knew he wasn't good enough for her on a moral scale. He'd wanted to try to be and see where this could go because every second with her seemed worth it. But this? Pointing a gun at his head that she knew could kill a demon was enough. He let the remnant of the soul he had taken seep out of his eyes until they were cold and dead.

"It's called trust, Miss Dorley. Either you believe me, or you don't. But if you choose not to, a couple of rather nasty demons are going to remain in Halifax. I assure you, the choice is yours, but if you decide to be wary of me, take note that there will not be another time coming. This will be our farewell encounter. Mating mark or not, there will be nothing betwixt us." He didn't wait for her. If Seraphina was indeed watching his every move on the streets, he needed to make it look real. Killing a demon really held nothing but energy for him, and if he was going to put on a show, he might as well prove to his mate that his mind tricks were indeed deadly.

Just as he went to lean against the wall, Eliza pushed past him and walked straight up to the couple. He felt as if he'd swallowed a lead ball as he watched. He'd seen plenty of hunter strikes, and frequently it involved a rush of arms and a display of strength, neither of which he was certain Eliza could pull off. He walked behind her just as she approached the two whores, pulled some coin out of her skirts, slipped her hands into the black haired female's hand and walked to the alleyway.

It took every breath in him not to charge after her. He had to assume she knew what she was doing. A flare of light came from the alley as he reached its opening and an inhuman shriek followed. Dropping to the ground, he let himself feel the two illusion demons, both fearful of a Thrasher Demon they owed money. His eyes closed, and without a second thought, he conjured up the scrawny, yellow, deadly demon in the alley. He didn't need to do anything else, just stay focused on holding the illusion long enough to make it effective.

The next scream he heard was distinctly Eliza's, and he wished he could shout to her, to warn her that it was okay, that it was just him. But doing so would mean letting go of the trance, something that may just happen if she didn't stop screaming loud enough to pierce his eardrums.

Lucius squeezed his eyes shut, color mixed with the blackness from closing them so hard until he could once more focus on his own illusion, his fear hallucinations. The creature jumped on the first female. His nails sliced through her throat and dropped her lifeless on the floor. Blood spilled and trickled, even though all that had done the demon in was fear. Then, the other female lunged at the Thrasher. She slipped right through it without noticing and merely turned around and went to use her own claws against the image. However, it was too late. The hallucination of the demon dragged its enormous nails upwards through her torso, and the body dropped to the rocky alley floor—dead.

Lucius absorbed the energy and felt the incredible sense of power as their souls began to depart their bodies. He reached out with one hand, and as if magnetic, they came to him. He didn't relish in the kill as he normally would.

Instead, his eyes flew open. He pushed off the ground and ran down the alley. He cursed when he saw Eliza. She sat, her red dress curled up around her, her back pressed against a building and her hands over her head. Whatever she'd thought she could handle, the Thrasher Demon hadn't been on the list. He sprinted the short distance to her and squatted down, tugging her against him.

"I couldn't have known Thrashers were a fear of yours as well. Otherwise, you should have seen nothing, Eliza. Shh, shh, Eliza. I'm sorry. It's just me. I promise it's just me." He stroked a hand over her head, over and over again trying to calm her down. She wasn't making any sounds, she wasn't moving.

Slowly, she lifted her head, and her voice trembled as she spoke. "What else can you do?"

He kissed her then. Just bent his head down and captured her for his. She was hot and needy as she wrapped her arms around him. Her body was warm from the air, and she mewled as he ran a hand down her back, more to pick her up than anything. Lust burned in his gut, but this wasn't about that. It was about letting her know who he was and that she was safe and cared for. So once he'd picked her off the ground, he held her and kissed her as if he'd almost lost her.

Finally, when he felt the thrumming of her heart calm, he pulled away. "I'm so sorry, love. I should have warned you. I should have told you how it worked."

She looked back up at him, her eyes radiating lust and her body pressed against his. She pulled her hand back and slapped him. The sting was minimal. She was far too dainty to hurt him, but he recoiled his head to make her think it had been a devastating blow.

"That was for not preparing me." She slapped him again, a bit harder this time, but still, the sting didn't last more than a few seconds. "That was for not letting me handle them on my own."

He pulled back, confusion marring his brow as he stared into her heated expression. "Not letting you handle them on your own?" His tone was laced with incredulity.

"Yes." She took a step back from him, touched her hair and pulled on her dress. "I had thought to have a go of demon hunting, which means as the Alliance does it, not in some uncivilized fashion."

Her words stung, she didn't realize it, but the insult ran deep. "Love, might I point out that you screamed and your shot hadn't damaged either of them?"

Eliza huffed, glared at him, opened her mouth agape and then closed it. "I didn't get a fair chance." She crossed her arms over her chest, pushing her lush breasts up toward him. His body, still on fire from simply touching her, growled at him to take her. But it wasn't time. She wasn't ready. He could tell she didn't trust him. Not yet.

"All right, love, you tell yourself that. Now, in proper Alliance fashion, where do we dispose of the bodies?"

The color drained from her face, and he thought he saw her gag slightly. The demons were exposed, showing what they truly were. Little brown bodies, covered in black lumps with beady white eyes. He wasn't positive if their sight was what blanched her color, or the idea of disposing of bodies.

"We would dismember them. Chop them up into small enough sections that they could fit in burlap sacks, attach them to cycles and take them to the incineration room in the Alliance." She nudged the nearest body with her foot. "But we don't have anything to do that with."

She rolled up the red sleeve of her dress and revealed the communicator he'd seen the hunters use prior. Interesting that they all received them. When he'd assumed she had one on the train, he'd thought she'd snuck it out. But if she could contact the guild with it, then she was allowed.

Damn what I wouldn't give to know how half of this bloody shit works.

"Love, what are you doing?"

"We have teams in various areas, most outside the London Guild are recon and intel, but they can do the cleanup. My communicator wouldn't know the proper vibrations to reach them, but the guild will be able to help."

His mind couldn't even grasp how it worked, unless an Angel had helped them, in which case, all of their mysterious technology made a lot more sense. He watched as she twisted a number of knobs, and he saw there were gears on the underside just above a purple crystal.

Interesting.

"Master Agardawes, I know this will not please you, but I've come across some demons. Illusion Demons. They're dead, but I cannot fathom how to dispose of them."

A gnarled, older voice came through the device, and Lucius took a step back, not really knowing why.

"Eliza, we will discuss your insolence at a later time. You have my thanks for neutralizing a threat. Give me your location, and I will dispatch a team. If you are level headed enough to take on demons for your first time alone, I should say your leave is over." The voice stopped, and the crystal ceased to glow.

He heard Eliza mumble something, but he wasn't sure what. His mind was already two steps ahead of hers, contemplating what a cleanup crew would mean for him.

"Love, these hunters that will be coming, they'll have that darling technology that allows them to sense demon blood or energy or whatever it is you lot lock onto?"

Comprehension took hold in her eyes, and she gasped. "We have to get you out of here. Go."

She shoved his arm, and he growled. "I am not leaving you alone in the night. Your Guildmaster might be foolish enough to think you did this on your own, but we know the truth, and I will not leave you unprotected." He swore he heard her growl back before she responded.

"Go to the shops at the end of the alley, once you leave this side street. On the corner, Finnegan's pub. An obnoxious Irish family runs it. I'll be there, and you can watch over. I'll wait at the front of the street, off to the side. It's a weekday, and unlike London, Halifax will not be bustling with people so late in the night."

"There's no way around this. I'm learning that with you. That when you get that little hitch in your voice and put your hands on your hips, like you are now, that I can't win."

He kissed her quickly and strolled out of the alley. For some reason, he felt things were going incredibly well. She didn't realize it, but she was looking at him differently now. Less like he was going to grow a second head and more like someone she wanted to touch, and not just in the heat of the moment. Her eyes had been playful much of their walk.

He smirked and pushed open the pub door.

TWELVE

HER STOMACH FELT as if she was sure to lose the contents of her supper at any given moment. She looked behind her, at the small demons that lay dead on the ground. "You always wanted to do that." She blew out a breath in hopes that it would settle her stomach. Wanting to fight a demon and then thinking she was about to be killed by one of the most brutal she knew about were two separate matters.

Things had been going along fine enough prior. She hadn't been able to stop wondering what he'd meant about the mating mark, hadn't been able to stop wanting to strip him naked and find the bloody thing. Her body heated as she thought about it.

He'd only touched her to comfort her. She knew that in hindsight. But his body next to hers, his hands on her back and his mouth on hers was not a sensation she was likely to forget. She looked down toward the pub and smiled as she saw him pressing his face against the glass to look at her. She laughed and lifted her hand, giving him a small wave. He returned it but didn't stop watching her.

She would be the last one to want to have found a lover in a demon. Even after Felicia had found herself with one, even knowing there were potentially more decent demons out there. She'd wanted to please her parents. She'd always had hopes that she would be able to bring a dashing noble to them one day. It hadn't been entirely farfetched, as they were the ones that funded the guild and the Alliance of Silver and Steam. But that didn't mean they walked down the same halls as her, ate in the same rooms or slept beneath the same roof. Still, it had been her fantasy.

After spending time with Lucius, her desires had shifted away from that dream, and it was him she wanted. She could tell, based on his character and charm, that he wasn't the noblest man in the world. Charming men were normally quick to run from a fight.

But he didn't run away tonight, she told herself.

He'd been on her mind since she'd run away on the train. Her thoughts were an alternation of lust and disgust on a never-ending loop that was likely to drive her mad. Being with him that morning and seeing the concern in his eyes over her tears had been the start at overriding her disgust for him.

Really, had she not known what he was, she would have been enthralled. He was handsome, had some sort of money, was charming and brought her to a release the likes of which she'd never known. Her resolve had shattered when he'd looked at her as if she mattered. His grand gesture hadn't meant anything to her. She almost was upset by his betrayal of his kind. But she wouldn't tell him that because she didn't understand why she even felt that way.

She hadn't really expected him to save her if the situation had come up. She hadn't wanted to need him too. She'd gotten so much more than that. She'd learned exactly what he would do for a kill. It scared her. All that power, the ability to unleash a fear and have someone drop dead from it, it scared her terribly. But he didn't.

The man, the demon, she wasn't sure what she saw him as anymore. It was like a watercolor painting that someone tossed a cup of water on before it dried. Everything was dripping, running together and changing the picture that once was. She was ready to see what would happen. He'd saved her. That was something she would always have to remember because she had a feeling, if she chose him and found some way to persuade the Alliance to leave him alone, that it wouldn't be the last time she saw the demon he was.

"Miss Dorley?"

She almost jumped at the sound of the voice. She'd been so busy staring into Lucius' eyes that she'd gotten lost in them. "Yes."

The man stuck out his hand. "Bradely Kempton. I'm the one they sent to clean up."

She motioned behind her, and he whistled low.

"But how are they just dead? These guns pack a punch and leave evidence." He lifted his weapon, the gun, and put it away as he walked around them. He pulled out a hatchet, and she flinched. She'd never understood how Felicia, or any one of them really, could do this part.

"I assure you, I did nothing extraordinary." The lie slipped out effortlessly, possibly because she hadn't done anything, so it wasn't a lie. She held up her gun, hoping the green crystal would throw him off since Kellan was the only other person who had one. "It stuns, stops the heart from beating. Just like that." She bit the inside of her cheek to force the actual lie out.

The hunter was already slicing into the demon closest to her. The sound made her queasy, and she felt her dinner threatening to make an appearance.

"Interesting. The transmission mentioned you designed these guns. I'm not usually in the field, I'd love something I could stun one with and see what makes it tick."

Ahh, so he is intelligence. Eliza's stomach dropped because she had a bad feeling she now needed to figure out how to make such a gun.

"If you don't mind, I'd like to get back home." She started to walk away when the familiar noise of a communicator stopped her.

"Kempton here."

"Kempton, this is guild leader Morely."

She'd heard the name a time or two around the London location halls, but she had yet to meet the man in charge of the Halifax sect.

"We've picked up disturbance from one badass demon out there. A Fallen; if the graph pulled it in right. It appears to be, well, ironically near the citadel. North Park Street and Cogswell Street."

She had some soul redeeming to do after cowering in a corner anyway and taking down a Fallen might be just what she needed.

Kempton said nothing as he ended the transmission.

"Mind if I tackle that one?"

He raised a brow at her.

"I want to see what these guns can really do. If you want, come a ways behind me, for protection." Now all she'd need to do was knock him out and persuade Lucius to take on a Fallen.

"If you'd like, Miss Dorley. As I said, I'm not typically out here. I was going to run to the quarters and see if I could fetch help. Best if I do that. You head over, but do not get seen."

She nodded obediently. He nodded back and took off on the cycle, this time, she heard the loudness of its departure and was momentarily bitter about the fact that the quieter one had blown up in her face.

She walked hurriedly to meet Lucius, but he was quicker and met her halfway to the pub.

"Remind me, I do not like seeing you alone with men." He grabbed her, right in the middle of the street, and kissed her until she could hardly remember her name.

"Lucius, I—" She said nothing else, rather tugged him down and kissed him a second time, relishing the taste of him—something dark and spicy. She let his shirt go, and his black eyes smoldered at her. "We aren't done. There's a Fallen. I want to see how serious you are."

His face contorted, and she was concerned he was going to unveil everything was a big lie.

"I can't. I can't work my skills on a Fallen, Eliza. We can track it down and try your gun, or better yet, let me use it. But if it gets ugly, you run. Understand?"

He grabbed her chin and tilted it up. His eyes bore into hers, and she almost cried out at the passion, not lust, she saw in them.

"You run like hell and get out of there. Now, where is it?"

"Cogswell and North Park. We need to be quick, though, I only found out because of the other hunter. Well, he's not really a hunter he's intelligence, but anyway, he was called to look because he was out."

Lucius didn't say anything. He just nodded and grabbed her hand. Not even thinking for a moment that someone might see, she let him tug her along.

They didn't speak as they walked. The frivolity of the earlier portion of the night seemed to have drained out of them. She liked him intense. More, though, she liked the way her hand fit into his and how safe she felt next to him. So long as the Fallen didn't turn out to be a trick, a friend of his, she would be done second-guessing him. She wanted him, and she wasn't going to let his species get in the way if other people could look around it. Besides, he looked human, felt human and had all the human parts. She knew that first hand.

Her feet were beginning to tire just as Lucius jerked her arm.

"Very slowly, look up."

She wanted to tell him to stop ordering her around, but it didn't seem to be the appropriate time. She'd never seen a Fallen before. Very few people had, and being an indoor sort of member, she wasn't among the ranks. Eliza wasn't prepared for the splendor of the creature that was perched on the rooftop a building to the left. He was shirtless, wearing only black pants. His body looked as if it was molded from fine clay and slathered with preserving oil. Every ripple of muscle, every inch of skin was a deep brown, almost black, and it called to her. His head was shaved, and she was unaccustomed to such a look, but it worked on him. No wings were sprouting from his back, which she supposed made sense, given he was not an Angel anymore.

"He's stunning, Lucius."

The demon next to her, her mate, scoffed his disgust and utter disagreement.

"I'll let that go since Angels by design are an appeal to one's senses. It's part of the reason why humans don't see them for the demons they actually are and think they're something special."

She narrowed her eyes at him, wanting to lash out for some reason and contradict him.

"Any sort of compulsion you feel, any desire to act out against the normal, is Angel born. Easily pushed aside once you're aware of it, but I can see by the daggers you're throwing at me with your eyes that you're keen to protect that Fallen, even get into a row for the creature. But I need you to close your eyes and shake it off. It's a visual allure."

She didn't want to, but she closed her eyes. It was as if someone dumped a bucket of freezing water over her. All the warmth and protection she'd felt vanished. She gasped, and her eyes darted open, but instead of looking up, she kept her eyes on Lucius.

"That's it, love. Just focus on me. I need to know how that gun of yours works. If I'm to fire it accurately, I need to understand what the desired effect is."

"When you pull the trigger, it's much like any other gun shooting bullets, like the guard uses. However, the trigger depresses into a set of four cogs and the pressure pushes them into motion, which causes them to grind—"

He put his finger up to her lips, and for an overwhelming moment, she wanted to suck it gently into her mouth. But she didn't.

"Love, I mean what is it supposed to do."

"Oh. It will fire a concentrated ray of light. It shouldn't be able to travel much over two-point-five meters, so you must be relatively close. You cannot get an effective shot with him perched upon the roof like a gargoyle."

"Bullocks. I should've known it wasn't going to be easy. Here's what we are going to do. I'm going to take the nice gun from you, and you're going to walk into the street. I want you to make as if you know the Fallen Angel is there."

"You want me to do what?"

"I need you to antagonize him. Pure Angels do not like to be bullied in any fashion. Fallen have never appeared to enjoy it much more. You're going to wait until I'm in place. It may take me a little. I'm going to walk round back of those houses and come out in the alley over to the left and just behind this spot." He was pointing in various directions, but that had never been her strong suit, the words flew over her head.

"How will I know when to begin?"

"You'll see me in place. Just watch that spot, right over there."

He didn't stop to kiss her, which disappointed her on a large scale.

"And, Eliza?"

Her head raised, and she looked into his eyes. So many times, they'd shifted back and forth from dead inside to alive with fire. They were alive now, and she could almost swear she felt his hand brush her cheek.

"Yes, Lucius?"

"When we make it out of this, when I'm done proving to you that this creature will never have my loyalty because it's yours for as long as you would like it. I'm taking you to my inn, and I'm locking you in until I've explored each and every meter of your tanned skin with my tongue."

A shudder raced through her body, and she nodded, unable to form any thoughts—which was fine because he hadn't waited. She watched as he appeared to scamper through the night. He moved so silently, so swiftly, and yet, she was able to follow his movements until he disappeared behind a house. She felt vulnerable without her gun, even if she was untrained in using it.

Being unable to defend herself and unable to even look at the Fallen without compromising her logical thought was unnerving. So she focused on Lucius. On the way, his hair fell just into the center of his eyes. His entire torso seemed to bounce when he laughed, and on how his laugh made her feel. She wasn't a believer in true love. Love took time and learning of the other person. But she could not deny the strength of emotion she felt for Lucius anymore than she could breathe without air.

The thought should have sent her running in the opposite direction, fleeing and leaving Lucius to fend for himself. But she couldn't and wouldn't do that. He was proving himself. They hadn't spent mountains of time learning one another as she'd hoped, but she did know him, from the train ride. He hadn't been falsifying himself. He was daring and charming. She also knew that he knew a woman's body and was ready to be loyal to her if it meant she would trust him.

It all felt as if it was happening so fast, and yet, it was as natural as courtship season as it had begun more than three months before when he'd first entered her dreams. It was early September, and the dance had begun sometime in May. She was ready for him, and she wasn't going to let anyone's opinions get in her way, even if they were the Alliance leaders.

A noise to her right jerked her from her thoughts. Twice in a span of two hours, she'd allowed herself to drift so far into thought and be startled. She looked and saw a rock. Another came flying at her. She looked up and saw Lucius, getting ready to toss a second in her direction.

He stopped when he realized she was looking, raised his hand and counted down from three to one. When his index finger lowered, she stepped out from the house she'd been hiding against. The street was quiet, thankfully. Taking a deep breath, she pulled her dress sleeve up and raised the arm with her communicator on it.

"I'm at the location. I have seen no sign of the Fallen. I have no backup, and I would appreciate assistance from at least the local inspector."

A hiss filled the air, and her blood ran cold. It had worked. As she turned to look behind her, to see if Lucius was ready to fire, a shout came from the other direction. Her head whipped around, the blonde strands streaked across her eyes painfully, and she saw Bradley. He'd managed to catch up.

"Miss Dorley, get down, your weapon did not work. Step out of the way."

As he drove up on the bike, two others fell behind him, another male and a female. However, they were clearly regular hunters. They wore attire similar to the London branches—the female in a corseted top and long skirt, and the male in a black shirt and trousers. Both donned radiation glasses, and for a moment, she thought she might be sick.

Lucius didn't have anything to protect his eyes from the toxic smoke the crystals gave off. Her eyes widened as the three bikes sped past her, all firing their weapons at the Fallen. She was almost too stunned to notice the brush of the demon's hand through her hair. The familiar sound of the crystal burning emanated through the night, and she didn't hold back a smirk as she saw a hole burning into the demon's arm from the corner of her eye.

The effect of looking at him was instant. The goggles have protected the other three, but she was fighting an urge to chase after the hunters, to tackle them to the ground and save the Fallen. Instead, she was the one that hit the ground. Her chin cracked onto the dirt road, and she cried out, only to have a hand slide over her mouth at the same time as she felt someone trying to lift her.

"Eliza, it's me. Don't fight me on this. Let me take you out of here before the demon sensor thing you lot dreamed up points to more than just the Fallen. Let them handle it."

"But I can't just leave them."

He hefted her up into his arms and proceeded to toss her over his shoulder. With every step he took, her head bashed into the lower portion of his back. His arm was wrapped securely around the back of her knees, and he moved quickly behind a row of houses before setting her down. She let instinct guide her as she balled her hand into a fist and punched at his chest. He sucked in a deep breath on impact, and she bit her lip to not cry out at the jamming sensation that jolted up her arm.

"I've told you. I will not back your line of employer. I protect you.

I will always protect you, and I have. I watched the way they fought, they know what they're doing, do they not?"

She nodded grumpily. "Yes, two of them were most definitely hunters."

"Then do not make me pick you up again and carry you in my arms back to my inn. Do not think to tell me no. We're alive. Your chin is bleeding rather badly, but we are alive, and I made a promise to you."

A bell tower chimed twice in the distance. It was two in the morning, and the streets of Halifax were about to become a battle zone. It would only take one wrong noise being heard. They hadn't even attempted to take the fight to some place secluded.

Suddenly, the night went quiet. Everything stopped. She pushed off Lucius' chest and ran for the road, splatters of blood coming from her chin. She stopped at the corner and sighed. They'd taken down a Fallen. One appeared to be limping, but the other two were working on dragging the dead demon off. It may have taken three to one odds, but she found comfort in knowing that the worst of the demons wasn't enough for humans and their weapons.

Eliza walked slowly back toward Lucius. He stood right where she'd left him with his arms crossed. She stopped a few meters away and smiled at him, pressing her hand to her chin to stop the blood.

"Yes, I believe you did make me a promise, sir."

He was on her in a flash, scooping her into his arms and moving as quickly through the streets as he could. She wasn't worried about being seen. By then, her parents would have retired to bed, as had any other citizen that would matter. Drunkards and whores lined the streets at such a late hour, and she cared not if they saw her. She wrapped her arms around his neck as he moved, doing her best to tilt her head back so as not to leave a blood trail, but the pain was intense as she blinked back tears.

Lucius didn't stop until he was outside the inn. His hand jerked over the front of her dress, tearing it and causing her breasts to be slightly visible.

"Lucius!"

"Be quiet. If I'm to bring you to my lodging, you must appear to be a whore, as I did not come here with a wife."

She bit her lip and said nothing as he took her hand and stumbled through the doorway of the inn, pretending to be intoxicated. She did her best to giggle absurdly and fumble her steps as well. They made it past the night guard without incident, and as they reached his room, she realized her chin was no longer bleeding. He opened the door and gestured for her to walk before him.

The room wasn't big. But it had a large enough bed for two, a table with a candle and a small sink. A door led to what must be a loo, and she was grateful that they were in an area where niceties were typically demanded by travelers.

"Come here, by the candle. I want to look at your chin." He turned the water on and dipped the end of a towel into it.

"My chin is fine. It has stopped, the pain will as well in time."

Lucius walked over and tipped her head back, inspecting her chin before slowly rubbing the towel over the wound. The fabric was coarse, and she flinched back.

"I'm sorry, they are a little rough." He rubbed as gently as he could to disinfect the wound. "I'm sorry for tackling you as well. You looked as if you were about to run headlong to save the Fallen."

She flinched as he ran the towel over her face again. He was so gentle, so not demon-like, it would be so easy to forget he was more than a man. But it was not possible. He was so much more. He was a demon willing to give up on his own species for her. Each brush of his hand over her skin sent a buzz through her body. His eyes never met hers, and the frustration she felt built and built as he continued to tend to her. Finally, after her body was all but humming with need, he took a step back.

"That should be okay for the evening. It looks like a severe abrasion, but if it starts again, we must find a physician to look at you."

She reached up and caught his hand as he dropped the towel. "Lucius, you're shaking."

"I was worried. Afraid I would lose you and then worried because I hurt you after promising to look after you."

"Mistakes happen. I can forgive you for that one little lie." She smiled and winked at him as she put her hand on his chest. "But I can't forgive you if you break the promise you made before setting off to find the Fallen. That would be a bargain breaker." The candlelight hid his expression from her as she leaned up and kissed him.

His lips blazed trails of heat over hers, and his growls sent shivers through her body. The day dress suddenly felt too hot for her liking. Her whimper sliced through the small room when he pulled back. She bit her lip to not protest. All her senses were on fire, screaming at her to take him, to surrender herself to him and let the mating mark win. His hands dug into her hair, and his mouth took hers again, hungry and demanding as he licked, nipped and sucked on her tongue and lips.

He walked them, still entangled, over to the bed. When he pulled back to lay her down gently, Eliza smirked at him and pushed his body backwards onto the bed. "I have a better idea, Mister I-Know-My-Way-Around-A-Woman's-Body."

She unfastened the buttons down the side of her dress, and his hands found the edge of the hem without being prompted, tugging it over her body causing a sultry sensation as it pulled over her body. His lips captured hers and released after a few seconds, trailing kisses down her neck as his big hands pushed kneaded her breasts. Briefly, her thoughts were on how she would get home with her clothes in such a condition.

Then his tongue flicked her nipple and heat streaked through her body so hard she trembled. She arched into his mouth, even as her hands worked at his slacks. His heated, thick cock sprang out into her hand. It was just as it had been in the dream, long and thick. Her fingers trailed over it, even as her head spun with pleasure from his mouth and the way his hand squeezed her other nipple. Pleasure built and wetness pooled betwixt her legs. His free hand wrapped around the frilled petticoat and yanked it down. She fumbled as she stepped back from the bed to step out of her undergarments. She was as naked before him as she had been in her dreams, but that had been nothing like this.

His eyes trailed over her as if he was seeing her for the first time as he sat closer to the bed's edge and tugged her to him. His hands sent shocks through her as her body came closer. His cock rubbed against her core, and he pulled her down to him, making her cry out with need. She was done waiting for the moment they'd already shared so many times in their dreams.

She pumped her hand up the length of his shaft before she tugged his head from her breast. Kissing him, she climbed up on his waist. The action pushed his cock deep inside of her, and her sigh mixed with his groan. He stretched her inner walls, and her body clutched at his thick shaft as she continued to slide down the length of him, taking in every last centimeter until their bodies pressed together. She bucked her hips once and arched her chest toward him, the rocking motion a mere start. He pulled her to him, and his mouth latched onto her throat. A scrape of teeth had her hips bucking and her speed increasing.

She shivered as she rode him, taking him in and out, over and over. Her body trembled, not with a release, but merely from the desire. He growled and bit her neck, hard enough it shot pleasure through her, and she cried his name into the silence of the room.

His powerful body rolled to the side and tucked her underneath him, never breaking the rhythm of their thrusts. Her praises passed betwixt them in small gasps of pleasure and demands for him to continue, to go faster, deeper. She was wild with need, and as her body pulsed and rocked against his, she threw her head back— panting and digging her hands into his back. Her heels locked around his arse, grinding him even harder into her body. She couldn't get enough and wasn't aware of anything but his body driving into hers.

His finger reached betwixt them, and he rubbed his thumb hard over her clit as he pounded into her with the wildness of his own need. Her arms flailed, and her hips bucked faster and faster until the rubber band of pleasure broke.

"Lucius!"

Her head thrashed to the side, and her mind spun with ecstasy. Her body clenched and milked his cock as he continued to thrust into her. Her hips moved with his, wanting to help him feel what she was feeling. She felt as his hips slammed into hers, and she watched as the chords in his neck tightened. His grunt of pleasure made her smirk, as did when he collapsed carefully on top her, panting hard. She could feel his cock twitching inside of her, and it set off tiny sparks of pleasure.

He was careful not to drop his full weight on her, and she wound her arms around his neck and kissed him deeply. When they finally stopped, his eyes were such a deep black it frightened her. Without thinking, she jerked back.

"Don't be alarmed, Eliza. I promise they get darker and wider when I come. I swear I'm not having thoughts of murdering you. In fact, the only ideas I'm having are of doing that again. And again." He lowered his face into her neck and nuzzled it.

The action tickled her, and she laughed and relaxed. There were so many questions she still had for him. "As much as I want that, my parents will send out every copper in Halifax if I do not return and be awake prior to them."

He sighed, pushed up off her and slid free from her body. She bit her lip to not cry out at the loss. She felt empty, colder. She shook her head, trying to remind herself there was a mating mark, and that was the cause. Not that she was falling for him, at least not for certain. Things would be different. Felicia had warned her of that.

And she was certainly correct.

Her head still spun with pleasure as he pulled her into his side and wrapped his arms around her.

"Mmm, do I have to return you? You know there are Changeling Demons who steal people away in the night."

She laughed and rolled closer to him, putting her head on his chest. "You do. But only after you show me this supposed mating mark, mate."

She grinned up at him, and he sighed before pushing her to the side and standing up.

"Do not give me hell. We have no control where the thing shows up. Don't forget, you've seen it before, in our dream meetings." He stood up from the bed and walked to the edge, his body slick with sweat and his cock still erect.

A shudder passed through her thinking about wrapping her mouth around the purple, swollen head, and she swallowed, pushing the longing back. "I see nothing, Lucius. Not even the marks of a warrior."

He grimaced, and she wondered if she'd offended him, but he slowly turned. Her eyes traveled up his well-muscled body with appreciation, but the half-gasp, half-laugh slipped out as her eyes found his backside. She put her hand over her mouth to try to stop it, but it was no use.

"Oh."

He jumped back into the bed, pinned her hands above her head and kissed her quickly. "I said you are not to laugh, Miss Dorley."

She only laughed harder, and tears formed in her eyes. His mated mark was on his arse cheek, and she most certainly did not remember that.

He stood up again and picked up his clothes. "We do need to see you home quickly. It must be close to dawn, and I'd like to be back here and rest before then. Plus, I may have made a mess of your dress and no mate of mine will be seen half hanging from her clothing."

They laughed and spoke a little as they dressed and returned to her home. The inn was only three streets over, and she was shocked. She'd never known one could be within an hour's walk when the plots of land, gifts from the king, could span so much space. Her hand wrapped around the black gate, and she stopped to kiss him again.

They'd been stealing kisses the whole walk, and she was upset that this would be her last one. Sometime in the course of the night, betwixt when she'd been thrown to the ground outside and when she'd screamed his name in pleasure, she'd come to realize that it was most definitely more than lust on her end as well.

When they pulled back, a smile was on his lips. "Goodnight, Eliza." He winked at her.

"Lucius, come back in four night's time. I want to try that power of yours on my parents, but we have prior engagements."

His face lit up as he picked her up and twirled her in the air. Somehow, she hadn't pictured him as the gleeful type.

"Anything for you, Eliza. I will see you in four days." He set her back down on the ground and kissed her cheek.

"Oh, and don't miss me in my dreams tonight." She smiled wide and pushed open the gate, leaving him standing near it, grinning like a fool.

THIRTEEN

SERAPHINA CLOSED her eyes and rolled her head. Her muscles were stiff and sore from a long night with Muriel. She'd thought the Angel would be ready far sooner than appeared to be the case. Letting her out of her demonic restraints had led to a battle she hadn't anticipated. But it was over now. Angelic blood of both varieties had splattered like flung paint on the floor and the walls. Her chest rose and fell from the exertion, but Muriel lay subdued on the floor. One wing jutted up from her body at an unnatural angle, and the demon restraints were back in place. She ran a hand through her hair and gently massaged her head where the little bitch had slammed it into the floor before walking over and squatting down in front of her old friend.

"Did you really think you could best me, Muriel? It's no secret that flight aides the Pure, but nothing is hampering a few months old Fallen." She gestured to the room. "I am in charge of this, of all of this. With power and control like mine, what chance did you stand killing me?"

Muriel's lip dripped ichor onto the floor, and her face appeared to be in a frozen grimace, likely from the wing. Seraphina had done nothing to try to untwist the broken appendage. There was no point since it was slowly going to be removed in its entirety before she left the room. She'd lost the patience to draw it out. She wanted Muriel to fall fast and hard to prove her point. That she would rule them all.

"You will never win, Seraphina. You can tempt me with Izazal's body all you want. He is of no appeal to me now."

Seraphina reached a hand out, moving her fingers toward the short feathers on the broken wing and jerked. The Angel's body lifted off the floor as her howl radiated through the dungeon like room.

Seraphina continued on that wing, taking clumps of five and six feathers at a time, for the course of the next five hours. Each and every scream of pain and curse pulled from the beautiful Angel's mouth was a potent drug for her.

"The last one on this wing, Muriel. The very last one."

She reached out and grasped the last feather on the broken wing. Once she pulled it, blood would spill. The feather connected all the rest, the rooted feather. The most painful to remove and the only one that if not removed could generate a new set of beautiful white wings. She dug the tips of her fingers into the bloody mess surrounding it and jerked the root feather out in one swift motion.

"No!" Muriel's scream was elongated from the pain, and she writhed around the floor, her body convulsing from the pain.

Seraphina knew the hurt as well. She knew just how long and how excruciating it would be as the powers and skills that made Angels special drained from half of her body. Forty-four minutes. Forty-four minutes of screaming, shaking and crying. The grin on her face was cruel, and she pushed the heel of her black shoe into the oozing mass where the feather had been.

Muriel whimpered and cursed, but she didn't try to get out from under Seraphina's heel. She was broken, bloody and shortly going to be begging for the taste of Izazal's blood.

"I'll leave you to your misery. And trust me, I know the misery. Don't bother believing that because I leave the door to this room open, you can escape. I'm sure you can already tell movement won't be an option. Try not to miss me too much. I'll see you again when you're ready for more. If it's one thing I learned from my own fall, it's that the body can only endure so much blood loss and pain before it shuts down. Whilst I would love to see your body an empty shell on the floor, I need more warriors. So my advice is sleep to ignore the pain. If you can."

She patted Muriel on the head and rose to leave the room. True to her word, she left the door open. A temptation, a hidden initiation that she would love to watch Muriel struggle for if the pain did not make her pass out. She nodded to the guards and continued to her office, where once again, the Stranglehold duo waited for her. Only this time, it was because she had summoned them.

"And just how did it go last night? Was it only last night?" Her time had melted away as she'd been with Muriel for the better part of the last day and six more hours today.

Dean spoke up. "I am not sure what you had planned, Seraphina, but Marquese is dead. We watched and did not interfere as you ordered."

She narrowed her eyes and nodded her head. "Interesting. So you watched the entirety of the matter?"

"Every moment, your highness," Arial answered for his brother.

She smiled seductively at him. She enjoyed how reverent he was in regard to her position.

"Then tell me how an inventor and a Nightmare Demon succeeded in killing one of my Fallen warriors." She had promised Lucius some help. She hadn't expected him and his play-toy to be able to destroy her own. However, if they had, it was knowledge she needed. Lucius would have been next to useless in trying to fool the mind of a Fallen, but perhaps that inventor had tools up her pretty silk sleeves that gave her an advantage.

"They were not alone. Three others joined them. Alliance members. I thought they only hunted in London. I thought you said that's why we could begin to move out in other areas. Are we sending our people, our family, out to die?"

She had her dagger to this throat before he'd finished his sentence. "Dean, I'll remind you politely not to take that tone of voice with me." The blade bit into the demon's neck, and the blood trickled over the silver edge. "You will not question me, and in fact, you two are dismissed. If I so much as see you lingering in this side of Hell, I will personally see to it that you die and your souls remain with the others dear Lucius is obtaining." She pulled the knife back, relishing the slick slurping sound as it drew a slightly thicker line of blood. "Out!"

Both demons fumbled to get up and shuffle out the door. She closed her eyes and breathed, trying to calm the rage. A Fallen with untempered anger could level a whole city with their strength and then, using the compulsion that seeped from their pores, trick the inhabitants into thinking they did it with. Unfortunately, only humans were susceptible to it.

"So you had help, Lucius." Her words echoed in the empty expanse of space. "It would seem there are more players in town, and if Lucius doesn't hurry, I'm going to have to take matters into my own hands." She walked to her chair and sat down, but gazed into the mirror hanging on the wall. Her eyes blazed, and her fangs were distended from her anger. Muriel wouldn't be ready for another round, so she would use the time to plan and see if perhaps killing the Alliance members wouldn't be as useful as converting some of them.

SHE'D GROWN LOST in her planning. Documents spread across her desk of plans and profiles of the guild. She hadn't realized how many days had gone by since she'd gone to Muriel. When Izazal entered without knocking and put his hand on her desk, she hadn't even blinked as she tossed him into the far corner wall. His grunt didn't even cause her to pick her head up.

She had a plan. If Lucius were to fail at infiltrating the operations of the Alliance, she would have no problem executing him for his failure. There was now a way for her to get inside, a way that she'd been too cautious to try prior, but if the Alliance of Silver and Steam was not limited to London, measures needed to be taken. It was only a matter of time before the truth in the actual number of demons would be something of public knowledge. There would be a day when that was knowledge she would release, but not until she had enough Fallen, and now enough Alliance members, fighting for her. Fighting for Hell.

"Seraphina, my liege." Izazal was back in front of her again, down on one knee with his head bent in the subservience required of the Angels to their leaders.

"What, Izazal?" She spat the words, but dropped her eyes back down to the profiles of the few hunters she had, trying to pick the right one to break first.

"Seraphina, it's been three days since you left Muriel's door open. She almost walked right out this morning. Had the guards been any less than Fallen themselves, she would have succeeded."

She let her fangs slip out further and hissed at him. "Do not tell me how to do my job." Though, she was annoyed at herself. Three days of planning was too long. Muriel's fight could start to return. She would need to finish it, quicker than she would have liked. The pain from her wing being destroyed would have vanished days ago, the wounds all healed from the torture as well. She would still be weak, but Seraphina had lost the advantage of playing with the Angel now.

"Thank you for the message, Izazal. I apologize for the outburst. Please ready yourself for your part, and I will see to Muriel's final fall."

Leaving her work behind, she transported to the cell, and Muriel twitched where she lay on the floor, hands still bound together.

"I was beginning to hope someone had killed you and I would be rescued." Muriel's voice was soft and weak, but clearly filled with misguided hope.

She wasted no time and took her dagger to the remaining wing, slicing deep into the flesh and cutting out a quarter of the feathers. "That's the problem with hope. It doesn't get you anything." She punched Muriel in the nose and smirked as blood trickled. She had to give the Angel credit. Despite the bite of the blade, she'd said nothing and hadn't moved at all. "Think you can remain quiet this time?" She blew Muriel a kiss and slammed the dagger to the hilt into the woman's shoulder.

Slowly, she dragged the blade down, feeling the pull and tension as it sliced messily through the root feather. She wasn't prepared for the elbow that slammed backwards and smashed into her teeth.

"Bloody hell." The dagger slipped, but it was so deeply embedded into the flesh that it only drooped, instead of falling out.

Muriel thrashed, slamming her own head once and then twice into the ground. Her body shook even as the screams ripped through the room. Seraphina took hold of the hilt once more and continued to pull it through flesh, curving once she'd passed the middle of Muriel's back, and then slicing upwards. The Angel's cries were loud enough to temporarily deafen her, but she didn't mind. In the future, she would not be the one to strip an Angel, only special cases like past combat brethren who had forsaken her, like Muriel.

Finally, reaching the top of the incision again, she jerked the blade free, not even moving back as the chunk of flesh, muscle and root feather tumbled backwards onto her foot. A line of blood sprayed into her mouth, and she only grinned wider. The screaming continued even as she stood up from behind Muriel and tossed the mess into a bin. Before passing Izazal in the doorway, she turned to look at the convulsing form of the Angel on the floor.

"I warned you, Muriel. All those years ago, I told you that you would pay for letting Demetrious die. Consider this the beginning of your penance."

Seraphina pulled Izazal's mouth to hers and kissed him, purring as she rubbed her body against his. She made certain his erection pressed into her stomach before slowing the grind of her hips into his and the dance of her tongue inside his mouth. She pulled back and ran her tongue over the seam of Izazal's mouth once more. He had been such a good lover, but he would be tainted after sleeping with Muriel, no longer a suitable bedmate.

He groaned, and she whispered into his ear, "Feed her until she's able to move again, and then fuck her until she can't remember anything but what a pair you two were."

He nodded, and she smiled to no one at all as she took the final step out of the room. *Sometimes it's just too good to be me.*

FOURTEEN

NIGHT WAS FALLING OVER HALIFAX, and nothing could wipe the grin from Lucius' face. Eliza hadn't been around to see him for the past days. He'd stood guard, quietly outside her home each night. When she'd finally returned from the feast, or the guests had left her home each evening, he'd felt her slip into sleep and had joined her from outside. His prick stirred as he stuck his head under the running tap to cleanse his hair. Just the thought of spending the night with her was enough to make him solid as a pole, and they didn't even always start in bed. They ended there, naturally, but it wasn't just about the lovemaking.

The first night in her dreams, they'd taken a walk along the Thames, the upper part, nearest the Royals. It had been a lovely evening. No demons were attacking them, never were in her dreams because he controlled them. He would never let the negative thoughts in at night for her ever again.

At first, he'd felt he was manipulating her until Lucius remembered that it was her desires and wants just as much as his that dictated what happened when he entered her dreams. That, and the knowledge that she woke up every time he left her after he'd been certain to pleasure her like no other male ever would be able to because she was his.

The next night, she'd forced him to sit through a dreadful opera, but her mouth had found his cock and sucked him intently whilst they'd listened.

The last night had been a session in her labs at the guild. He'd marveled at how they looked, at the use of crystals instead of candles for light, and she'd abruptly sealed off access to those details in order to work on a crystal motorbike that had literally blown up on her and caused her holiday to Halifax. She'd been all crazed and sexy as she'd flown about, tinkering here and there. That moment had done him in. At that moment, watching her hair covered in soot and grease as she babbled about a frequency of some sort, he fell in love with his mate.

He whistled as he put on the black suit and grey cravat that he'd worn the first time he'd met her on the train. He felt as if it would be a good omen because he was going to tell her he loved her. She'd already asked him to pretend to court her, so they wouldn't have to sneak around Halifax, but he was going to press the matter until she allowed him to truly ask her father for permission to entertain his daughter. His steps were lighter as he walked down the familiar path.

He was running a little late. Seraphina had sent a new demon with a message and a target. Though it sickened him, he found a drunk in the light of afternoon and took his soul for her. There had been no questions from Seraphina of his intentions, no demands he move faster. So, he chose to believe his ruse was working. Soon, he and Eliza would be free, and Seraphina would run rampant with false information, giving the Alliance a chance to end her reign. He really believed that, with her exterminated, the order would return to what it had been. Demons would still be topside, and humans would still die, but it would be as nature clearly intended it to be and not a full scale, dual species war.

The familiar tree loomed in the distance, and his grin widened. The night would be perfect. So perfect, she wouldn't be able to say no. They hadn't broached the concept of a mating, or him being a demon since the first day, and he was grateful, but sticking one's head in the sand was not how things got done. He leaned back, crossed his feet at the ankles and fixed his bow tie.

It was late, and he could feel the energy patterns of so many sleeping people around him, including Eliza's. Not wasting any more time, he closed his eyes and sought her out. He found her sitting in the same room with lush golden sheets and luxurious curtains as the night he had taken her body for the first time against the glass window.

A different location, but the same room. He wondered if her thinking on it meant anything. He was so busy looking at the room, he didn't notice her sprawled out on her back on the bed, stark naked. One hand was playing with her breasts, and her legs were spread, slender fingers dancing across her glistening core. An invitation if he ever saw one. She groaned and tossed her head back chasing away the plans he had to do this right and proper. His cock punched out into his pants, and he closed his eyes to not jump on her and startle her. "Eliza," he rasped out whilst making sure his clothes were gone as well. There would be no need for them with what he was going to be doing to her.

Her eyes opened slowly, and he was hit with another surge of lust as she blushed.

"No, no don't do that. Don't ever do that." He crossed the room in two strides to where she lay on the bed.

He pressed his mouth to hers as his hand took hold of hers and moved her fingers in a slow circle across her swollen clit. She cried out into his mouth and arched off the bed even as her free hand raked across his chest. She'd been adventurous of sorts in bed, but seeing her pleasure herself had his own release pounding through him, and he had to bite his tongue to force it back. If she was already willing and waiting, this was going to be all about her.

He left her mouth and pressed kisses down her body, still running his fingers over her core. The desperate moans rising from her knocked him off his game, making his mind spin with lust as he laved his tongue over her pebbled nipple and bit down on it. He let her hand go and pushed it aside as he slipped his finger into her wet sheath. He blew hot air across her nipple before continuing to kiss his way down her body, stopping at her core. He licked a path up it whilst his finger continued to work in and out.

"Oh, Lucius. Yes, Lucius. Yes."

Her voice was hoarse, and she trembled beneath his mouth as he let his tongue slip inside and swirl around as his finger continued to thrust in and out. Her panting was driving him mad, and he dragged his cock into his hand and squeezed the head of his shaft before pulling back from her body.

"Love, touch me. Stroke me whilst I taste you more."

Her hand folded around his length, and his hips bucked into her hands. He returned his head betwixt her legs and slipped a second finger inside, scissoring it with the first as he licked her folds over and over.

Her hips were frantic, and her touch on his erection grew strong and stronger every time he pleased her. He was as relentless with his tongue and two fingers as she was with his cock, fisting it with both hands and creating a friction so potent, his cry broke through the room at the same time as hers.

He didn't stop, though, his tongue continued to lick, flick, swirl and thrust into her until her knees clamped around his head and her hand let go of his cock. Her fingers dug into his hair as she rode his mouth. Her second release jerked through her body so hard, he felt the pressure on his cheeks.

"Lucius. Oh my god, Lucius." Her voice was sultry, her legs unwound from his head, and she went from clutching his hair to running her fingers through it. "You weren't supposed to see that, but you were late, and you were all I was able to think about as some rich Englishman pawed at me all evening."

He saw red at the idea of another man sitting anywhere near her, let alone touching her. He kissed a trail back up her body and swung his body over hers, dragging his still erect cock across her core, letting just the tip slip inside as he nuzzled her neck.

"Love, it was the most beautiful thing I've ever seen. The most erotic. The most amazing. And I'm going to make love to you now if you think you can handle a third round of pleasure." He winked down at her and sank his shaft slowly inside her body.

She moaned and arched up to meet him, shoving her breasts near enough to his mouth that he kissed the swell of both. "If you stop, I shall have to find a way to torture you for weeks on end, Lucius Willan." She laughed, ruining the threat behind the words.

He gyrated his hips, sheathing himself inside her fully. "Well, we can't have that now can we, love?"

He claimed her mouth, and his hips started a slow and sensuous slide in and out of her. He saw her hands fist the golden sheets, and he smiled despite himself. She was saying his name like a mantra, as if he were sacred, until suddenly, she was screaming it, but the tone was all wrong.

"Lucius! Lucius help me! Help me!"

Her scream sliced through him. One minute he was fucking her slowly, and the next, she was gone, and he was laying in a mess of sweaty sheets.

He slammed his mind back into his body, taking himself out of the trance. Frantically, he forced his brain to function. Something had happened to his Eliza. He leapt off the tree he was leaning on and sprinted across the cobblestone road. He stared in transfixed horror at the wrought iron gate standing open, and the blood tracked along the gravel path.

"Eliza!" he bellowed, not caring if the neighbors overheard him.

His shoes sent gravel flying as he raced up the path. The front door was closed, and when he wrapped his hand around the gold plated knob, it swung open. The smell of blood and death mixed in his nose. Fear gnawed away at him as he looked. The blue sofa was flipped over, blood streaked across it like a path to the woman lying on the floor. She was dressed in finery, save for the slice that went from ear to ear. Blood drained from her neck, and though she was gone, he needed to know by how much. Her cheek was warm to the touch, but cooling ever still, and he suspected the woman had been dead only minutes. Her hair was the same spun blonde as Eliza's, and she'd never spoken of visitors, which meant he was looking at Eliza's mother—dead and bloody on the floor.

"Eliza!" he roared as he began to race through the halls.

One night, she had shown him her home in his dream, all but her bedroom, the one room he needed to locate. He took the stairs two at a time, in some instances three. A man in a butler's outfit lay curled in a ball, blood running like a river down the steps from his stomach. His mind spun with fear was not his Eliza, but he had no clue of what he would find. He turned onto the second floor and blew through the open door in front of him. A large bed draped in expensive linens held another body. Another man lay in sleeping clothes, and the cover had been tossed off his body. No blood marred his form, but his face was frozen in shock. He'd been strangled to death.

"Dean and Arial."

He cursed and ran out of the room. How many more dead would he find? He frantically checked the next two doors, screaming for Eliza until he finally heard her shout his name. His heart was pounding like a mass of carriages trampling through a city. His eyes darted from left to right, taking in the smashed pottery, the torn wallpaper and the shattered window fragments that covered the floor.

Everything had all happened so quickly, and whilst he'd kept her all but trapped in a dream, she'd been in danger. How many blasted demons had been sent there and how was she still alive to call out to him?

"Lucius, please. I need help."

The fear in her voice tore him in half. He turned and ran from the room. Following the sound of her sobs, he ignored the next door and stopped in front of the final door in the hallway. It was open, and he could see her. Fury ripped and clawed at him. He felt his eyes go a deadly shade of black.

She wore a lavish pink sleeping gown as she lay on the floor, leaning against a luxurious oak, four-post bed. Tears tracked down her face, and the gown was marred with a giant red stain across her stomach. Her fingers clutched desperately at the wound, and he was by her side in a flash.

"What happened, love? Who was here? Who did this to you?"

He could tell Arial and Dean had been there, but slicing a victim open was not their modus operandi. Something else had been there. Something had needed to come through the front door.

Could Seraphina have caused this? He growled at the thought and did his best to calm down, for Eliza's sake.

"Please. Need my communicator."

She lifted her hand off her stomach to point to the strange communication device. The blood flowed slowly from the wound, and he sighed in relief when he realized it was deep and painful, but hadn't nicked anything serious or the blood wouldn't be moving as slow. He'd killed many dreamers through gutting, he knew what it looked like, and she would be okay. That would not stop him from tracking down every creature responsible, even if he died from his lack of physical usefulness in a fight in the process.

Lucius scrambled up and placed a kiss on top of her head before grabbing the device. "How do I make it work, Eliza? What do I do to get help to you?" The blasted thing looked like a watch wrapped in a piece of leather with a shit ton of external knobs sticking out from the sides. He was momentarily grateful she had it to use, so there was no need to leave her side to find the police.

"Pass it to me." She held her hand outstretched, and he put the device in it.

He watched as she pushed a series of knobs and spoke weakly into the device when he heard the man from the other night.

"Guildmaster, I need help. Demons attacked my family. My family, oh my god." Her voice shattered, and a sob wracked her body.

He wanted to pull her against him and tell her it would all be okay. But, truthfully, it would most likely never be okay when she

NIGHTMARE IN STEAM   151

realized she was possibly the only survivor. There was a floor above he had not checked, but of the three bodies he happened upon, it was clear that she was the only one not intended to die.

"Miss Dorley, I need you to be calm. Are you all right?" Concern was evident in the tone of the man on the other side, presumably the man who ran the Alliance of Silver and Steam. The man responsible for getting her tied up in such things.

No, that was all you, Lucius.

"I believe so. A Thrasher demon was here, he didn't come alone, and he was very deliberate, sir. He sliced slowly through my stomach, once I was awake enough to know what was happening, and then left. Please, I have to see my family."

His stomach lurched, knowing full well two of the three bodies had been her parents.

"Thank God. Remain where you are. I will get in touch with the few members there, and they will alert the Metropolitan Police. We must make sure this is handled to appear to be nothing more than an attack. Do you understand me, Eliza?"

She nodded slowly, her eyes hadn't left Lucius' since he'd come flying into the room. "Thank you, Master Agardawes. Thank you."

She turned the small knobs on the device, and he heard the distinct turning of gears before she set it on the floor. Tears shone from her beautiful brown eyes, and she blinked, sending them down her cheeks.

"Oh, Lucius, what have you done?"

FIFTEEN

THE PAIN TRAVELED through her body like a current. Her vision was blurry, and her eyes watered, but it wasn't entirely from the pain. Lucius wasn't all that he had appeared to be. The betrayal stung worse than the wound the Thrasher demon had given her as it plunged a long claw into her side. He was by her side, his eyes staring into hers, and she wasn't certain if she wished to strike him for lying or beg him to hold her until the Alliance members arrived to give her a tonic for the pain and some stitches for the wound. She could feel the blood leaking out slower now. She would be fine, but her heart was damaged beyond repair.

"What happened, Eliza? Tell me that first, and then I swear to you, we can talk about anything you wish."

"Oh, but they are one in the same, Lucius."

Her voice had a nasty bite to it, and he flinched.

"You are the reason this happened, and that is why we need to talk."

He tried to reach a hand out to caress her face, but she pulled back, the motion sending a new rift of pain through her abdomen.

"I don't understand. Eliza, who was here? What did this?"

"I need to know what you saw as you got to me, Lucius. It's important."

"Love, there is nothing more important than knowing who attacked you so they can be found."

She shook her head, fresh tears stinging her eyes. She'd heard the sounds as they'd moved through the house. Even as she'd been lost in pleasure with Lucius, she'd vaguely heard something. Once the demon had woken her with its claw, she'd heard the sounds in the rest of the house. She'd heard her parents.

"There are. Like my parents. You weren't here, Lucius. You didn't hear what I heard, what I'll always hear in my nightmares."

The tears were falling at an alarmingly fast rate, and she squeezed her eyes shut as tight as she could to stop from crying, but she could feel them traveling paths down her cheeks and dripping off her nose, anyway. She didn't pull back as he tucked her against his body, his hand stroking through her bed-mussed hair.

"Eliza, it wasn't pretty. I do not know who is who in your household, nor will I pretend to." He paused and let out a deep breath. She exhaled on a cry, already anticipating the direction of the conversation. "There was a woman downstairs in the parlor who did not make it, she was a member of your family based on her appearance, of that I am certain. The door at the top of the stairs, whose is it?"

Tears tumbled down her cheeks, but no sound came out. Her mother was the only woman in the house apart from the cook. It was as if her vocal cords were paralyzed when all she wanted to do was scream, throw things and hit Lucius. The tears continued, and she struggled to make herself vocalize the words.

"Father," tumbled out.

"I'm so sorry, Eliza. So very sorry."

A shudder traveled through her body, and her scream of agony was loud enough to leave her throat raw. The tears fell faster and faster as she listened to him tell her about the man on the floor, and the condition of the house. She listened, but she didn't hear him speak. Her mother and father were truly not the best parents, but they were hers, and in the end, they did love her. They were gone because she'd fucked around with a demon. Because she'd allowed herself to trust the depths of kindness and passion she'd witnessed in his eyes. Solid black eyes that could look just as soulless. She'd never know how he was able to fake such emotion, but she would never trust another demon, perhaps not even Greyston or a Pure Angel.

Her body shook with tears, and her throat grew hoarser from her incomprehensible screams and sobs. Minutes ticked by before she remembered that she would need to speak to him. Give him one last chance, one time to prove her wrong and give the Alliance information they would need to take Seraphina down and set forth new laws for all demons. She forced the air out of her lungs in shaky breaths until the crying stopped. She pushed away from him, not having even realized he was holding her again.

"Lucius, I need to talk to you before the Alliance comes."

Should this all be a lie, he would need time to flee from her home and get far enough away that a crystal tracker wouldn't sense him. If it wasn't a lie, she would be forced to keep him there for the Alliance to dispose of, regardless of how terribly the idea made her heart cry out in pain.

He nodded his head, his eyes still filtering anger and concern. Odd that he was still putting on an act for her.

"Who did this, Eliza? Tell me so I can stop them from ever doing it again."

"Friends of yours, actually. Though they told me there were at least eight demons loose in the manor."

"I'm sorry, what?"

"Dean and Arial. Stranglehold Demons, I believe, based on their prominent brow and larger than life hands. They were terribly talkative, Lucius. Which means, now you will have to be." Her voice was steely, and she watched as the color drained completely from his face.

Confirmation received.

"Damn it! Bloody fucking hell!"

He launched off the floor beside her, and she watched as his fist punched into the wall, shattering the plaster and sending small flakes of it the floor. Tears began again, this time for his betrayal.

He turned then, his eyes a wash of fury. "What did they tell you, love? What lies did they try to use?"

"They said this was your mission. That you had been assigned to infiltrate the guild and the Alliance through me. That the mating mark was branded onto you by Seraphina." Her voice shook with the tears, and she flinched as he smashed the wall again. "Is it true, Lucius? Don't lie to me, not anymore."

He didn't come any closer. In fact, he appeared to back towards the door ever so slightly. "That is a lie. That mating mark on my arse is real."

He clenched his jaw, and somehow she knew he wasn't lying about that. Maybe it was the tension in his face or the anger that he probably wouldn't have at being exposed if it were a lie. He could easily pick another victim, even an apprentice who wouldn't have too much knowledge of the demons and the clock workers were kept utterly in the dark.

She nodded, her eyes dry. "You neglected to speak on the rest, Lucius."

His shoulders rose and fell as she watched him inhale deeply. "I did it for us, Eliza."

Confirmation.

"I swear it."

"Please explain to me, as quickly as you can whilst I pass judgment on your actions, how using me to get information to the bitch that we fight is for us." Her tone was laced with ice, and she inhaled as a wave of pain crashed over her. She slowly moved her hand and saw the bleeding had begun to come quickly again. She must have moved in such a fashion to have opened the wound further. He must have seen what she did because he took a step toward her.

"The Alliance will care for me. You've lost any right to that. It's deep, but it will not kill, and someone should arrive soon. It's been almost a half an hour since the mayday was placed. My head is woozy, though, blood loss and all that, so I suggest you explain quickly."

She hadn't lied. The room had been growing fuzzy and dim. Her head was swimming with pain, but she hadn't realized it until she'd been able to calm down. She didn't know how much longer she would last, or how she'd made it that long, as she'd known others to pass out far quicker.

"I was given a choice. Seraphina has spies everywhere. Something I damn well should have known but didn't. She found out about you and told me to use you. She owns me, Eliza. I messed up and got caught, and if I don't obey, every demon I've ever fucked with will be allowed to have a pound of flesh from me. Then she'll kill me." He walked back over to her but didn't sit next to her. "I was selfish, Eliza. So selfish, I'm over a thousand years old. I wasn't in the mindset to wish to die. I'm a demon. I was simply doing what I do for a boss. Much like you do at the Alliance."

She hissed at him as if he'd struck her. "We don't kill for anyone."

"Your hunters kill every demon they encounter without so much as seeing who and what they are, with the exception of the rare Angel, I presume. That is killing, love."

His voice held its own bite, and she recoiled as his words sunk in. He wasn't wrong. Felicia had even tried to kill Greyston when she'd met him, but the pheromones from him being an Incubus had messed with her mind. Then it had been too late. Were there other demons out there, like Greyston, hunting their own kind? Lucius wasn't one they would have saved before. He was making that abundantly clear, but the demon he was now had humanity. Killing him on sight would seem cruel now.

"Fine. I will not argue that even though I had never realized how potentially wrong we were until now. But, that doesn't answer my question. How is using me to betray both myself and the Alliance not an issue?"

"Angels, even Fallen, are held to their word. It's just how they are. I struck a bargain with Seraphina that, if I did it, she would release me from her service and never go after you."

She felt her face turn a frown, and he rushed to continue.

"I was going to do it. Only I wasn't. I wanted to tell you once we were safely inside your home where no one would be able to interfere. I wanted to feed her false information and then take you away."

She nodded as the information processed. *How can I tell if this is the truth, or if the version told by the demons he seems to know is the truth?* She closed her eyes as the room spun. She couldn't trust him ever again, but he didn't deserve to die. She knew he wasn't the same demon from a week before, probably even from three months before when it had all begun. But he'd crossed a line, and it was the end.

"I believe you, Lucius. I honestly do." Relief flooded his eyes, and she held up a hand. "You need to come with me to the guild, to the Alliance, and let us know how we can reach Seraphina to take her out of the picture."

"I cannot do that, Eliza. You lot wish to eradicate demons from the face of the Earth, and we have been around, just as you and every animal, for a purpose. I had every intention of sending her in circles, throwing her plans off and alerting The Alliance so they could handle it. But I will not aid in the destruction of my species as a whole."

Her heart broke. They did need to reevaluate something, but one thing was certain. If he would allow the creature that was behind the slaughter of her family to exist, there was nothing left for them. She looked at the carpet, stained a vicious red from her blood, and nausea swept through her.

"Then you need to leave, Lucius."

"No. I will make you understand. I'm not leaving you."

She was eerily calm as she looked up at him. "Yes, Lucius, you are. You crossed a line and showed me who you really are, deep down. But I've seen another side of you. A side that deserves to live, despite it all, because I choose to believe you will only harm those you have to until you can find a way out. I don't even know if you will find a way out, but the demon that I love would." She hadn't realized that she did love him until the words came out. It was natural really that she'd finally found someone who was right for her, who made her happy, and he would be a demon with a past too dark and corrupt to change.

"I love you, Eliza. You have to believe me." He sounded so different, pathetic even.

"I do, Lucius. I do not doubt anything you've told me. But I cannot be with you, and the Alliance is coming, at least I have to hope they will be coming soon because I don't think I will last much longer. You need to get out. You need to make sure that you keep on living. For me." She wanted to kiss him, just one last time, but she didn't.

"Eliza I—"

"Get out. Get out now, Lucius!" she shouted as best as she could and closed her eyes. The urge to sleep was overwhelming. She felt a shift in the room and heard him turning. Whether or not he would actually leave, she'd never know. With her eyes closed, her brain took over, and she breathed in deeply as she surrendered to unconsciousness.

SERAPHINA COULDN'T HELP but smirk as Muriel strutted past her, obviously well sated from a good fuck and blood addiction after a full day with Izazal.

"Not an ounce of self-disgust I notice?"

The newly Fallen stopped and turned back to her. A day had passed since the fall had been completed, and thanks to having Izazal's blood, which contained some of her blood, Muriel would maintain loyalty to her. She wasn't the first Angel Seraphina had tried it on, but she was the first one from her combat unit that she'd managed to find. Izazal had fallen on his own. The stupid fool had decided he was too in love with human women, and it was forbidden to mix blood. As the most powerful of all demons, Pure Angels had a strict code of conduct.

"Very well, Seraphina. Feel free to gloat. I was wrong. I do not agree with your methods, but there is something in Izazal's blood keeping me here, demanding I belong. I'm enjoying it, I must admit."

Agitation broke out on the woman's face, and Seraphina couldn't help but notice how unflattering it was. A grin curved on her lips and she clucked her tongue at Muriel. "That would be the cost of Fallen blood." She enjoyed the look of confusion that passed over Muriel's eyes. "It's addicting. It forms a bond as dangerous as when a human looks at us directly. A compulsion."

"But that doesn't make any sense. How? We share blood to strengthen connections all the time on the field of battle, and we never feel an urge to appease the commander."

She stopped before giving anything more away, and Seraphina noted the new information. Before she'd fallen, blood had only been shared amongst partners—it was sacred. Hearing that they were ordering all warriors to do so with a command leader could mean one of two things. One, that they were facing subordination, or two, their numbers were dwindling so fast from her random mass demon attacks that they needed all the strength they could get. Either way, it was a positive sign for her.

"The answer to that is something I can't explain. It's just something that happens when we fall, the manipulation of the blood from pure to pure evil. But as you're experiencing right this moment, it works. Exceedingly well if after only one day you have lost the urge to fight me and my command. But I promise you, as you grow to know the Alliance and the humans as I have, you very well may find the fall worth it."

A look of distaste passed across Muriel's face, and Seraphina couldn't help but think about how truly sweet it would be when the Angel agreed with her. Fallen fell for all reasons, mingling with humans and murder were only the most common. Hatred, however, could drop the feathers right from an Angel's back just as quickly.

"I'm done with you now. Enjoy your time learning your new home. Fallen go above ground only when I say so. Find your little space in Hell and enjoy it."

Seraphina shouldered passed Muriel, thumping her arm into the other woman's and walking away. She had a meeting with a Thrasher Demon that could not be missed. She hated venturing outside of the region designated for Fallen. Some were downright disgusting, filled with nothing but demons screwing each other. But others, like the Fallen and the human sections, were pleasant. An afterlife that mimicked much of what they had known in life. Thrasher Demons were the former.

She sneered as she stepped through the ridiculous doorframe that led to their location. Blood and body parts lined the ground. The Thrashers were almost impossible to contain, and working with them was only possible because of a bargain she'd drawn up, allowing them full freedom once she was in charge of the topside. A bargain she'd had no intention of keeping, but there was nothing she could do until the real victory had been won. She needed the Thrasher Demons for their brutality.

Stepping around the carcass of a gutted Thrasher, she scrunched her nose at the smell emanating from the residence she needed to enter. Well, the one which she was going to call the resident from. She would be a fool, even with her strength, to go behind closed doors with one of the creatures.

She raised a delicate, pale hand and rapped gently on the door three times. It swung open, and the almost two meters tall, yellow-skinned demon looked down at her. They had no names for one another. Instead, they used a series of grunts and snorts that formed things they could call one another. Seraphina had no intention of simulating such sounds with the big male demon.

"The attack?"

"All are dead, except the girl."

The raspy voice was so garbled and guttural she had to strain to make sense of the words that were strung together. She really hated working with the demons.

Seraphina wanted confirmation of which girl, but Thrashers weren't the most intelligent, and they didn't like it when what little intelligence they had was questioned. So she bit her tongue.

"Delightful. Where are my two pet Strangleholds?"

He didn't speak this time. Instead, he stepped to the left and allowed her to see into the hovel he called a home. In the corner, two large humanlike creatures were heaped on top of one another, blood circling their bodies on the stone floor. She nodded, pleased that he'd been able to handle two of the brutes at once.

"Good. Did they deliver my message to the girl?" She'd needed a way to get rid of the Stranglehold brothers, but she'd also needed something that could articulate properly to speak to little Miss Eliza.

"They did. She seemed to believe them rather quickly, my Queen."

Wonderful. That meant Lucius hadn't been doing his best to seduce and fool her. Never the matter, she was done trying to infiltrate the Alliance through seduction. There were much easier ways to gain entrance, such as turning one of the hunter's into a demon.

Very few demons had transformative powers, but for some, it was the only way to keep their breed alive. She was still seeking out the best to use for her purpose, but for now, the only thing that was clear was that Lucius would be coming home to do exactly what he'd been doing for fifty years, killing and bringing her souls for her collection.

"You have my thanks. You are a trusted and valued component of this war, and I am more than happy to share the spoils of our victory with you."

"As you have stated," his graveled voice actually irritated her ears, "but when will this day be? We have been fighting the humans under your orders for almost fifteen years."

Seraphina bared her fangs at the demon and hissed. "The time will come, but not until we have the resources we need." She didn't want anything further to do with the Thrasher, and she half suspected he was going to turn on her any moment, so she transported herself out.

She immediately felt the drain on her body. Fallen couldn't just pop in and out as their Pure counterparts could. It put a massive strain on them, and that wasn't ideal since she still had to pay Lucius a visit. One that may or may not end in his death by her hands. Finding him was not the issue. She had a blood contract with any and all of her servants. A single drop of blood mixed with her own and released into a small vile that she kept in a cabinet on the same wall as her bed.

One moment, she was in her chambers, and the next, she was standing beside Lucius. The sky was still black with night and twinkled with stars. Large manors lined each side of the street, some close to one another, but many further apart. This was what she was looking forward to. To stealing residences such as these and living as the humans did, parading around their grounds thinking they were so superior.

She snarled, and it drew Lucius' attention. His head whipped around, and she felt the press of a dagger against her throat as her back crashed into the ground.

Her laughter was a rich, loud sound, and it filled the quiet of the night. She knew they weren't near his precious Eliza's house. By then, the Alliance, and even the human police force had been called in, so he must have run from her already. She put her hands on his chest and pushed up, launching him into the air. As he crashed to the ground, she rose up, her eyes sparkling with mischief.

"Not happy to see me then, Lucius? Such a pity." She walked to where he was and pouted down at him. His hand wrapped around her ankle, and she counter-acted, whipping her foot to the right and breaking his hold. "I'll take that as a no."

"You bitch!" He flung himself at her again, and the dagger connected with her arm. A bright stain of red instantly seeped from the shallow wound. It didn't hurt, but it had been a whilst since any had managed to injure her. She was almost impressed.

"Oh do sit down, Lucius dear." Again, she put her hands on his chest and used her strength to force him to the ground. He snarled at her, but she held him tight. Her strength was waning from two transports in a close range of time, but she was still easily able to pin him. "I take it your little human mate wasn't thrilled to learn of the secret you were keeping."

"If you think you can push me to talk, you're wrong. Aside from Eliza keeping Alliance information very well guarded, any desire I had to help you is certainly gone now."

She wasn't sure what he was doing as he closed his eyes, but she figured he was trying to calm himself, knowing that attacking her would surely be his last action if he did it again.

"It's no matter to me now, Lucius. I have another way into the Alliance, and your services will not be needed. However, if you would like, you may return and finish out the contract for your disastrous lifestyle. I was going to kill you, but there is really no need to lose a soul collector. I do have plans for them after all."

She'd expected some sort of response from him, even if it was another disgusting curse that caused her to twist his head from his neck like a grape from the vine. But he did nothing. His eyes remained closed as if he was ignoring her.

"Seraphina."

The voice slid over her body and sent goose bumps over her flesh. Her whole body tensed, and she took her hands off Lucius' shoulders. Slowly, she turned behind her, and her knees almost gave out at the image.

"Demetrious." His name wasn't much more than a whisper as he took a step closer to her.

His crystal eyes sparkled, and his long hair blew behind him in the wind. His hands wrapped around her and pulled her close. She sighed and sagged against him, except she didn't. She slipped and connected with the wall just behind her love.

"Demetrious." Her mind wasn't working right, or she would've remembered that she'd destroyed his soul a century before. All she could think of was how good his hands running up and down her back felt. She was so lost in the fantasy that his words cut deep.

He stepped away from her and laughed. "You vile, disgusting creature. You think you can place your hands upon me? That I would allow your filth and evil to contaminate all that I am? You are a plague, Seraphina, and you have no use to anyone."

No one had even known what had happened betwixt them so many years before, and the words were like hot pokers in her side. She felt herself lose control. She screamed and lunged herself in his direction, just as she had done when he'd spoken those words to her a century before. Her body passed right through him, and she slammed into a fence, the pain ricocheting through her body. She turned chest heaving with exertion and found herself looking at only Lucius—eyes open and a smirk on his face.

"Getting weak, Seraphina? Allowing me to slip into your mind like that. And now that I've done it, now that I know the thing you fear most, there's nothing you can do to stop the nightmares I can unleash on you."

Lucius laughed, and her eyes widened as the realization of what had happened sunk in.

She'd been weak from transporting and so focused on gloating that he'd been able to get inside her mind and see her fear. The encounter with Demetrious hadn't been fear exactly. But his reaction to her when she'd fallen to save him was enough to haunt her dreams without Lucius interfering. She would have to rid herself of Lucius now. With that kind of power over her, he would be impossible to control. It had been the real reason she had done away with his kind. She truly feared what they could do in an attack on her. It would have been nice against the humans, but she hadn't wanted to do anything that could put her in danger.

"Congratulations, Nightmare Demon. You've earned your freedom. I realize that any attack I try on you now would need to be swift, and without my dagger, I cannot kill you quickly enough for you to be unable to unleash my personal hell on me once more. Do not think this means that you are safe, Lucius. I can send others after you. You are weak."

He took a step closer to her, still leaving a respectable enough distance before he spoke. "No, you see this is how it's going to go. I have pissed off my mate protecting you because, to a small degree, I saw use in your cause. Our kind is slaughtered by the Pure Angels and the Alliance of Silver and Steam. I am not wholeheartedly against an attack on them, though I am beginning to think your side will lose. They have incredible stamina and a drive to protect one another. I witnessed it the night your Fallen attacked, and three hunters who didn't know Eliza appeared to save her and the residents of Halifax."

He took another step closer, and she saw the cold deadness of his black eyes.

"So here is what is going to happen. You are going to see to it that, in twenty-four hours, the demon you allowed and most likely ordered to attack my mate's family comes to me. Tell him, her or the whole fucking tribe of them, that I have Felicia and Greyston ready for transport, but that you can't make it topside. I will kill them for what they did in your name, and then you will leave me alone, or I will find the handful of Nightmare Demons still alive and share your fear with them."

His breath was hot on her face, and she realized he'd fully closed the gap betwixt them as he talked. Her body wanted to shake with fear at his words, but she would never allow a lesser demon to see weakness.

"It would appear we are at a stalemate, my friend. In exchange for your freedom and delivering the Thrasher who did this, you will never concern yourself with demon matters. You've chosen a human, and I won't get into a conversation with you about the disgust that fills me with since you really are a talented lover." She pulled back from him and turned to walk away.

She half expected him to attack again, but he didn't.

She was going to be stuck there for a time until her strength returned. They were too far from the nearest actual entrance to Hell, and she knew of more than one lesser demon she could intimidate into giving her lodging.

SIXTEEN

Lucius was torn betwixt a feeling of outrageous fury and gayness. He'd done the impossible. He had not only broken into a Fallen's mind for control, but he'd also freed himself from Seraphina's grasp. Even if it meant looking over his shoulder for some time, sooner or later, she would forget him and move on.

The anger that coiled in his gut like a viper ready to strike was at war with his elation. Eliza was hurt, not fatally, but if her guild didn't get there soon, it would be. She'd also likely never trust him again. Seraphina getting off with only a slight mind fuck didn't seem to be justice enough, but there would always be room for retribution later. For now, all he wanted was the Thrasher demon's head on a plate and body parts spread across the world. Regardless of what she thought of him, he loved Eliza, and she loved him. No one was ever going to hurt her again as long as he lived.

Nothing would ever hurt him worse or cut as deep as the look in her eyes when he hadn't been able to say that the demon that'd attacked her had been lying. It was as if every iota of hope she'd been holding on to had been shattered with a mallet and flung from her eyes at him. She'd trembled and bit her lip, and there'd been nothing he could do to erase the betrayal. Well, there had been one thing. He knew now that, had he agreed to help them catch Seraphina, she would have forgiven him. She loved him. She'd said it and had never taken it back. He hadn't even been able to enjoy the sound of the words coming from her properly because of the situation they'd been in.

He hadn't been ready to turn over Seraphina. Not because she didn't deserve it, but the persecution of his species would continue even with her out of the way. He didn't really care what happened to humans, so long as that human wasn't Eliza. But now, he had to wonder if it had been the wrong answer. If he'd said yes, would she have allowed him to remain in her life once they'd returned to London?

The answer wasn't one he would ever know. He wasn't like Greyston. He wasn't a good guy in the body of a bad one. He was a bad one, and every demon detector would always go off near him. He'd seen the way she'd spoken of the guild and the Alliance. It was her home, and he doubted she would leave it for him.

"It was a lost cause either way then, wasn't it?" Who had he been fooling with the belief that they would make it simply because he had managed to make her love him? He should have known better than to hope to live a dream. "You can't live in a dream if all you've ever done is walk through nightmares."

His fingers wrapped around the device he'd slipped into his pocket on his way out of Eliza's house. The sun was officially up, and he felt the strain of it in his body. Though he'd walked two streets over from Eliza's, he wasn't going any farther. He'd needed to get away from her, needed to go somewhere where he wouldn't disobey her wishes and piss her off further. But he'd taken that communication wristband of hers.

It felt like nothing more than a supremely thick leather strap in his pocket. But if he ran his hand over the front side, he could feel the smooth glass and the knobs across the top. There wasn't any part of him that knew how to use the device. He'd watched Eliza push a series of three knobs in and tug one out the two times she'd used it. But he wasn't certain he wished to speak to the gnarled sounding older gentleman who ran the guild or was at least in charge of Eliza.

Lucius yanked the device out of his pocket and brought it close to his face, turning it over slowly, staring at every intricate detail and looking for something that might indicate a working knob. The leather was a rich cocoa brown, and the clock face a snow white. It was then he noticed the hands didn't appear to move on the face of the watch. No second hand ticked an annoying beat, and the face didn't contain numbers.

There were symbols in the place of the main numbers—twelve, three, six and nine. At the top was a symbol resembling a cog and gear, to the right, the medical symbol, on the bottom sat the letter "A" in script, and finally, the last image was of a beaker.

"Hmm, I would bet these need to be set to reach certain people." Turning the strap around, he laughed at the small etch work on the smallest knob. On the button's end was the letter "F," which he could only hope stood for Felicia. That was who he wanted really, Felicia and Greyston. The demon hunter may dislike him greatly, but he was relying on her mated bond to a demon and love of a close friend to send her his way.

He closed his eyes and pushed the knob in, nothing happened. None of the strange rumbling or clicking came from the device. He grimaced, and eyes still closed, wrapped his forefingers around the knob again and pulled. He felt a strange vibration coming from the device in his hand and heard the clicking noise he'd heard when Eliza had used it. A part of him was curious how it worked, and the other part was so delighted that it did, he wasn't going to question it. He just hoped that the tiny 'F' stood for Felicia.

"Eliza! Are you all right? Master Agardawes reached out to me. Greyston and I will be coming to transport you back to the Alliance." Felicia's voice was speedy, obviously upset for her friend.

He let out a breath, relieved that it had found the proper destination. "This isn't Eliza."

He opened one eye, and then the other, breathing out a sigh of relief again. Lucius began to walk back in the direction of Eliza's as he spoke. He'd only left due to the rising number of gatherers, he'd never intended to get distracted with an unwanted visit and stay away for so long.

"Don't cut the connection."

There was a moment of silence, and then Greyston spoke. "Lucius, get out of where ever you are. You can't be seen with her. They'll know what you are, and you don't stand a chance in hell." Greyston's voice was clipped. Clearly, the fiery redhead was not interested in dealing with him. No doubt she blamed him for whatever had occurred, even if she had no idea what it was.

"I took this, whatever is. I'm not with her. She kicked me out." His voice lowered with the admission and hurt crept its way back into his heart. There would be no making peace with this choice. He was a demon, and it was appropriate that he had finally damned himself.

"I'm not going to pry. Felicia tossed my arrogant arse to the curb too. And then she came crawling back and made love to me like the mate that she is. Ow!"

Lucius smiled, he had a decent feeling Felicia had just hit Greyston fairly hard.

"What are you calling for then, and you'd better get this back to her. They're specifically keyed for certain frequencies. Don't ask me how they learned it, but I'd stolen the tech awhilst back for my own use when I was a vigilante."

"I need you both here, in Halifax. We're going to take down the demons that did this to Eliza, and from the looks of her house, it was a small army of them. I'm going to need your skills and your fiancé's gun."

Seraphina hadn't told him how many had attacked the home, but there was no way it hadn't been a simultaneous hit. Noises like that would have easily torn Eliza from the dream, even if she'd been enjoying herself. The screams hadn't gotten to him either, which

NIGHTMARE IN STEAM   171

meant the demons hadn't played with their victims. They probably had known there wouldn't be time.

"Are you certain this isn't a trap? And if you've been with Eliza this whole time, how did you allow her to get attacked in the dead of night when you're supposedly at your strongest?" Felicia cut into the conversation. "And we are coming, anyway."

"We were otherwise engaged during the attack. There's nothing to explain. Seraphina arrived to gloat, and she was weakened from something. Weak enough that her mental guards were down, and I was able to force a nightmare hallucination in."

"There's always more to explain when a demon is involved. Just look at the mess Greyston can get into, and he's Captain of the Guard. Your kind has a way of stirring trouble and getting noticed, but that isn't the point. So what if you scared her? She isn't rotting six feet under, or you would have led with that comment. I hope." Felicia almost sounded bored.

"Once a Nightmare Demon knows a target's fear, they can take them down anytime, anywhere. Seraphina knows that. The problem is she is still too strong as a Fallen for me to kill. I can make her life hell, though. So it was decided upon. She would give me the demons that did this by tomorrow night and my freedom from servitude, and in exchange, I leave her alone."

"You can't be fucking serious? Leave her alone? Leave alone the single force responsible for the unleashing of demons on Earth?" Irate wasn't the word for Greyston's female.

"Felicia, you cannot understand demon matters. Some things must be done, and cannot be undone." Greyston's tone indicated he wasn't too happy with Lucius using his bargaining chip and allowing Seraphina to get away. However, he clearly understood why, or at least he wasn't going to question it. Lucius heard Felicia grumble something under her breath.

"You are both arriving, yes?" He had a feeling one went where the other did, but if this crew of hunters wasn't aware of a demon in their midst, it might make things tricky. However, Greyston's Incubus scent had easily overridden the hunter's concern in London, or they would've known what he was more oft. Eliza had explained the royal connection to the Alliance, which meant they'd worked with Greyston before, at least some of them must have.

"Yes, we are coming in on an Alliance transport. The bikes are not yet fast enough or discreet enough for daylight. However, there is a train that runs far more rapidly than the simple steam engines because it's powered by the crystals. We'll be on that."

"Felicia, will you help me when you get here?" He stopped walking just off the side of Eliza's house. There was a ruckus of coppers talking loudly, and he saw Alliance members slip through. He hoped a physician was among them. When he'd left Eliza thirty minutes before, the blood had been still flowing from the wound, and she looked as if she might pass out. Leaving had torn him apart, but he'd had to place hope in her guild, in her family.

"We will help. For Eliza. Not for you. When we get there, I want all of the details. These transmissions aren't powered for long. Meet us at the station at half past seven tomorrow evening."

"Why the delay? She's been injured and is left unattended." The growl slipped out. How dare they leave his mate alone overnight? What could her people be thinking?

"Calm down, Lucius. The physician will need to grant her leave to travel before we can move her. Our people are there already. We do not leave our own."

"Thank you, Felicia. I promise, you will understand everything, but only if it doesn't interfere with getting to the demons who hurt Eliza."

"Understood, Lucius." Her voice was fainter, and he wondered if the power supply was running low. "This had better not be a trap, Lucius, for any of us."

The clicking sound came from the device again, and he had a distinct feeling that the communication was terminated. "Well, isn't this little thing helpful."

He placed the device back into his pocket and narrowed his eyes to block out the sun. The past few months, he'd been spending more time awake, when he should have been resting, and his body drooped with the need to sleep. "No one can burn the candle at both ends."

He wasn't going anywhere, regardless of the exhaustion seeping slowly through his body. Not until he could know for sure that Eliza was all right. The number outside her home was growing, people opening doors and windows of neighboring residences to see the latest gossip. He growled low in his throat when he heard one of them mention that the daughter had brought lowlifes back with her from London. Then he realized, in a way she had—him.

His growl grew louder, and he smashed his hand into the brick wall he was next too. Pain lanced through his knuckles into his wrist. When he looked at it, the small scratches and blood did nothing to ease his anger. He had done all of this. Every single second of her pain, every member of her family and serving staff lost, was his fault.

Anger pumped through his body and began to override the need for sleep. He'd fucked up. He shouldn't have sided with Seraphina, shouldn't have even considered letting her walk away from their encounter. His fists were balled, and tension shot through his arms, down his torso and into his legs.

"All my fault," he whispered.

He'd felt remorse like that once before. When he'd gotten his breed killed. He didn't like the way the regret wrapped around him and sank its teeth into his neck. It drained him, leaving him feeling hollow and alone, and for the second time in a century, he was.

He'd spoken too loudly as an onlooker looked over their shoulder at him. When the man did so, his face twisted in horror before he turned around quickly and shouted for the Constable.

"Bloody fucking hell."

He knew what he must look like, what the mask of rage had probably done to his face, and with his outburst, the man most likely thought he had been the killer. He may as well have been.

The man had reached the nearest copper and was waving his arms frantically. Lucius looked up at the window he knew was

Eliza's. It had been opened, and he could see the shuffle of people inside. His heart longed to know if she was all right or awake because he couldn't sense someone's energy if they were unconscious and not asleep.

He shook his head and forced himself to slowly turn and calmly walk away. He couldn't afford to be a suspect. Mass hallucinations were almost impossible at full strength, and he hadn't had a refill in four days. If they took him in, he would be a sitting duck if Seraphina decided to come after him, anyway.

He needed to sleep. He needed to make sure that, when Felicia and Greyston arrived, they could come up with some sort of strategy. He didn't doubt the human's fighting skills, but they'd never fought as a group, and fighting was as much an art form as dance. The wrong partner and the enemy would get away, likely with your life.

"I'll make amends, Eliza. I swear it." He shoved his hands in his pocket, forced himself to place one foot in front of the other and returned to the inn.

Lucius' foot tapped impatiently on the wooden platform. He was still early, long before the train was due in, but he'd been on edge. Fire had danced in his veins when he'd woken up, knowing that retribution and revenge were on the agenda. Staying away from Eliza the past day had been a test of willpower that he did not think he would pass again.

He'd gone back to her home the previous night and had seen them walking, the Alliance members, with their strange crystal weapons. They had kept him from even attempting to get close enough to see her in her dreams, to check on her in any fashion. Getting caught wouldn't do them any good,

Felicia and Greyston would never know where the rendezvous point was if he were caught, and that wouldn't do any of them any favors. All that mattered was killing the demons that had done this.

After that, he would go to Eliza and let her people do what they saw fit. He'd been wrong to tell her he wouldn't hand over the Queen of the Demons, he was ready to do that now, but he knew nothing of her newest plan. He was useless.

He heard the sound of a train chugging in the distance, heard its eerie scream as steam was released. There was a time when he'd thought the latest modes of transit were mind-boggling. Now, with everything he knew of the Alliance of Silver and Steam, well, something as mundane as a steam-powered vehicle wasn't as awe-inspiring as it had once been. The sound vanished into the warm summer night, and he continued to pace again. Twice, he'd tried to speak with Felicia again, and every time nothing had happened. For all he knew, the piece had broken whilst trying to communicate for so long the morning before. His fingers curled and uncurled, and he cracked his neck over and over, but nothing took the edge off. He wasn't concerned about meeting the demon, that creature would be ordered to wait as long as it took since it was supposedly bringing in Greyston and an Alliance hunter. It was simply the idea of having to wait.

The toe of his boot caught in a knot in the wooden planks, and he lunged forward, enough to smash his wrists into the nearest support pole.

"Lucius, it's a wonder you've survived this long. You can't fight and can't even fucking walk some days," he mused. "But typically, there's a hefty dose of booze in your belly and fine women in your bed."

That last thought wiped the smirk from his face. His old way of life had been appealing before he'd known what having a mate was like. Now, nothing would ever bring him joy the same way. He was not throwing life away. He'd heard of plenty of creatures who survived without their mate, it just didn't mean he was going to enjoy the world as he once had. Even without having to bow down to Seraphina's every whim.

His mind went blank then. There was nothing left to think about. No point in fantasizing all the ways he would put down the filth that had attacked Eliza. No reason to think how much he loved her, how she'd actually changed him. Nothing mattered if the damn train didn't hurry up and arrive. Which, thankfully for him, it did.

He stood off to the back of the platform, nervous that other hunters might be on board. They were. Six people, Lucius recognized from some of his nightly stays in those first three months poured out of the train car prior to Felicia and Greyston. His lip pulled back in a curl as they walked up.

"A warning might have been nice," he hissed under his breath at Felicia.

"Yes, well, you leaving Eliza alone after my initial warning did not happen. Why should I have wasted my breath on a second?" She raised a brow at him, and the trio descended the stairs from the platform.

"Because getting me captured thanks to one of your little hand-held ichor detecting devices going off would be a waste of everyone's time since I'm the only one who knows who did this." His voice echoed as they walked under the platform and away from prying eyes and ears.

Greyston gave him a displeased look. "Well, you shouting things that loud isn't going to alert everyone to what you are now, is it?"

He saw the dominant simmering under the surface. Incubi, by nature, didn't like to be ignored, and they were sexual masters, ordering their bed partners to climax and do other devious acts; something that many women found appealing in the bedroom, but not Lucius.

"It doesn't matter who hears me. What are they all doing here? Did you alert the Alliance that you mysteriously knew what had happened?"

"No, and that is precisely why they are all here."

Felicia turned her nose up at him, and he got a distinct feeling she likened him to a patch of dirt beneath her slipper.

"An attack this brutal, where a surveyor can pinpoint its demonic nature, would demand for all hunting teams to be out in London and any other area."

"About that . . . ."

"Not happening, demon. Just know we are in other areas. Halifax is a small offshoot because of the Halifax Slasher. Otherwise, none would be here at all."

She may not have wanted to tell him, but she had just revealed that smaller locations were demon safe. Information he tucked away, so should Eliza forgive him, they could run to those areas and be free of the Alliance and Seraphina.

"Now, what happened? I want it all, Lucius. If I think one bit of information is left out, I'll let Greyston know just what nightmares you gave me last week." Her eyes narrowed and stared him down.

He sighed and stuffed his hands into his pockets. There was no way Greyston wouldn't kill him when he found out he'd put images of Greyston having an affair into his mate, and bride-to-be's, dreams. Let alone that the second set was of his death.

"Before you assume that I did try to trick her, Eliza, and I had talked everything out. But Seraphina knew about her. We'd made a bargain. If I used Eliza to get inside information, she would tear my contract up and let us be free. Even as a Fallen, she has to keep her word."

He saw the gun almost before Felicia squeezed the trigger, and a purple beam sliced past him, missing him my mere millimeters.

"You son of a bitch!" Felicia snarled.

She advanced, and Greyston wasn't stopping her. The big demon's hand wrapped around Lucius' neck and lifted him from the ground. His hands darted his neck to try to give himself a chance to breathe, Greyston's fingers slipped slightly, but not enough. Lucius continued to struggle, his legs flailing perilously in the air. He choked, trying to do anything to drag air into his mouth, and by the grace of luck, his toe caught Greyston on the inside shin and the left ball. He growled, and his green eyes flashed black, but he dropped Lucius.

His throat screamed as he took in air and rubbed his crushed neck. Greyston was still doubled over, and Felicia had run to him, dropping her gun in the process. Lucius grabbed it off the floor and fired it right beside them.

"Will you two stop it? And for fuck's sake, where did your female learn to talk like that, Greyston?"

Greyston was up and advancing.

"I was going to double cross Seraphina. Feed her false but seemingly true information and get out with Eliza. Truth." He held the gun still trained on Greyston and hoped his friend would stop. He didn't want to hurt him.

Felicia put her hand on his forearm. "Greyston, stop. I think he's serious. If that was his only way out, well, I can't say I'd blame him. I've slept with demons for information. It's not that dissimilar."

Greyston gnashed his teeth at Lucius once before the black turned back to its normal green. When he was clearly in control again, Felicia kept talking.

"That doesn't explain the attack."

"We hadn't been able to see each other for a few days. Eliza had society functions with her family. So we'd been consorting in her dreams. That's when the attack happened, whilst she was asleep. It was strategic. Seraphina planned it, so all the deaths were simultaneous. No way to scream and alert the sleeping target then. She'd used it to tell Eliza her version of the truth. And I'm sure you'll be pleased to know that, whilst she believed my truth, she kicked me out anyway."

There was no need to bring up the whole kicking him out for not turning on Seraphina thing again. There were only so many times he could piss the couple off before it proved to be fatal. He passed the gun back to Felicia, and she took it from him, sliding it onto a loop on her long black skirt. How she could hunt in that was beyond him, he much preferred Eliza's pants and shirt. It was so much sexier on her.

The stars were starting to show, and the sky was changing from dusk to twilight by the time they'd hashed out what was going to be done. It was a simple plan, almost too simple to work. They would each take a demon, no focusing on helping the others until they were gone. It was very self-serving, but Felicia told him that it was how they survived. Two people fighting one demon could be attacked by another they didn't know was there, and if there were going to be a group, it would be more efficient. She balked when he produced the black rope, however.

"Felicia, if they are to believe the ruse, they will need to arrive and see you captured. Otherwise, they will attack us." He was distressed. They'd been going around in circles for the last quarter hour on the topic.

"I don't understand why we have to wait for them to show. If we stand there, ready to attack, we have a much higher survival rate."

"Felicia, this is my con. My arse is on the line if we fail. I'm not going to pretend as if I don't need your help. We need to be at my inn by eight sharp. That is when they arrive. If we are not there first, we then need to struggle on the way to them. It will be harder."

"You speak as if you know what we are going up against."

"Thrashers."

The color drained from her face, and she tipped backwards, barely making contact with Greyston's outstretched hand. Her whole body shook, and her eyes were unfocused. Greyston didn't take his gaze off her as he spoke.

"A potential group of them? Bloody hell. Lucius, she was captured by one last winter, and her father had his throat ripped out by a pair of them on her birthday. You should've told me." The last sentence was a growl.

Whilst he felt bad, he knew it wasn't her worst nightmare, so he couldn't care. This wasn't about her.

"Then pass me the guns, and I'll go down fighting on my own. There's no more time for this. Either we leave now, or I go now. Either way, this is the only chance we will have to make sure they never find Eliza again." He was already walking away when Felicia caught up to him next to a waiting carriage, one she'd called in before they'd begun planning.

She climbed in, Greyston following behind her and Lucius last.

"Fine, tie the damn rope, Lucius. So help me, if this goes wrong, it will be all on your head, and Eliza won't be happy that the girl she made Fido for is dead. We bonded whilst she explained her ability to create things to me." She shoved her hands into his face, wrists touching so he could tie them.

The carriage ride felt long after that, no more talking happened once he'd tied their wrists and supposedly taken their weapons. They'd brought an extra gun and sword for him to hold whilst they concealed more weapons. Thrashers weren't stupid, but all they thought about was killing, they wouldn't even think of extras.

The carriage stopped without a word from the driver, and as they were stepping down to the alley next to the inn, he saw them coming. A line of five Thrashers stood against the wall of the building next door. Their eyes glowed both red and yellow. A male and a female.

Much to their credit, Greyston struggled, and Felicia swore at him as they crossed the small space. It was up to him to say the right phrase, indicating for them to slip their thumbs into the loop and untie their hands.

A phrase he may not remember to speak. His eyes enlarged—the black even deeper with his rage. These were the demons, and one specifically had dared to touch his mate. He stopped walking and almost ignored the rasped question from the largest one, one he knew to be in Seraphina's graces.

"We've been watching you, Miss Gannon. Ever since you were six and ten, and we put down that hunter father of yours. We've been watching. This time, there won't be anyone to save you. There's no one else here." He acknowledged Lucius then. "Let them go. I have orders to bring them to Seraphina."

He breathed heavily in and out of his nose, trying to control the impulse to shove the sword in his hand into the gut of the demon. "You can have them as soon as you answer who attacked the girl in the manor last night."

The creature howled with laughter, his black pointy teeth dripping saliva. "Well, that would be me, of course. That bitch could scream too."

Nothing passed through his mind. It was an absolute blank. No saying the right sentence. No torturing the demon for what he'd done. He lunged forward and impaled the Royal Guard's sword deep into its stomach. The creature wasn't laughing then. Its hands tried to pull the blade out, but they were too slick with its own blood.

Lucius growled as he twisted the sword to the left, then the right and finally jerked it from the Thrasher's body. The leader hit the ground with a thump and blood splashed onto Lucius' pants. He was breathing so hard, and anger bubbled in his ears so loud, he didn't hear Felicia yelling at him for messing things up.

He turned sideways just in time to see another Thrasher coming at him. Its claws tore across his shoulder in a blaze of pain. He let the sword clatter to the street. It was too big for the small alley. He grabbed the crystal gun and fired, sizzling a hole through the thing's chest, even as it stuck a claw into his other shoulder.

Blood poured down his arms, but he couldn't care. Thrasher's had no fears, nothing he could latch onto and kill them with. So there would be blood—his and his enemies. A beam of purple light flared to his right, and he heard a demon scream. Felicia whizzed by him, a flurry of arms and legs, and threw herself on top of the wounded demon.

He stopped what he was doing and watched, blowing, yet again, another portion of the plan. She didn't move off the creature, didn't flinch or stop pummeling it as it sliced a claw down her upper leg.

"This one's for my mother!" She grabbed the gun off the street where it had landed in her assault and fired it directly against the Thrasher's head. Blood flew everywhere, and chunks of the demon fell on Lucius' boot.

With three down and two to go, his prick suddenly began to twitch with desire. He turned and snarled at Greyston. "Fuck you, Greyston. Fuck you for this."

"Not my fault, Willan. I can't help how we kill." The Incubus's hormones were flooding the tiny space.

It amazed him how Greyston had used it to attract women as Captain of the Guard, pretending to take down the bad guy with just punches. Truthfully his scent was strong enough to distract anyone, any creature—even most Fallen.

Greyston's hand wrapped around the creature's neck, and he grabbed the sword off the ground and hacking its head from its shoulders. It bounced off Greyston's chest and rolled a few feet away.

Felicia screamed out, and both men turned. An angry, scarlet trail shone on her neck where the last demon had gotten her. Her fingers squeezed the trigger on her gun, but nothing happened. The creature slashed at her cheek, the action knocking her backwards, and it made a move to mount her. He didn't waste any time, and neither did Greyston. Two beams hit the demon in the chest and knocked him off Felicia, leaving twin holes steaming on its body.

Greyston ran to Felicia and swept her up, slamming his mouth over hers as he ran his hands everywhere over his mate's body—most likely checking for non-visible wounds. Lucius cleared his throat, and Greyston set her down. All three of them were breathing hard, and only Greyston was walking out of the battle unharmed.

Both of Lucius' shoulders were screaming in agony, but it didn't matter. It was all over, and Eliza was going to be safe because he'd made sure no other demon would ever come within a meter of her. Lucius dropped his hands to his knees as his chest continued to heave with emotion and depleted air. When his breathing was under control, he picked his head up and looked at the pair still standing in the alley with him.

"Oh, you two are nuts if you think you're getting this gun back." He grinned wide, and they all laughed, letting the tension from the whole day slide off their backs as they cleaned up any sign of what had gone on in the small back alley. None had come out during the fight, and none interfered as they removed each trace of blood and flesh from the ground. All that remained were scorch marks from the handy little crystal guns.

SEVENTEEN

THE LIGHT slowly streamed down onto her face and splayed a pattern over her eyes. Eliza winced and tried to roll over, only to find she couldn't. She felt a tug on her arm as she tried to turn left, and her eyes snapped open.

The suspension, Lucius, the attack. Her parents. A cry tore from her throat as everything came rushing back all at once. Images danced in her mind. Lucius and her on the train, her fighting with her mother, the two large demons talking to her, and the blood sliding from her stomach wound. Over and over, different variations of the same scenes bombarded her.

She sat upright in bed, her knees bent and her head tucked betwixt them as her hands went to her sides, and she rocked as the tears fell down her face. The tug from the medical monitoring device she was hooked up to snagged, and she felt the small blonde hair on her arms tug, but she couldn't summon any reaction. There was too much in her head, too many memories. Too many mistakes.

Her body rocked, and the tears fell for quite a whilst before she heard the knock from the other side of the room. She grimaced that anyone at the guild, or the Alliance, would have walked in on her during such a moment of weakness. Inventors and scientists weren't supposed to feel. They were expected to be cold, calculative and analytical. Which she was, but she did feel.

Her body shuddered one last time as she inhaled and exhaled a series of deep breaths. The tears wouldn't give up, though. They continued to stir in her eyes and pour down her cheeks to the point where she feared she might never stop. Her eyes squeezed shut of their own volition, but she forced her head up, though it still shook side to side as if her denial her family's death and Lucius' betrayal of could be gone like the wind extinguished a flame.

"Eliza."

The voice was soft, feminine. Slowly, she forced the irregular breathing to stop and focused on the room, the crystal glow beside her and the way the sun let so much light into the chamber. It must have been past midday.

"Eliza, I don't want to push you. You have to believe that I don't. But we need to talk."

Felicia's hand ran down her shoulder and had Eliza not opened her eyes to see it, she wouldn't have even known it was there. How could she be so incredibly numb and be drowning in a storm of emotions on the inside? She didn't even remember being brought back to the guild, though it made sense that at some point they would return her to London. She was alone now, save for an Uncle in America who wasn't known for having the most stable mind. All she could remember was the made up images of her parents and the stolen moments with Lucius.

Lucius. Her body burned with desire and the need to pin this all on him. To force his hand as the blame for her tragedy. But she took this position long before him. None were to blame but herself for becoming involved in a dangerous way of life—even if it hadn't appeared to hold any danger for a simple inventor until recently. She thought about that final row with Lucius and wished there was a way to take it back. To not ever hear that he chose that demon bitch over her. But she supposed that was a part of life. All of this was and placing the blame on someone else did nothing except give her false absolvement from her own problems.

A cold metal flicked across her hand that was over the bed, and a harsh bark filled the room. Jessabelle was back. She scratched her hand over the dog's head but said nothing. Jessabelle wasted no time jumping on the bed with her, which caused a streak of pain. The dog happily put her head on Eliza's chest and wagged her tail for attention.

"Eliza . . . ."

"I heard you, Felicia. Did it occur to you that I just might not be ready?" she snapped at her closest friend and felt no remorse.

"Eliza, you've been asleep for two days. If not for the designs Antonio knew about stashed in your desk, draw you might be dead. You lost a tremendous amount of blood, Eliza."

The statement should have shocked her. She could remember the pool of blood beneath her legs and the way her fingers had been stained red with a dripping, steady, wound. The designs must be the ones for a transfer. She'd been playing with the idea of blood transfer since she learned it was blood that powered the strange crystals that allowed them to track and detect demons. With a small metal tube and twin needles powered by the gems, it would be far faster, better to heal those in trouble than the invention of Mr. Blundell a few years back. That it worked, well she was shocked at that.

She turned to face Felicia finally and recoiled from the bright sunlight. Much of the guild was interior only, especially the labs, and she was beginning to feel a bit like Lucius, with his weakness in the sun. "I'm tired, Felicia. I lost quite literally everything in that attack, what could there possibly be to speak about to you as opposed to the Guildmaster's and Master Agardawes?"

"I want to know how much you care for Lucius."

The statement took her off guard, and she stared, mouth open at her friend. "I don't see why that's any matter of yours."

"Because the demons that did this to you have been killed and Agardawes is going to want to know how Greyston and I were able to track them down. Lucius is prepared to turn himself in for his crimes, Eliza. I never thought I would say this, but it would appear a demon can change, for the right reasons."

Eliza didn't quite understand the information. Lucius had tracked them down for her even after she'd kicked him out? But why, and why turn himself in when he loved life and freedom so much?

"I'm not sure I understand what you're telling me, Felicia."

Her friend pushed up off the small cot bed and sighed. "I've been here you know. Almost literally where you are now. Only I hadn't had months to learn the truth, a few days at best. To tell you the truth, it's been such a short time, and yet the only thing I remember from Greyston is the first time he took me, against the alley wall. Life without him is such a blank, I can't even fully remember the attack on my parents."

She swallowed hard. She'd forgotten that Felicia had gone through this at a much younger age. That she'd witnessed the brutal slaying of her parents, parents she was close to. Eliza exhaled a contrite sigh, mad at herself for her inconsiderate attitude. "I had forgotten you know, that you've been here."

Felicia walked over to the window and looked out. "There's no way to heal from this without Lucius, Eliza. So I suggest when Master Agardawes gets here you don't give him up. He's a wanted demon, Eliza, not like Greyston." She turned back to Eliza and offered her a small smile before the knock rapped on the doorframe, and the familiar old man filled the space.

He inclined his head to Felicia who quickly scurried from the room, away from her adoptive father, with Jessabelle close behind. Master Agardawes blue eyes were laced with concern, they seemed to lack any sort of the crystal clarity she always saw in them. He gently closed the door behind him and walked to stand next to her bedside.

"What are we going to do with you, Miss Dorley?" He sighed and shook his head, she could swear she heard the weight of the world on the Alliance leader's shoulder. "Two times in a little more than a week I have to wait by your bedside with a heavy heart and low spirits and pray you will awaken."

She flushed at his statement but found the courage to respond. "More than your hunters then, isn't it?"

That earned her an honest chuckle and some of the clouds cleared from his eyes as his laughter resonated through the small medical bay room. "Yes, my dear, it truly is. Though they all have added to this mess of grey hair at one time or another." He smiled and winked at her. "I'm not nearly as old as my coloring would have you lot think."

It was her turn to laugh. When she stopped, the room was quiet, he was looking down at her, but saying nothing. Felicia's words, her warning, ran through Eliza's head. Was it possible he would have somehow found out about Lucius? Would he actually order Lucius' death?

"I have no reason to put this off any longer, Eliza. I need to speak with you about what happened that night. I do not need a recap, the blood on the floor told stories I have seen a thousand times, and your wound tells all it needs to of your own injury." He walked away from the bed and scrubbed a hand over his wiry beard. "The problem is I have a report from Bradley that you told him you were out testing new weaponry."

She went to cut him off, to try to explain, but he put his hand up and silenced her the way her father used too. A pang of pain tore through her thinking about him but now was not the time.

"I do not wish to know why you told a lie, or why you were out hunting when you're not trained. Those are disciplinary problems, and I will see to it that when you're fully recovered, we take action for them." His voice was calm, he didn't have a threatening tone, just very matter of fact.

"I understand."

"But what does need to addressed is that when you ran away from the Fallen you weren't anywhere near qualified to be near, he reported that a man tackled you to the floor, a demon to be precise."

He turned his gaze directly to hers, and she felt the world closing in on her. She couldn't lie to the man, she couldn't lie to anyone, really. But how could she condemn the person she loved simply because he was what he was born to be? She'd come to terms with his genetic background over the week, not his betrayal, but at least the knowledge that he was who he was and changing a person for their birth is disgusting.

She took a deep breath in and closed her eyes causing a tear to slip down her right cheek. Another deep breath in, and another tear fell before she opened her eyes. "I was in the company of a demon, I cannot deny it."

"I see. Can you tell me why you were doing such a thing? Following him perhaps? Or is he the reason behind the attack that left your family dead and you severely injured?"

The tears felt like acid as they ran down her face in hot streams. She didn't wipe them away, though, the truth could be painful. It didn't mean you swept it under the rug and hid from it. "I need to know what will happen to him before I say anything, you cannot track down someone when you haven't an inkling of who they are."

"You've properly damned him just now, my dear. But since he means something to you, and I regretfully now have experience with this idea, I will be forthcoming. He will be put on trial. There will be no hope for his escape. However, he must have helped Felicia and Greyston the other night and for that, there is a small debt of gratitude. As well as a small hope he is decent as Greyston is. But if he doesn't answer he will be taken to the few rooms we use for torture."

She didn't blink. She'd had no idea they had ever done such a thing to demons. She'd always assumed they were slaughtered and taken care of outside. *But how else would they have learned so much without studying them? Did it have anything to do with the Angels that Lucius had brought up?* "And of his death?"

"His cooperation will determine his sentence."

Fear for her mate was a lead stone in her stomach. He hadn't been willing to betray his kind for her, did that justify her giving him up to the Alliance? Would he talk for them or would he be tortured and killed?

"Eliza, I need your answer. If you do not wish to help me, I can go to Greyston and Felicia."

"He is my mate." There was no shame in her voice, no sense of regret and she realized she didn't regret it. She may not have found the ideal person to love, but she had loved and been loved for a short period of time. She would let nothing spoil those memories. Even how it all ended.

"I see. That means my actions against him will surely trigger something from you. Whilst you've been sloppy, you wouldn't be top inventor if you didn't have something the others did not. The countless future tools we could lose, the secrets you could tell the other side..."

Her vision burned red at the accusation. "I would never tell Guild or Alliance secrets. This is my home, and I am loyal." She wished she had the nerve to slap him for his insult, but that was not how she was brought up, and she would not tarnish her parent's good name by acting like a hooligan.

"I was hoping you would answer that way. But you need to understand, I had the same fears with Felicia, and I knew what sort of man, demon, Greyston was from his position within the city. I have nothing but a theory from Bradley as to what this demon is, save for that he may rescue you."

"I am not interested in sharing more information. I have answered the question that yes; I was working with a demon. And yes he is the reason I was attacked. Seraphina wanted him back, and I suppose because he and I were, are, in love it was making that impossible." When the Guildmaster didn't flinch at the name Seraphina, she wondered how long he had known it since Eliza was fairly certain Felicia found out when she did.

"That is fair. I will be speaking with Felicia and Greyston and by the way. She brought your communicator back. It's been completely checked and resonated with demon energy. Which means your mate had stolen it from you at some point and used it to contact them. So you can be certain I will get the information from her as she is not as invested in the demon as you are." He walked to the door and said one last thing before disappearing through it. "We will be fair, Eliza, Greyston has taught this old mind a lesson or two. But if he is a problem, the Alliance of Silver and Steam will do what the Royals pay us to do. We will protect the city from him."

Eliza hadn't the slightest clue where the bravado came from, but she knew it would be her only chance to say something to him and she wasn't about to miss the opportunity. "Master Agardawes, just know that one day you will have to stop keeping secrets from the Alliance. I don't know how long you've known about Seraphina, but we had a right to know we were dealing with organized attacks and not simply random acts of demon nature. And about the Angels? We all know that an Angel told the Royals what was going on, but there has to be more to it, and we deserve to know. One day you will have to tell us."

There was no response from the man. No tightening of his shoulders, no sign of annoyance. He just left the room. And it infuriated her. She was tired of secrets. There had been enough of them going around, and whilst she understood not starting a worldwide panic over the actual existence of demons, she was never going to tolerate another secret betwixt herself and the Alliance ever again.

The hot fury she'd been feeling was simmering now, fear intermixing with it. She thought about what Felicia had said minutes before. If Lucius turned himself in, it would be the end. But if she could get him to run, to leave London, perhaps he would get to keep the freedom he had just earned.

She looked around and room and saw the communicator sitting on the chair across from the bed. She wanted to be mad that Lucius had stolen from her, but she couldn't bring herself to be. He'd done it to get help seeking revenge. Whilst she didn't like the idea of adding more faults to his shaky character, the idea that he'd done it for her, for love, made it a little better. But she couldn't let him turn himself in. She needed to see him one last time, though, tell him she wasn't angry for his choice and say goodbye. She wouldn't be able to stand it if he just vanished, and she wasn't interested in some dream dalliance. She wanted a flesh and blood interaction.

Eliza didn't notice time's passing as she thought over her choices, her possible actions, and their outcomes. A dinner tray had been brought and left, but she had yet to eat it. Her mind was torn. Lucius had fundamentally spelled out that he loved her, but not enough to choose her. That would never stop hurting, but she couldn't hate him for it. She'd contemplated leaving the guild, leaving the Alliance and running away with him. Not to tell secrets, only to live. But that idea hadn't appealed to her either. This was her home, and more importantly, she was doing what she needed to be doing, inventing and helping take threats off the street. She couldn't trade that in, her work was too important to her. After a lengthy debate with herself, the only thing she did know was that she was tired of lying in the tiny bed and that she was going to meet with him.

The issue was getting the communicator; it was like it was purposefully left where she couldn't reach it though it would work on this level of the Guild. Carefully, she tugged the wired up needle out of her arm and let it dangle. If she were up and moving with no real pain, she wouldn't need any blood, anyway. Her legs shook as she put weight on them to cross the floor, but she kept going. It felt like minutes later when she finally put her hand on the leather strap. Suddenly, she was sidetracked. What if she could make Lucius one prior to his leaving? Would they work no matter how far he went? She knew certain locations had to communicate through paper mail, but maybe if he didn't go too far, just some place remote, it could work. Hope drove her as she activated the knob for Felicia's own communicator and she held her breath as she waited.

"Yes? Is this an emergency? My soon to be husband and I are having a rather fitful row over the flower colors for the wedding."

She wanted to laugh but somehow didn't. "It's Eliza. I just need a minute."

"All right but I recommend hurrying so I can get back to informing this ridiculous dominant man of mine that pink roses would not make him seem less of an Incubus Demon - especially since half of the guests will not know he's a blasted demon in the first place."

"I want to see Lucius. I want you to come and get me to him. He can't come back here, and I have a way he can remain safe for however long he lives."

The voice on the other end took her breath away. He was there.

"Eliza, I'm not running away. I need to face my sins and be someone who might be worthy of you when I come out the other side, still a demon, but one with morals and a heart because of you."

EIGHTEEN

"You can't Lucius. You just can't."

He flinched at the pain in Eliza's voice. Felicia looked away and then patted him on the shoulder before leaving the dining room. The pair of them had indeed come a long way from the last two interactions regarding Eliza when she'd tried to kill him. His heart broke at the pain he heard, pain that he'd once more caused.

"Eliza, I have to do this. You made a valid point, I don't have to be a murderer anymore, not of the innocent. I still have to kill, it's the only way I'll survive. But I can continue on as I was doing, and if I'm executed for my crimes, well, then at least I know I would have made you proud."

He meant every word. He'd been out for himself his entire life. Even when he struck the bargain with Seraphina to infiltrate the guild, he'd been thinking about his own freedom more than being left alone with Eliza. He was always going to be a demon, but Greyston Westham was not the only demon fighting for the side of humanity. Angels were, he was far from a Pure Angel, but he'd bet there were others out there as well among the lesser demons who'd taken a stand.

"No, you don't!"

Her voice rose considerably, and Fido whimpered in the corner of the room. The poor metal dog probably thought the shout was at it since it wasn't intelligent like Jessabelle.

"Lucius, listen to yourself. They may not kill you if you come in, but they're certainly going to strip your freedom."

Keeping his tone calm was almost impossible, he wanted to shout to the skies that his mate still clearly wanted him safe despite everything. But keeping himself peaceful was the only way to comfort Eliza.

"It'll be all right, love. I've lived a very long time, and I've never taken responsibility for my actions. Revenge was not enough this time. I'm going to do what's needed to atone for what happened to my mate. You all believe demons to be vile, evil creatures and for the most part we are. We're selfish and thrive on things like murder and sex and blood. But lesser demons are also human in a way. We look human, and we have to pass for human each and every day of our lives if we want to survive. Let me have this chance at pretending I'm human."

There was a pause on the other end. He wasn't certain what she was thinking, but Lucius would bet they didn't have much longer to discuss the matter.

"Lucius, I need to see you. I need to feel you touching me again, especially if you're going to turn yourself in."

Inside he was screaming with joy and sighing with relief. To her, he only said, "Yes, I'd like that, Eliza."

"I'll have Felicia get me. I can't let you try to come inside. Every crystal would sound, even if Greyston walked in right beside you, it would be impossible to ignore your eyes, Lucius. I don't know how they ever marked you as anything else, but your eyes are so very demon sometimes."

"How is your stomach?"

"That's your response? Are you sincere, Lucius?" her voice raised, and he hoped she wasn't near listening ears.

"If you're going to come to me I'm not going to let you leave untouched, Eliza. I need to know your body is healing before I do that. Don't argue with me. It's important."

"I've been given blood. My head doesn't appear to be in any pain, and I have been very adequately stitched up. If Felicia wasn't exaggerating, I have been asleep for two days. My body is still weak, but it is not fully broken, it's had a little time to heal, and the stitches are sound. I've moved plenty and yes it's hurt, but nothing has torn apart."

He nodded, forgetting he couldn't see her. His body surged with lust, and he almost forgot to say anything at all. "Then let me tell Felicia. I do not want to wait any longer."

Nothing else was said and when he looked down the glow of the crystal had stopped, he'd exceeded whatever power source kept the communication going once more. His heart was pounding. Did he really stand a chance to fix things with Eliza? It had sounded like it, but demons didn't have cause for hope and he wouldn't allow his emotions to get the best of him. Cool and detached had worked for so many years until it landed him in Seraphina's employ at least. He stood up and walked out of the dining room, the swinging door almost clipping his arse when he didn't move fast enough.

The parlor was empty, save for Steven who gave him a dirty look and pointed up the stairs. Sooner or later, he was going to have to get that Incubus Demon laid because the man was a thorn in his side. He stopped at the bottom of the stairs, not wanting to interrupt anything.

"Felicia, Felicia I need you to come down please."

No response came after several seconds, so he walked to the top of the stairs. To the left would take him to the offices, both Royal and Alliance. To the right, he'd stumble onto the bedrooms and potentially something more. He turned toward the offices first. He'd learned over the past two days that when Felicia and Greyston were occupied, he could hear his friends bellowed commands or Felicia's moans. Something that had him dumping a glass of ice water into his trousers. He had no idea how Steven could live here full time with them, particularily as an Incubus himself.

He rapped on the first door, the Royal office door, and heard nothing from within. He heard a muted voice from behind the door that held the secrets of the Alliance, and Greyston's initial work against the demons.

"We're in here. The alarm went off, and Greyston didn't want to miss anything." Felicia called from just down the hall.

He walked into the room, and Felicia leaned in and whispered, "Which is code for he doesn't want to deal with anymore wedding details. He's long since lost the ability to order me around anywhere but the bedroom. Be grateful you haven't heard us fight yet. That is one demon who doesn't like to be told no."

They both laughed, and Greyston picked his finger up off the map of the city he used in his own makeshift tracking system. "If the two of you are done laughing, this demon is about two seconds away from throwing you both out. I'm Captain of the bloody Guard, of course, I need to have my orders followed."

Felicia stopped laughing, but Lucius could tell that any fear the orders of her future husband used to hold was long since gone because she knew he would never harm her. He, on the other hand, shut right up.

"Sorry to interrupt, but I need you to bring Eliza to me." He'd expected a chorus of reasons why that was a bad idea from them both. But he got none.

"Getting her out is going to be rough if the Guildmaster is around. He knows we are aware of something," Felicia admitted.

"The Guildmaster, this is the same man that runs the Alliance or no?"

"He is, not all the masters at the guild have a spot in the Alliance, but this one does. He raised me after the attack took my parents' lives and because of that, I'm watched heavily when I'm there. I promise I'll get her to you, though." She put a hand on his shoulder and actually smiled at him.

A low growl from Greyston had her pull it off.

"Felicia, I realize the power I had over you has lessened in the past months, but if you continue to touch that man, friend or not, I'm going to throw you over my shoulder and take you to a private room and have you begging to come so badly your whole body will be trembling before I allow it."

Felicia squeaked at the comment and Lucius cursed as his prick roused to life a little at the idea of doing the same thing to Eliza when she got here.

"We have a mission to run first, and then I'm going to hold you to that. In fact, if we go near the Thames I have a very good idea of where you can take me."

She winked at Greyston, and he adjusted his pants and muttered something about women. Lucius was amazed to see how his friend really had changed thanks to this tiny little woman. It was amusing, but if he looked in the mirror, he had a feeling he wouldn't recognize the demon he had become. He was ready to turn himself over rather than look out for his own arse. A new concept and one that he wasn't entirely convinced he liked but knew he had to do.

"Do you think it could be this evening? I don't want to drag things out. I will lose my nerve, and now that she knows I want to try to be a good demon for her, the last thing I want is to change my mind and run for the hills. At least this way I go down with the love and respect of my mate. Funny, I never wanted one, and I got one who is appalled by my means of survival and yet, loves me and not just for the mating mark."

He shook his head, honestly amazed at everything. Everything had been strange and awkward, from how the mark appeared to the last time he saw her. But there was no way to deny the love he felt for her and how grateful he was for the ability to have a mate — the highest demons, the Angels, didn't have that option and it made it all the more special. The one thing a lesser demon was granted that those more powerful, more respected among their kind, could not have.

"I don't think there would be any other chance." She walked over to Greyston and showed Lucius the marked paper indicating demons.

Little black dots lined the southern side of the city. "It looks like it's going to be a busy night at the guild. Who knows, maybe some regular guild workers will get the thrill of their life and learn about the demons." Felicia took the paper back from his hands and headed out of the room.

He turned to Greyston. "How on Earth do the workers of the guild not understand what they are covering up for?" The idea was preposterous, there was technology throughout many of the halls that couldn't be seen anywhere else, surely they noticed.

"They believe it's all new work. That what's being done down-stairs is the promotion of a lifetime that awaits them if their clock working skills are top notch. Poor sods." Greyston tucked the paper in his pocket. "Well then, we'd best be off and get your mate. Why don't you grab some of the wine from the cellar behind the house, she may need a glass to dull the pain from transport. Plus Steven is going to come out with us, it's time he learned more than just pissing me off."

He had a feeling Steven had pissed Greyston off earlier, but that it was to give him some time alone with Eliza. There was a lot to smooth over, and after witnessing the Incubus scent in the air, his member might have trouble waiting for the talking to be done. He shifted his pants again and headed to the back to see about a bottle of wine.

HER HANDS WRUNG TOGETHER in her lap. It had taken almost an hour for Felicia to get Eliza out of the guild. An attack near the lower Thames left the Alliance scrambling to send hunter teams out. They hadn't been able to get a read on the creature, but there had been so many points of contact coming in, Master Agardawes had dispatched nearly everyone - all using the new and improved weapon Kellan had. Felicia wasn't even with her because of it. Her friend had been grabbed almost the second she'd stepped over the threshold onto the marble floor. So the silence of the carriage car was unnerving. She could hear her eyelashes softly tapping against her cheeks, her breath and the small tapping her foot was making on the carriage floor.

Everything had seemed quite simple earlier. Eliza was going to go to Lucius and beg him not to turn himself in. Then she'd explain exactly how a communicator worked and pray that it worked whenever he surfaced again. She would never fully forgive him for his actions and decisions. But it wouldn't ever stop her from loving him. She was all right with that. She would figure out a way for her life to continue without him.

The carriage stopped, and she took a deep breath. For all the waiting to arrive, she was not certain what would happen when she finally did. He'd made a promise to her over the communicator, and it had set her body on fire for the better part of the night. She'd done nothing but think of his powerful body above hers, driving into her as their mouths danced together and her own body thrust to meet his. Or of his cock sliding in and out of her mouth, her tongue trailing across it as her lips sucked him deep. She'd worked herself into a fervor of desire, one touch from him may be enough to send her screaming over the edge. But would he still feel that way when she arrived? Her heart pounded as she stepped out of the carriage and thanked the footman, telling him he would not need to stay and wait for her. She only hoped sending him away wasn't presumptuous. A small piece of parchment with horrid penmanship was sticking out of the door. Carefully, she freed it from the door crease and squinted her eyes, trying to decipher the writing that was so difficult to read it may as well have been in code.

ELIZA,

Parkes will be on the hunt with us, please let yourself in. The key is in the bushes to your left.

- Greyston

SHE THOUGHT it strange they hadn't told her that in the guild, but maybe they'd been concerned someone might overhear that she was stepping out. She looked to the left and saw the two perfectly trimmed bushes in the grey porcelain pots. She couldn't bend at the waist because of the injury, so she bent her knees and stuck her hand down into the pot, blindly feeling around until she felt metal. She pulled out a loop with two keys; one golden and one silver and suspected the locks to use them in were colored similarly. She slipped the silver one into the top lock and smiled as she felt the disengagement of the lock as she turned the key. She did the same with the second key and then pushed the door open.

Her face fell when it didn't immediately open and reveal Lucius standing on the other side. But this wasn't a silly fantasy, this was reality; no matter how fucked up it was with demons. She stepped inside and tugged the door shut behind her. The smell of pheasant cooking touched her nose, and she salivated a little. It had been so long since she could remember eating, dinner the night her parents were murdered. She inhaled the scent and sighed, it was delicious, and she detected pepper and oregano too. Someone had set out to cook, or perhaps she was simply smelling the meal Felicia and Greyston had eaten. She continued to walk toward the kitchen area, anyway.

"Lucius. Lucius, are you still here? Tell me that you're still here." She couldn't help but smile as a memory of Felicia's came to her. Almost seven months ago Felicia had been chasing Greyston down after thinking she couldn't be mated to a demon. "Well, this situation is a little different now isn't it?" she muttered under her breath.

"Different than what?"

Lucius' voice startled her as he walked from the kitchen, a towel around his hands.

Her breath caught in her throat at the sight of him. His hair was almost all cut off now, hardly acceptable for society, but perhaps perfectly so for a demon on the run. His eyes almost sparkled, gone was the coldness she saw so oft in them. Her eyes traveled down his bare chest to the pants that hung on his hips. His body was scarred on the shoulders, and she couldn't help but wonder if he obtained them when he got vengeance for her family. The idea of him being hurt for her didn't seem proper. His feet were bare, and his toes wiggled in the fine carpet beneath him when he realized where she was looking.

"Oh, Lucius." She wanted to drop pretense and run to him, to wrap her arms around his neck and pull his head down to kiss her senseless.

When her eyes pulled back up to look at his face, the sparkle was gone from his eyes, replaced by a heat and a hunger that sent wetness betwixt her legs. She wanted him, now more than ever, and she didn't know if she could wait to speak with him to do so. He moved first, his legs making long strides to close the gap betwixt them. His hand reached out and tugged her by the wrist into him even as his other arm reached to wrap around her body. He kissed the top of her head and rested his chin there. She could feel his heart pounding in his chest and the way his cock was beginning to swell beneath his pants.

"Love, I can't tell you how happy I am you are here." His voice was quiet, almost as if he was embarrassed to say it to her.

She kissed his pectoral muscle and trailed her hands down his back. "Lucius, I don't think I want to talk right now." She pressed her body into him and gave a small roll of her hips. His growl made her body tense and turn to liquid all at the same time.

"Then we won't talk as soon as you answer one question for me. Are you all right?" He tipped her chin back, forcing her to look him in the eyes. She tried to turn away, but his fingers held her face firm. "No, love, you answer this, or there will be nothing more."

"I'll live, Lucius. I told you that prior. My stomach is sensitive, yes. My heart feels like it's been torn out of my body and the rest of my body is burning for you. So stop asking questions, demon."

She punctuated her sentence by trailing her hands down his chest and sliding one under his waistband whilst the other worked with the leather belt and metal buckle. She felt his hips buck as her hand slid over his cock, hot and steely under her grasp. She stroked him, even as she worked with the other hand to take the belt off and shove his trousers down. She gasped slightly as pain shot through her stomach from the motion. Lucius growled, and she stroked his cock faster. "Do not stop this, Lucius."

She sank to her knees, felt the hard ground under the lush carpet and shifted her weight slightly. Her right hand slipped from his prick and massaged his balls. A drop of liquid glistened at the end of his erection, and she wasted no time suckling the tip of him into her mouth. She groaned at the salty taste of him, and he growled. Her tongue swirled a circle over his erection's head as her mouth slid down, inch by inch. He stretched her mouth the same as way as he stretched her body and she hummed against his cock. Desire pooled betwixt her legs, and when his hand rolled her nipple through her dress, she cursed the corset. She had not dressed alone due to her injury, and if she couldn't feel the heat of his hands on her flesh soon, she was going to kill the physician that helped her when she returned.

He fumbled to shove her dress down, and she felt the corset release its grip on her torso, but she did nothing to stop her strokes on his cock. Over and over she slid her mouth down it, sucked the tip, nipped at it and rolled it around in her mouth like a sucking sweet. She ran her tongue up the bulging vein that ran from the tip of his cock to the base. Her cheeks hollowed as she sucked him harder. She wasn't certain whose moans were louder, hers or his. She felt his hands tug on her hair as she sucked him. He didn't force her head about, simply held onto her hair and thrust his cock into her mouth, sending it even deeper than she was able to on her own. She arched her body into his hands as his cock hit the back of her throat and she felt his thrusts hike in speed. Everything was a whirl of thrusts and moans as his hips circled hard and fast into her mouth and her hands stroked his balls in the same rhythm.

She felt him explode into her mouth before she realized he'd grunted her name. His hips still pumped into her mouth and she didn't stop licking and sucking. The salty taste fueled her desire for him to seat himself inside her body. Her hips bucked slightly, desire overruling her sense of judgment and she felt the pain from her injury but didn't give in to it. Lucius' thrusts slowed, and she pulled him from her mouth with a pop and swirled her tongue around the head of him, licking up the last bead of his release that lingered. His cock was thick, red and pulsing. She moaned again, needing to find her own release.

His hands gently pulled her up and his mouth covered hers. His kiss was deep and hot, filled with promises so erotic she was ready to burst then and there. He pulled back and pushed the strands of hair that had fallen from the bun back behind her ears. "Love, I don't want to hurt you." He swept her up in his arms, her dress swishing behind him. He laid her gently down on the table and went to work removing her dress. He placed a kiss on her shoulder, and she shuddered.

"Lucius, please."

He didn't respond as he slid the plain tan dress from her body. "I don't like these as much as the fancy ones you were wearing. Not as much for me to bury my head in."

He winked, but his voice was thick with lust and didn't have the same playful tone she'd come to recognize in him. He pulled the dress past her knees, and let it fall to the floor, her corset following suit shortly after. He placed a kiss on the angry red skin around the stitches, and she flinched. Not from pain, but because she hadn't wanted him to see it.

"I'm sorry, Eliza, I'll be careful. I promise I'll never hurt you again."

True to his words his hands gently splayed open her legs. One finger brushed the wet curls betwixt her legs, and she threw her head back on the table and groaned. When his hands wrapped around her and tugged her so that her legs dangled off the table, she almost didn't notice the stab of pain she felt. He nudged at her entrance with his shaft, and she pushed off the table a little further, eager to have him inside of her.

"Oh, Lucius, yes."

He slid in and out of her so slowly it was maddening. She wanted hard and fast. But she knew she wouldn't get that from him, not right now. His body stood betwixt her legs against the table, and the erotic image filled her mind, and she bit her lower lip. Colors began to dance across her vision as his thrusts went deeper. Their breathing was loud, the sound of their bodies hitting together a rumble against the table. Her body thrashed as his finger swept over her clit. She arched off the table again and hooked her legs around his waist. He gasped that time, and if she hadn't been so overwhelmed with need she might have laughed at the startled look in his eyes as she tried to take over. Her backside rocked against the table, and he slipped a hand under her, lifting her body and stopping the way she was bashing into the table.

His cock slid deeper in, and she tried to angle her hips up, allowing him to go deeper still. When he thrust in next, it felt as if he was seated to the hilt and she sighed at the thought of his entire thick cock pounding in and out of her body. She couldn't focus on anything, couldn't even open her eyes as his body moved in and out of hers, and his finger circled her clit over and over again.

She squeezed her eyes shut tight, and she felt Lucius' second release come and fill her. Desperate to reach her own she tugged his head down to her and ran her tongue up the side of his neck to his lips and slipped it into his mouth when he opened with a groan. He kissed her hard and fast even as his release took him and continued to go slower than she would like. She almost wasn't ready as the wave of pleasure crashed over her body. Her hips jerked, and her core milked his cock as he continued to slide in and out, wringing every last moment of pleasure from them both.

When he finally stopped, she unwound her legs, took her heels from off his arse and breathed hard. But he didn't move. She could feel him, still twitching inside her body and the sensation was delicious. She never wanted him to move, never wanted to not feel this connected to him ever. He leaned down and placed a kiss on her breast, and she shuddered, squeezing his cock with her muscles again.

"Love, I hadn't intended to destroy their oak table."

She flushed and shifted her body ever so slightly, groaning as the action took him deeper. "Oh goodness, Lucius." Her body was a mass of nerves, and he ran his hands down her torso, his fingers sending sparks where they touched. Her body quivered around him, and she closed her eyes, suddenly embarrassed by how much she wanted him.

"Never close your eyes again like that. I want to see the desire in them every single time."

The way he spoke, it was if he knew there was going to be more times to come. Her head swam with possibilities even as his fingers pinched her clit. She gasped and twitched, and her eyes opened to see him grinning down at her.

"Dinner is going to have to wait, love. I'm not done with you."

He picked her up and her legs instinctually wrapped around his waist, and she bit her lip to stop from crying out with pleasure each time he took a step. He laid her down on the couch and covered her body with his and showered her just how much he wasn't done with her, for the course of the next hour.

NINETEEN

Lucius' hand gently stroked through Eliza's hair. Her breathing was slow, and she was quite content in her place curled up against his chest. They'd made a mess of the couch, having strewn the cushions about, but neither of them seemed to care. She certainly knew she didn't. Her stomach pulsed a little, but the feeling of absolute fulfillment that buzzed through her outweighed the discomfort. Sooner or later they were going to have to rise, clean up the mess and have the right and proper talk she'd come here to have. The smell of the meal had long since vanished in the air, and her stomach's low growl took her out of the moment. When Lucius laughed her head bounced on his chest.

"Sorry, love." He continued to stroke her hair, and she forced herself to rise up off his chest and sit upright to speak to him.

"Lucius, we need to talk."

"No, love, we do not. We've had a fantastic night. Let me make a scrumptious meal and then we will go to the guild together, hand in hand. If you would allow it." He took her hand and placed a soft kiss on the back of it.

Kindness, gentle kisses, consideration. All things she would have said were impossible for a demon. Yet, Greyston was in the world, as was Lucius. How many more like these men could there be? She hoped for many as to show they weren't all evil, but her concern rested with one this eve, and only one.

"You cannot turn yourself in, Lucius. I spoke with the Guildmaster. I know what they have planned for you." she sounded panicked, and she was.

"Really then, tell me, what is in my cards, Eliza?"

He sounded jovial, and his tone irritated her. "Can you not take this seriously, Lucius? This is not some con to be won or gambling cheat to pull off. I thought you cared for life?" Her tone was haughty, and she pulled away from him completely.

His eyes darkened, the light and laughter clearly extinguished. "I take you seriously. I take us seriously. Your life is serious. I am hundreds of years old, and I have not been the sort of creature you would want. Yet you do, and for that, I am serious about protecting you. Turning myself in protects you from lying to your family, from running in the dark with a creature they want to destroy."

Her throat went dry. His words touched her soul and infuriated her all at once. "Life isn't something to throw away, Lucius. Not a week ago you were talking about your own skin and your own importance. I refuse to let you throw your life away for mine. I'm not asking you too. In fact, I'm asking you to run. Just run."

He ran a hand down her face, and she cursed inwardly as she felt herself melt against his touch. "Eliza Kempe Dorley, would you have me be an honest man so that I might one day seek to make amends and court you?"

The question came from nowhere. Eliza momentarily stop breathing. What did she want from him? A week ago it would have been to see him killed. A few hours ago to see him safe; but now? She realized it with a sudden clarity that she couldn't ignore. She did want him to court her, but she didn't care what sort of man or demon he was when he did it. What mattered was who he was when he was with her.

"Yes."

A grin spread across his face, and the twinkle returned to his black eyes. "Then tell me what awaits me when I turn myself in to your Alliance. There will be no more talk of it, Eliza. It is still a man's world, and you are going to have to accept my nobleness because I find no shame in it and there is nothing that can be done to stop my actions now. I have already asked that Felicia and Greyston tell your Guildmaster I will be arriving in the morning, of my own volition."

She was surprised to find his words didn't anger her this time. Perhaps it was his grand and silly declaration, but how could she stop him if he wanted to be someone the Alliance didn't want to put down on sight. "Very well, Lucius. Do not think it will be easy for you. There will be a trial. You will be put before a jury of men and women who would no doubt love to put a bullet in your head for just breathing. But being as you are my mate, the trial will be peaceful should you cooperate. Should you not, well there are cells beneath the street level in the guild, and they are not peaceful, Lucius."

He kissed the top of her head, an action she found she rather liked the more he did it. "Then we have nothing to fear, love. I am going into this ready and willing."

She heard the words, but there were no means to process them correctly. "And what of Seraphina?" She was skeptical of his ability to answer her question.

"I was wrong to protect her. Your people need to realize Greyston isn't an anomaly. In fact, many lesser demons love humans for what you give them. Food, ale, women. I am a killer, Eliza. I have always been one and will remain so. But not all are like my kind and if Seraphina needs to be destroyed to prove that to your Alliance then so be it."

Stunned wasn't the word for her reaction to him. He was ready to give it all away for a chance to prove to her he loved her. Tears sprung to her eyes, and she sniffed them back, not wanting to ruin the majesty of the moment. She forced herself to breathe, to remember there was more than just herself and Lucius at this time.

"Eliza, love, are you all right? Is it your wound?"

"I am fine, Lucius. Merely trying to comprehend the change in you, in my mate." She put a finger to his lips and laughed. "And do not tell me it is love, Lucius. Love is a wonderful concept and a truly wonderful feeling, but this change starts within you. For that, I am without words. I am so sorry you felt you had to change for me. I regret that I was so narrow-minded, but by your own admission, you were exactly what the Alliance needed to keep off the streets." She hung her head, ashamed to throw such a statement back in his face.

"I was, Eliza. I was a cad, and I enjoyed every second of it. But no longer. Plus there is something to be said for the energy a truly vile person gives off." He smiled at her, and she laughed. Deep down he might be changing, but he was still the same charming man she'd met so many months ago in a bar in her dreams.

"Let's not dwell on anything. If we do, I am going to start to mourn the morning, and whilst your cooperation is unexpected and appreciated, it will not mean your freedom by any stretch. So let's fix this room before Felicia and Greyston know what we have done and eat that dinner you were making."

Lucius chuckled as he rose and she raised a brow at him. "What is so funny?" She couldn't help but admire the firmness of his bottom as he bent to grab a cushion.

"Greyston is an Incubus Demon. He can smell sex days after it's been had." She paled, and he laughed again as he tossed a cushion her way. "Don't worry. Felicia will get a very good morning out of this. She'll probably thank you for fucking me out in the open...three times."

That time her face turned bright scarlet, and she cried out a little. "Oh heavens! Lucius!" She launched at him and flinched at the small pain and punched his arm as hard as she could muster. "That is for not taking me to a bedroom. Oh no, on their table! Lucius." She groaned, and he laughed.

They finished rearranging the couch and moved into the dining area. Eliza couldn't look at the table the same as she waited for Lucius to bring out the meal. They ate, and they talked and when the sun rose he placed his hand in hers.

"It's time for you to call your Alliance now, Eliza, the dawn has already touched the sky. Do not give me such a look, your face is likely to freeze in that position." He popped her on the nose and smiled at her.

She sighed and went into the other room to call for the carriage. Twenty minutes that felt all too short passed before they arrived and took Lucius away in cuffs in one carriage and her in another once again all by herself.

THE WOODEN BENCH PRESSED INTO LUCIUS' arse, and he did his best to shuffle side to side. The metal from the handcuffs bit into his wrists from the movement, and he cringed. The physical pain was still a bitch to bear for him. He looked across the small room, and his eyes landed on Eliza. *A bitch to bear, but one far worth it if it gets you your mate.* She sat across the way from him, guarded by two hunters whom he'd learned were Philippe and Kellan. A panel of Alliance leaders including Greyston, the Master of the Alliance, two other Alliance leaders and a royal sat directly to his left. None save for Greyston looked upon him with any concern or compassion. Had he known Greyston had a seat on a panel he would have demanded his friend not be put in such a position. But what better way to test loyalty than to damn a friend?

He wanted to force himself to not watch Eliza, but it was impossible. She was stoic and quiet. In all the time he'd known her, she had been shy, but never silent. She'd told him her mind more than once, and she couldn't run the inventions without telling men when and where to shut it and shove off. But here, she was a different woman. She was cold and untouchable. He knew why, though, any sort of emotional interest on her part might condemn him. The grey haired Alliance Master who also ran the guild, Master Agardawes, cleared his throat and looked down at him. The old man's eyes were teaming with intelligence and Lucius had a feeling he missed nothing that went on in his guild. His grey hair was cut short, and the beard and mustache trimmed neatly.

"Demon, we will begin this trial now." He wanted to remind the man that he had a name, but the look in Greyston's eyes squelched the need. To the rest of the room, the man continued to speak. "This demon is to be given no extra consideration for his unfortunate pairing as our own Eliza Dorley's mate." That, however, was more than he could handle.

"Fuck you, old man! She is a beautiful female and undeserving of being spoken about that way." He rose, and the chains on the cuffs pulled him back down.

"Enough!" Shouted the Guildmaster at the same time as Eliza shouted his name. "I was implying the problem lay with you. Your outburst will not earn you any favors, demon. We will continue now. Panel bear in mind that he has helped seek those who committed mass murder. But that he too has committed murder, freely and with no remorse. He is a demon we all had no knowledge of until recently, proof that there are so many more out there for us to rid the world of." His tone rose, and Lucius wanted to remind him he was remorseful or he wouldn't be here. But it was Greyston who spoke.

"May I point out I am a demon, and I was helping your people kill mine long before we ever knew the other existed. You asked me to be a part of this proceeding so that fairness could be attained. I am sorry for the incident with your daughter in The Americas. But Lucius is here, has always been here, and it is not appropriate for you to judge him for the actions of one. I will take his side forever should you walk such a line of hate. He has come, on his own, to help us in this fight. Much as I did when I knew I had no other choice. I fought against my kind for years in secret, and I do so by your side now. Do not make me regret the side I chose. Do not forget what Lucius is truly capable of." Greyston's chest was heaving, his face red from exertion, by the time he finished and sat back down. He had never known how deeply Greyston felt against other demons, or how highly he now regarded himself.

The older man appeared humbled, a frown crossed his face, and he ran it over his mustache. "Forgive me. Greyston is right. I will not let the actions of demons in another part of the world interfere again." He turned to Eliza. "I give you my word." He turned back to the room filled with people hanging on his words. Lucius wanted to know what the fuck had happened, but it wasn't the time, and it was sure as shit was not his place. "This demon is a Nightmare Demon. He can frolic in one's head whilst they sleep and pull images from your minds, your greatest fears, and use them to kill you. He can create hallucinations whilst you are awake, but I am told it puts him in great peril, and he will not try it in this room. He must kill to survive; it is in his blood to need the energy a dying soul gives off. Should we execute him, we save countless lives. Should we save him, he walks the streets with one of our own. Should we impression him, we must supply him humans, or demons, to murder so that he may live. We judge him now, for his crimes with the Fallen we know as Seraphina to enter this guild, to breach the Alliance secrets and to return them to her."

Murmurs rang out from the people in the room. The only ones not speaking were Greyston and Eliza. "We judge him now, once and only once. Do not let anything change your opinion based on the facts he will share in this room. All will have a vote, including Greyston and Eliza as Greyston is a member of our panel and Eliza lost her family due to this demon."

Nothing was said for a few moments and the one thing he wasn't expecting to happen, did. Eliza stood up from her seat across the room and began to talk. "He came to me in a dream. Sometime in the spring. I didn't know what he was, and I was seduced by him. I met him almost a fortnight ago on the trains and was once more seduced. I found out what he truly was from Felicia. When I confronted him with the knowledge, he came clean. He told me of his kind and that I was his mate. I will ask that you do not ask to see this marking on my mate as it is attached to his rear end, and that is mine to look at, mine alone."

He couldn't help but grin at her words. She still was emotionless in her voice and her eyes, but her words meant enough.

"In a show of faith, he hunted down three demons for me, without my knowledge. Demons I reported to you. Then we went out to hunt, I am not allowed, and this I understand. Put me on trial as well then. But we did. I have never been out in the field, and when we came across two Illusion Demons, Lucius used his own powers and comforted me when it was done. Shortly after he saved me from a Fallen. I fell in love with him. I will never apologize for that, but I will apologize that it was not sooner so that I could have been happier longer."

Again the room grew noisy, and she stood and waited for them to cease.

"I do not know when his deal with Seraphina was made, but I was attacked, along with my family by demons sent from this Seraphina. They told me Lucius was to use me to get to the Alliance. He told me it was true, but that he was going to give her false information and we would be free of her forever when he was done. I believe him. I've seen this man attack, make love and laugh. His words were true. But he would not turn his boss in, and that is where we fell apart."

Eliza said nothing else, no words in his defense, no continuation of the story. She just sat down.

"Thank you, Eliza. I know it was hard to keep personal feelings out and I will strike your assurance of his honesty from the records. Demon, it is your turn now."

"His name is Lucius. You will address him as such, or I will walk away from the project you have me working on." Eliza's voice cut through the small quarters, and the Guildmaster looked stricken. Lucius had no clue what she might be working on, but it was enough to make the older man scoff.

"Lucius then, go on."

He bit his inner cheek to refrain from smirking. His mate was something all right. "I make no claims different from what has been spoken. In fact, I will further it by stating that for the first thousand or so years of my life I killed with pleasure. The release of energy from a soul to a Nightmare Demon is the greatest pleasure a Nightmare Demon can know, next to having a family."

The talking started up, and he looked to Greyston who nodded and Eliza who smiled. They'd talked this part over prior to calling in. Every line and word from his mouth were rehearsed and set to draw the most positive response. But it didn't make them any less true.

"You humans have made a mistake with the demons. An error that Seraphina will undoubtedly take advantage of. You grouped us all together. You decided that we were all of one nature, of one mind. If one of us had black spiked teeth and yellow skin, we all hid that beneath the surface. If one of us kills for sustenance, not simply for a joy in a killing, we all do that. So where then do all the demons you DON'T notice walking around fit? The merchant who's secretly an Illusion Demon living with his mate. The ice and fire demons that contribute to weather cycles you humans enjoy? The Incubus Demon parading as Captain of the Royal Guard and married to one of your own? Where does that leave them?" He stood as best as he could with his handcuffs together and chained to the bench.

"It leaves them right where they already are. Safely under your radar and harming none. What about the murderers amongst human men? They are not put down on the spot. The thieves are not either. Am I innocent? Absolutely not. I am a Nightmare Demon, my friends. I like to cause pain and fear, and I have survived longer than most of your entire bloodline doing it. But I have found the one thing that can change a part of me that I never could on my own. I found Eliza. Everything she said was correct. Only let's cut to the part where now, since finding her, I've only killed when Seraphina ordered me too, a blood debt I have recently broken, and will kill for her no longer. Or to the man with alcohol on his breath that was about to rape a young girl running an errand for her mother, who now lies rotting in the Thames because I was there to serve justice. Or the thief who murdered someone in an attempt to get away with her jewels. I make no claims to who I was. I speak to who I have been since finding my mate, and who I will be to her once I am free."

The rioting from the small group of people grew so loud he dared to let the demonic cold seep into his eyes before he spoke the next part. "The Alliance of Silver and Steam is in place to protect the humans from the demons because the Angels told the Royals a story twenty years ago. You hunt, seduce, and kill without ever even double checking what we really are. Of the families who you, the humans, have ripped apart. We are no different from you. Some of us hunt to live, others hide to survive. You play executioner to all of us because you've never dared to look behind the curtain. So I'm daring you now. Look behind the human facade, see the demon I am and judge me. My sins are my own and my future is yours."

Lucius sat, and the room exploded. Shouts and curses rang out like firearm shots. They had not wished to hear of their own flaws, and he had shoved them into their faces. He sat back against the wooden back of the bench and his eyes connected with Eliza's. Fear spread across her face, but he was not afraid. He had done the right thing by his mate, and if this worked, then he would be a new person in her eyes and maybe have changed the way the Alliance of Silver and Steam worked. Her eyes widened just as he felt two sets of arms wrap around his forearms. He heard nothing over the screaming and fighting in the small room, but he felt the lock on the chain disengage and saw Eliza frantically telling him not to run.

Everything in him centered on the two men holding him. He crept into their minds and froze when he saw what they both feared the most. It was him. At this moment the two hunters that had been guarding Eliza were terrified of him. The knowledge seeped through him, and his eyes were closing into a trance before he knew what was happening. His hearing faded as he entered into the trance before he could stop himself. He wasn't certain what the room saw, all he was certain of was the truth staring at him from his mate's eyes. He'd crossed over the line. He'd forgotten to be what he'd promised he would. Instead, Lucius had become the creature they thought he was.

With a scream, he forced himself out of the trance and let the hallucination drop, never having seen through his victim's eyes to know what they truly saw him as. Or worse, what his mate had seen when he'd unleashed his power.

"That is enough! Get him the hell out of here even if you have to shoot him to do it."

"No! No, you can't!"

He saw Eliza as she shoved Greyston out of the way. Everything moved slowly as if someone had found a Time Turning Demon and reset the seconds. He watched as Greyston wrapped an arm around her waist and pulled her, violently, back against the wall. His eyes were solemn as he nodded his head at Lucius and Lucius put his hands up in the air. His eyes closed, pain streaked through him for his mistake. He almost didn't feel the weapon that cracked against his ankles and sent him crashing to the floor. He couldn't hear anything but the sound of his chance snapping like a twig beneath his boot.

Hands still raised in the air, Lucius laid his head on the green lined marble floor and did nothing as arms wrapped around him and something collided with the back of his skull, sending him into immediate darkness.

TWENTY

"Sit down, Miss Dorley, and quite frankly, shut up."

The harshness in Master Agardawes' tone threw her, and she found herself lowering into the chair. It was a deep, bellowing pitch that made her feel like a small child being scolded for eating an extra sweet after dinner. "It is by the grace of God that he is not dead as we speak. Your closeness with Felicia and her own mated demon are the only things keeping that creature alive, and I will not remind you again to watch yourself, girl."

She had never heard him raise his voice to anyone. For the entirety of the time she had been at the guild, she'd never heard him above a dull roar. He was intimidating, but never cruel or terrifying. He was both right now and had been for the last hour and eighteen minutes since she had stormed into his office with Greyston.

"He got overwhelmed. Don't you understand that? You heard the comments in the room. You saw the way Philippe and Kellan advanced on him! He was protecting himself. If anyone failed to do what they should have in that trial, it was you! You are the one in command, you could have silenced everyone, and you let them provoke him. Let them shout about his death being needed and how all demons were nothing more than abominations. You sat and watched as the room exploded into chaos. His mistake is on your hands."

Her whole body felt like it was on fire, being eaten alive with rage and the sudden urge to strike the man she'd admired most of her adult life. Her breath was coming out in quick pants, and her nostrils flared even as her nails bit into her palms. She felt the blood slide down them, just as she had the three times prior when she'd been driven to control her emotions by inflicting pain to herself.

"You have stepped out of a line, Miss Dorley. You must remember who you are speaking to."

"And you must remember that there is a demon in the room with us. One you damn near are about to treat as your own son. How do you think he feels about what was said? About your choices and actions?" Tears stung her eyes, and she let them fall. She had lost everything — her family, her mate, her respect for what she had thought was the greatest man alive — there was nothing left to lose and no reason to hide her fury and pain.

Thomas Agardawes' bright blue eyes slid to Greyston, who was standing in the corner of the room, blackness filling his own eyes. He took his spectacles off and put them on his desk. "What would you have me do?" The question wasn't directed at her but at Greyston.

She barely recognized the anger that blazed in his voice when he responded.

"I would expect you to be a leader. To open your eyes and see that whilst he lost control, so did every one of your Alliance members and that fucking Royal snob, Jacob. I do not disagree that he needed to be contained. A Nightmare Demon in a small room would have been fatal, regardless of what he wanted. I cannot speak for what everyone saw, but I have a pretty good guess that it was themselves. As at that moment every fucking one of us should have feared nothing more than that. Because we kill without asking, without remorse. We are no better than the demons we hunt. The only difference is as a demon I can tell who needs to be put down and who should be allowed to run free."

"Is that your way of telling me you've made your own rules for your job as both Captain of the Guard and a hunter?" Agardawes' tone was incredulous, his eyes wide with curiosity and betrayal.

"You're damn right I have. Do you know why? Because I. Am. A. Demon. I will protect all innocents the same and hunt all evil, regardless of what form it comes in, the same way. I am sorry for your loss, Thomas. But you are in London. You are the one running the show, and it is time to pull your head out of your arse and open your fucking eyes because if it's one thing I know, it's the lengths a mate will go to in order to protect each other. You and every other non-mated demon cannot understand the strength and force of the fated bond. It goes beyond everything deemed needed by your silly bible and laws. It is survival, and I can tell you this one right here, the beautiful blonde female shooting daggers at you with her eyes, is ready to unleash hell, Thomas. So it is your turn to pick. Do you fight your daughter's battle in America or do you be a damned leader and work with what's right here? I will never fail to protect this city and Felicia. However, this fight is not with me, and trust me, you do not want to make it so."

He didn't speak as Master Agardawes straightened up in the chair behind his desk. Emotions flew across his face that Eliza couldn't comprehend. But Greyston was long out the door, and it slammed shut so hard the hinges shook.

Silence fell in the room. Two occupants, both ready to do what they felt was best. "He is correct." Her mentor, Master and almost family member looked up at her then, astonished.

"Whatever do you mean, Miss Dorley? I fear he made more than one appropriate point. I am not apologizing for anything, I will not be questioned. But I am willing to hear what you have to say. Fifty years in a cell, with victims brought for him to slaughter so that you might retain your mate alive in some fashion is more than generous. He would have killed us all. I should see him put down, I really should."

She ignored everything he said. None of it mattered. Whilst she'd sat and listened to Greyston, she had determined her next move and the game would be hers. There was too much to lose for it to go any other way. "About what we will do to protect our mate. I am not saying he does not need a punishment of sorts. His actions were violent, but not unnecessary as he most likely felt we were going to attack him. Which ironically happened since I watched his limp body dangle from Philippe's arms as he was carried off to the dungeon. Before you tried to run to your office and pretend you weren't responsible. You know what he said was right."

"Nothing that he said was right."

His voice was cold, and Eliza recognized it from her own dismissal of his comments when he wouldn't help with Seraphina. But he wasn't wrong.

"We are no better than the demons. We ask no questions and slaughter the moment they talk, or they enter a room. Not all demons are Thrashers or Kappa Demons. We'd be foolish to think we have spotted out every demon, how could we without each and every type of blood to drop onto a crystal? I told you there would be a time when the secrets needed to come out. Well, an Angel supplied us with the crystals, I know that without a doubt, but I don't know the rest of the story. What I do know is that you have quite a lot to lose, Thomas." She folded her arms over her chest and leveled a stare at him. "You have an awful lot to lose."

"Just how do you figure that, Eliza?" There wasn't a semblance of worry in his voice.

She almost felt guilty before she got ready to speak. This had been her home when she wasn't good enough for her parents, and now it was the only home she had. But she would never stay if Lucius suffered death or fifty years locked away to be tortured and questioned and probably tested upon by the real alchemists that worked in the labs.

"No one, not you and not the Royals and not even the demons themselves want their lives to be public. I will make it so. I have

Greyston who would gladly bare his eyes and seduce an audience to expose the secret." She didn't add that they'd never actually discussed anything. This was a farce if ever she had told one, and if it was too transparent, everything was over. "If that did not work I have six pieces of technology hidden away at the estate, the task is being done even as we speak. It was set up long before Lucius and I arrived this morning, or rather before you dragged him in. Not including the motorbike safely tucked away with Felicia in a location that you will never know because she left her communicator, and therefore her tracker behind. I may fail to expose the demons, but I will not fail to start a revolution over the secrets the Royals have been keeping. You ask yourself, is that enough blood on your hands, Thomas?"

Genuine fear shown on the old man's face, fear that she had put there. It was the truth. She had not known if the plan was going to be needed when they'd thought it up this morning. Yet, Felicia had discarded her armband and taken a bike and two guns to a small area just outside London's main gates. Gates that had been put up by the guilds to keep workers and the society members apart. Even if Eliza never left this room alive, though she doubted her old friend would resort to murder, the plan would move forward. All that was left was one, stubborn, old man.

"What is it going to be, Thomas?"

He sighed, and she watched as years seemed to tear off him and grief settled in. His voice held none of the temper or bravado from a moment prior. It was meek and hard to even hear. "He must be punished, Eliza. What would you have me do?"

The smirk slid across her face, and she thanked her lucky stars it had worked. "Oh, I know just what you can do, Master Agardawes."

He hadn't been able to think straight. He'd woken up in a tiny cell, the smell of mold and water permeating the area and he had a feeling he was in the cells Eliza had told him about. They had stayed up much of the last night hashing out a plan that may have secured his freedom. What he'd done had most assuredly damned not only himself but Eliza as well. "Because you always only look out for yourself, Willan. You can't change just because you tell her you can." He growled, and he grabbed the cell doors and shook them. It was probably the fifth time he'd tried since regaining consciousness, and they were steady as a rock. If he didn't know any better, he would guess they were made with the same material used in Pure Angel's demon cuffs. It would make sense since there was no way of knowing what they would be holding down in the cells.

A steady drip of water was enough to send him spiraling into madness. Over and over he heard the obnoxious plop onto the stone ground. But that wasn't all he could hear. He wasn't alone down here. There was no light, and his eyes weren't meant for seeing in total darkness. But he could hear plenty. At least five pairs of feet had shuffled around down there with him. Heavy breathing and growling accompanied the steps but never talking. He had tried to communicate with whatever was down here and had decided either they had no tongues left with which to do so, or they were a demon without human speech capacity. Many had such limitations, and he wanted to believe that was the cause and not the former.

There was nowhere to sit but on the floor, and he slid down the lumpy stone wall, dragging his head as he went. The ground was cold under his arse, and he felt the mating mark tingle, the skin would forever be slightly more sensitive there. But he didn't want the reminder of what he'd ruined. She must hate him. There would be no way she could forgive him after he basically attacked a room full of people she was close too. There was no excuse for what had happened. He was a demon in the guise of a man, and he could not control what he was. Not the way that was needed. He'd heard the shouts to kill him, and his mate and his blood had boiled before he'd known what he was doing. There had been no exchange of energy so he could only hope that he hadn't succeeded in killing anyone with their own worst fears. But he was certainly a caged monster in all their eyes now.

He couldn't help but wonder what their plan was for him now. In the darkness, there was no way to tell how much time had passed or even what day it was since he had been unconscious at one point. His body was weary, and he'd assumed it was day, but it was impossible to know. He was left drained and with nothing to do except agonize over what he had done, over his failure to Eliza.

No one had been down to see him, and the idea of being left to die didn't sit well with his well-worn cowardice. He much preferred the idea of a quick execution to the alternative. Without soul energy, he would begin to fade away as a human did without nourishment. It would take him longer to die, about two months, and it would be slow and painful. He'd never done it before, but his friend had grown weary of killing and had done away with himself, much as many demons do after an immortality of the same thing. It became tedious. Perhaps that was why mates existed, to alleviate the routine. His skin would dehydrate first, and his muscles would lose mass. Within a week he would be unable to stand or speak, but he would still be very much alive and very much in pain.

The sound of a heavy door being displaced caused a tremor in the ground under him, and he jumped up, his legs shaking, but still able to hold him. Light blasted through the room, bright and scalding compared to the darkness his eyes had adjusted too. He was not the only one that hissed at the intrusion, but the door did not close. Footsteps moved closer, and the scent of lavender replaced the mildew. His heart leapt in his throat, but he didn't want to hope. Anyone could share her bath oils. The people, he could see the silhouettes of two, continued to walk toward him. His body began to shake again, but not from weariness as Eliza's golden blonde hair became visible in the bright light. The man that walked with her, he was one of the one's who'd grabbed him. Philippe, if he wasn't mistaken. He growled as the pair approached and he saw Eliza's arm grasped tightly in the man's hand.

Let him walk close to these bars with his hands touching my mate.

I'll yank his stylishly long hair through this cell and tear his head from his shoulders for touching her.

"Settle down, Lucius. I don't know how the fuck Eliza did it, but she's got something to tell you." Philippe's voice was heavier accented than in the trial, the French accent a little more prevalent, but still well hidden underneath the British diction needed to properly work in this city.

"I will when you take your hands off her arm, and I ensure you did not mark her skin." His teeth were bared, and Philippe shook his head and released Eliza. She stumbled forward for a second and turned to glare at the hunter.

"Think twice about who you come to for your next weapon, Philippe. You are only doing your job, but there was no need to be so forceful." She turned to look at Lucius, and her smile was wide. "You forget I hold all the cards in this gambling game." Her hands wrapped around the bars and he hurdled up to wrap his hands around hers. The contact sent a sizzle of lust through him, but more importantly a sigh of relief knowing where they stood.

"What are you doing here, love? Tell me you're not being tossed in here with me? Much as I would cherish your company."

She shook her head and laughed, a sound so light and filled with joy, he wasn't certain if she was mentally addled or if she had news to share.

Philippe snarled something from his corner, and she turned away from him to look at the hunter.

"How about you give me that key and leave us be? Stand right outside the entrance and even lock us in if you wish. I have no intention of going anywhere but right here, with my mate until the time comes that I cannot be."

"Eliza, that was not part of the deal." Philippe's agitation was written all over his face.

"There was no deal made, Philippe, save for the arrangement agreed upon regarding Lucius. You can stay if you like, but I have no problem telling you that once I can actually touch him, I'm going to.

With or without you in the room, Philippe, because I no longer care what any of you think. I will be loyal to my family, to the cause and to my mate. One of which is locked up and I need to assure him of his safety and my love. Your choice."

Lucius felt the blood rush to his prick at her words. He smiled too, she'd gotten so brave. Or maybe she'd always been this outspoken with the men.

"I think I liked it better when you were more respectful, Eliza," Philippe grumbled as he unlocked the door.

"Do not be daft. I have always spoken with men like this. Hunters just rarely enter the labs to hear me do so." She stepped aside as he opened the door to Lucius' cell and she stepped in and tugged the door closed. "As you can see I have no plans of escape. Lock us in if you wish, Philippe."

The man muttered something under his breath as he walked out.

The heavy door closed with a booming sound, and they were ushered back into darkness. His hands found her face and pulled her into him. He kissed the tip of her nose, quite by accident before his mouth found hers and devoured it. She tasted of sweets again, or maybe that was just what he associated her as being, sweet and special as a confections treat. Their tongues twirled together and her body melted against his, as it always did, as it always would. Her moan of need had his cock standing at full attention. Her hand reached betwixt them and undid his pants, springing it free into her hand. She wasted no time wrapping her fist around him and beginning a medium tempo stroke up and down his shaft. Her left hand joined her right, and he saw stars briefly. He nipped at her lower lip and pulled backwards. Their breathing was as loud as the creatures that occupied this space with him and realized they could possibly be seen, and that he had no idea what she was doing here.

"Lucius, they cannot see anything. The walls are stone with no windows. It is to assure no plotting can be done with visual cues. Guards are always outside should anything occur, but just the same, it's for the safety of the whole guild." Her hand didn't stop its sensual glide up and down his shaft, and he bit his lip to force himself not to thrust into her hands. "I think I want to play with you for a little whilst though whilst we talk." She went quiet as she let go of his cock and then dragged just the tips of her fingers up and down it. "You ruined everything, you know?" Her tone held no accusation, just simple fact as she dragged her nails back and forth, up and down over his prick.

"I'm sorry, love. The things they said—" he cut off with a groan when she pinched the skin under the head of his cock gently. "It's damn near impossible to think when you're doing that and I cannot touch you."

She'd been wearing the pants he favored her in, he'd noticed that when the door had been open. He felt her move closer to him and a momentary absence of her hand on his cock. When she pressed her body against his erection, he felt bare, wet, flesh and he groaned. She rubbed against him twice before he leaned down and suckled her neck, drawing a gasp from her this time. He let his hand trail down her stomach, lingering just above her core before swiping a finger over her folds. Her moan sent a jolt of longing through him, and he rocked his hips against her as she wrapped her hand around his shaft first.

"We have to talk first. Talk first," Eliza repeated herself as Lucius slipped a finger inside her body, moving it in a circle whilst his thumb ran over her clit in a slow manner. "Your sentence has been decided, and you owe me, mate."

"I believe I'm repaying my debts to you now, Eliza." His voice was husky, a perfect match for hers, but as much as he wanted to bury himself inside her, he wanted to know what would happen more.

She ground her hips on his finger and whimpered. "Yes, but no. You have a choice, Lucius. You may choose your—" she broke off with a loud moan, and she squeezed him tighter, causing his hips to buck for more. She was breathing heavy when she continued, her words punctuated with small gasps. "Fight with us. Help the Alliance and only kill those already sentenced to death and our punishment will be a week of you in the dungeon with me far enough away we cannot meet in dreams."

He noted the use of the words "our" and "we." His heart clenched because he'd known she would suffer, but hearing it made him all the angrier at himself. He slid his finger from her body and put his hands under her arse, picking her up and turning to back her against the wall. A part of him did not wish to put her beautiful skin on the wall, but she still wore a top, so he leaned her against it slowly, biting his cheek as her wet heat glided over his erection.

"What's my other option?" He held still, not wanting anything to cloud his judgment after she gave him his choice.

Her body gyrated gently against his, but it was as if she knew they needed to halt, to finish the conversation first.

"Remain down here for fifty years. You will be brought demons to kill, they will be drugged and ready when they are brought to you, and you will be expected to give information about your kind to the Alliance."

He growled and not because of how badly he wanted to slip inside her and forget everything but her body around his. How she could even think there was a choice was beyond him. "Love, there is only one choice that would ever do. I will fight alongside the Alliance, but I will not kill unless I have too and I will make sure my kills are never innocents when it is to survive." He felt her nod against his chin, and she lowered her head and playfully bit his throat. His cock swelled thicker at the sensation.

"That is what I was hoping you'd say," she whispered against his neck and shifted her body, angling the tip of his shaft inside her body.

He didn't need any other directions. He leaned Eliza back against the wall and put one hand beside her head, and he seated himself in her to the hilt and began to rock. He wanted to be mindful of the stone behind her head, but his hips were frantic, and he took her mouth with his as he slammed into her body. Their mouths moved in tempo with their hips, and he felt her body begin to tremble with each and every stroke. He felt his balls tighten as his own release neared and his thrusts sped up, he needed the friction of her body gripping his cock and he pulled out quicker and quicker. With each thrust, he pulled himself from her heat as far as he could without losing contact and sank back in. Over and over until her walls spasmed around his cock and pulled his release from him. They made no sound, not wanting to alert Philippe to what was actually occurring inside. But when they finished coming, when her body was no longer milking his cock, and he was no longer sinking in and out of her to prolong their pleasure, he slid from her, and she dropped down the wall. Or he assumed she did because he heard her feet touch the ground.

They were both breathing heavy, and she was the one who spoke first. "I love you, Lucius. I think I've loved you since that first dream when I was mystified how I'd imagined such a sexy man."

He wished he could see her. Wished he could hold her gaze with his, but there was nothing to see in the blackness of the supposed dungeon. "I love you, Eliza. I'm sorry for everything. I can't do a damn thing about any of it, but I will do better in the future." He reached his hand out and brushed stone wall and growled. "Damn it, I wanted to touch you."

She laughed, and it spread to him, a feeling of lightness that everything was over. He was free of Seraphina, and he got his mate. He may have trapped himself with another boss he did not want, but with Eliza by his side, none of that would matter anymore.

"There will be plenty of time for that. Philippe!" she shouted, and he was slightly saddened she was about the leave.

Light poured into the darkness again before he had a chance to even know if she was clothed. His eyes darted to her, and he sighed as he saw the black breeches perfectly back in place, not a hair messed up in the bun she always wore. How had she moved so efficiently in the pitch black?

"Done then?" Philippe looked from Lucius to Eliza, but his expression gave nothing away.

Eliza had told him what would happen when she was in the cell whether he believed it or not was not evident on his face.

"Very. I'm ready to go to Felicia's now." She leaned up and kissed him, a gentle brush of her lips, and he wanted to capture her face in his hands, but he knew there was no time for that. "I will see you in a week, Lucius. I promise."

He nodded, and when Philippe went to open the door, he stepped backwards, a show of his compliance. She smiled at him and even walked backwards to the door. "I love you, Eliza."

"And I love you, Lucius."

She went through first and then the hunter did. Yet, when the door closed, he couldn't be anything but happy. It was going to the start of a new life, with a new side to fight for.

Seraphina's eyes were blurring with exhaustion. Finding the best demon to convert a member of the Alliance of Silver and Steam was proving to be impossible. She had been at it for weeks and was no closer to having things narrowed down than when she had begun. Each species with a toxic ability to change a human, or a demon, into what they were had drawbacks. Some died quickly after the change, others lost all ability to converse in human speech. She needed the person, well people, she chose to be able to still function within the Alliance and report back to her.

She ran a hand through her hair and cringed as the perfect blood red locks tangled under her fingers. She'd not done anything but research. She'd bathed briefly, but only because she'd had a meeting with the Kappa Demons and had needed to impress. None had shared her bed, and the premise was actually making her irritable as well as tired. But she'd tried to fuck an Incubus Demon when she'd returned from Lucius' assault. Demetrious had appeared in the room with them. His cold eyes and body spewed words of hatred at her. She'd been so frozen with terror she hadn't even killed the Incubus for failing to make her come.

Every time she closed her eyes, her lover was standing next to her when she opened them. It didn't matter where she was, he was always there. His wings gleamed white and his eyes sparked with anger. The words never changed, and she was unable to ignore the hallucination yet. There was no one she could kill to make it stop. Lucius started it, but he couldn't hold an illusion if he weren't nearby. This was all her doing. Her hands crumpled the paper under them, and she screamed, and she tore it into bits and threw it to the ground.

The Alliance of Silver and Steam was growing, and her army was not. Muriel was successfully transferred, but the next attempt, Bastian, had failed. He'd slit his own throat with her knife to avoid it. She'd been distracted and had gotten too close. Time was running out and Time Turning Demons worked for no one. She couldn't even spot them out in a human crowd. They were as elusive as pure Angels but cared for none. Nothing could make them erase a moment they didn't wish to and the one time she'd approached one in the bowels of Hell it had used its own powers to escape her. She'd spent a year trying to find it again before giving up.

Her eyes flamed, a bright red under the crystalline grey blue. "Figure it out, Seraphina."

She picked up her crystal dagger from the table top, the one only Pure Angels could effectively wield and kill a demon with one stab. Its pointed tip slipped across her arm, and she felt nothing as the blood dripped out and steamed when it hit the table top. Bloodletting was frowned upon, but a simple way to relieve tension for any Angel. The tension poured out with her blood, and when she touched the crystal to her arm to close the wound, she felt better. More in control.

A knock at the door brought a smile to her face. She'd known sooner or later she would fail if she did not see to herself. Vanity was its own reward sometimes, and her body was preventing her mind from seeking the proper solution. She pulled the straps from her gossamer gown down and let the bodice of her dress fall just below her breasts before tugging open the door. The massive Inferno Demon smiled, and when she put her hand on his bare chest, he was already hot to the touch. She stepped up on tip toes to close the small gap and pressed her mouth to his. The heat from his body set hers on fire. His mouth devoured hers, and she pulled him inside even as he shut the door closed.

His body tumbled with hers onto the bed, and even as she threw her head back in ecstasy, her eyes landed on the figment of her one true lover in the far corner of the room. She closed her eyes as the hot demon's fingers entered her body and focused on finding her own release so that she could get back to work against the Alliance. But the whole time her body trembled with need and lust, her eyes were locked with her imagination's version of Demetrious.

EPILOGUE

HER HANDS WERE slick with sweat as she went to stand by Felicia's side, despite the autumn chill. The date had been pushed back due to Lucius' confinement, and she had never heard the end of it from her friend. The fate of their wedding day seemed to rest on Eliza's shoulders now as she walked down the center aisle of the palace.

The ridiculous flowing purple gown caused her to trip twice. Her face never hit the ground, but she could hear Lucius' laughter over the organ music. Felicia looked stunning as she walked down the aisle. It was strange, seeing her friend in a delicate gown when she was all hard edges and work. Her eyes shifted to Greyston, who looked dapper in a black suit and tails with a purple vest himself. A small red rose was pinned to his suit jacket, roses that matched the arrangements at the end of the pews. He looked as though the sun had just come out in the night sky as he watched his bride move closer and closer to him, even though it was first thing after Sunday services. Her hair was twisted into a knot, with white daisies interwoven in. Her gown was flowing, a silver silk instead of a pure white and perfectly molded to her body. Everyone could see all of Felicia's slender curves and Eliza could only imagine that Greyston was approving of their dress choice. The two of them had spent hours in the marketplace selecting the silk and finding the proper spinner.

Being Captain of the Royal Guard, the room was almost more stunning than the bride, with his highness sitting to Greyston's left. White rose petals scattered all over the stone church floor, and silken curtains had been draped over all the windows. Steven Parkes stood next to Greyston, and Eliza laughed softly as he pinched Greyston's arm when he didn't take Felicia's hand when she stopped at the altar. Everyone stood now, a sign of respect to the soon to be wedded couple. Gowns of all magnificence filled the room as did top hats and canes. Even everyone from the guild had gotten dressed proper to celebrate such a high society wedding.

When Eliza heard the Bishop begin, her eyes left Felicia and Greyston, beautiful as they were, she only wanted to look at one person during a wedding, even if it was not her own ceremony. She looked to the front pew and smiled at Lucius. He looked splendid, and she beamed with joy at her mate. He wore the same outfit from the day they met, only the vest was woven with black design work instead of a solid grey. His black eyes landed on hers, and he nodded so small only she would have been able to see his head moved. He mouthed the words "I love you," and she wished she could return them, but she would do nothing to take the guests eyes off of Felicia. She and Greyston deserved this day. So many in the room had no clue as to what the groom truly was, but it was a day for celebrations when a man such as himself took a bride. Their courtship had surprised all members of society, and they'd gone through hoops to shut those people up. Now it was time for them to celebrate, so she merely smiled back at her own mate.

Applause broke out in the room and echoed like thunder. Eliza turned her head and saw the pair locked in a kiss, Felicia's crystal veil being held back by Greyston's large hand. Everyone laughed when the Bishop cleared his throat, and the couple remained locked in a passionate kiss. There was no stopping an Incubus Demon and sooner or later Felicia would have to pull back or risk setting off a sexual frenzy. She laughed and stepped off the altar, walking toward Lucius who was already standing to grab her hands. He kissed her gently, he'd had impeccable manners that she had never seen coming.

"How is my lovely mate? Getting ideas of your own?" He winked at her, and she elbowed him playfully.

"Well, that would be impossible as it's been a little over four months since our first official meeting and someone has never asked." She smiled and leaned to whisper in his ear, "I believe he thinks he has this one in the bag." She winked at him as she pulled back and turned to look at Felicia and Greyston, who had finally broken apart in front of a very flustered Bishop.

Arms wrapped around her waist and she felt warm lips on her neck. "Well, if that's how you want to play it, love." He spun her around to face him and kissed her. His lips were warm and felt like coming home. That's what he was for her now, home. "How about you come and be my wife in the big old manor I purchased just doors down from Mr. and Mrs. Westham? I bet you ladies would love to sit for tea one day and demon hunt the next." He laughed, and it tickled her nose.

Her smile was all she was able to manage in the way of an answer, and she leaned in and kissed him, just the same way Felicia had kissed Greyston before the Bishop.

PREVIEW OF BITE OF SILVER

Keep reading for a preview of *Bite of Silver* (*Alliance of Silver &
Steam Book 2*), *coming February 8th, 2015.*

The smile on Seraphina's painted red lips was cold and yet, colder
still by the time it reached her eyes.

"It has been a pleasure. An absolute pleasure." Cruelty danced in
her eyes as she turned her back on the Kappa demon leader and
Lake Biwa.

"When will we have our payment?" The leader's voice was raspy,
much like the froglike creature he was.

She tensed at the question, as the ruler of Hell and all demons
aside from Pure Angels, she didn't get questioned oft. Her hand

twitched at her sides with the urge to simply kill him. But that wouldn't help her with her plot to turn an Alliance of Silver and Steam member.

"It will come when the job is done. When Philippe Clemis has been bitten, and I have proof, your kind will have a section of Hell to call home." She hadn't bothered to turn around and immediately flashed herself away from the serene Japanese lake and back into her chambers.

She reached out over the mental bond she had with her Fallen Angels. It was a bond she only shared with those she created from her own blood, and at present, there were twenty of them. She latched onto the link with her original turned victim, Izazal.

"I need to exercise out my frustrations. See to it that an adequate demon is sent to my chambers quickly." She would get no response from him, just his obedience, so she closed the mental link.

Her smile morphed into one that was decidedly more sensual as she turned and saw herself in the mirror. She trailed her hands over her body, delighted in the pleasure just the small touch brought her and sauntered over to the table beneath the mirror. She poured herself a glass of wine that was nearly as red as the paint on her lips and wrapped her lips over the glass and tipped it, drinking every last drop in one sip before gently setting the crystal glass down.

She stared at herself in the mirror. Her grey-blue eyes sparkled with delight, and it was barely after nine a.m. "It would seem you have finally outsmarted the Alliance, Seraphina." She grinned at her own praise.

It had taken her almost six months of research, but her dream of transforming an Alliance of Silver and Steam member into a demon she could have power over was delightful. The hardest part had been choosing the proper demon to do the task. She'd poured over her options for the better part of two months. There were so many options, but very few that had seemed undetectable enough to get the job done.

The Kappa demon, an old Japanese myth that the culture only

got half right had been the best choice. The small frog like creatures lived outside of Hell as they weren't a species that had earned their spot down there over the centuries. They lived in lakes and typically did nothing more than drown their victims. However, Seraphina knew that their bite could transform a human, and only a human, into their blood slaves. It was how their supposedly secured victims would come to the lake and the perfect way to steal a hunter. The blood slave would never change form and would have a decent amount of free will; until the Kappa demon that created them put out an order.

And the only order this one would be giving was to follow Seraphina's every wish. Her body flared to life at the thought of the sensual Philippe Clemis servicing her body and her cause—to rid the Earth of humans so the demons could live topside without persecution. A small moan escaped her as she thought about his shoulder length black hair splayed out over her thighs as he pleasured her with his mouth.

He was the perfect choice for this experiment, and she couldn't wait to hold control over his mind.

Made in the USA
Lexington, KY
02 February 2018